THE LETHAL EFFECT

Books by L.J. Sellers

The Detective Jackson Series

The Sex Club

Secrets to Die For

Thrilled to Death

Passions of the Dead

Dying for Justice

Liars, Cheaters & Thieves

Rules of Crime

The Lethal Effect

(Previously published as *The Suicide Effect*)

The Baby Thief

The Gauntlet Assassin

THE LETHAL EFFECT

L.J. SELLERS

THOMAS & MERCER

The characters and events portrayed in this book are fictitious. Any similarity to real persons, living or dead, is coincidental and not intended by the author.

Printed in the United States of America.

Published by Thomas & Mercer
P.O. Box 400818
Las Vegas, NV 89140

ISBN-13: 9781612186221
ISBN-10: 161218622X

Library of Congress Control Number: 2012911788

Cast of Characters

Sula Moreno: PR person at Prolabs
Tate Moreno: Sula's young son
Karl Rudker: CEO at Prolabs
Tara Rudker: Karl Rudker's second wife
Diane Warner: scientist at Prolabs/disappears
Robbie Alvarez: Karl Rudker's son/Prolabs employee
Paul: ex-hacker/Sula's best friend
Trina Waterman: TV reporter
Cricket: environmental activist
Allen Sebring: whistleblower at Prolabs
Jimmy Jorgovitch: private investigator
Emily & John Chapman: Tate's foster parents
Felisa Quinton: clinical trial director/Puerto Rico
Miguel Rios: clinical trial patient/committed suicide
Luis Rios: clinical trial patient/committed suicide
Aaron Despain: new friend/asks Sula on date

Chapter 1

Monday, April 12

Sula started to walk away, but the conversation in the conference room grew loud and pulled her back. Karl Rudker's salesman-smooth voice was stretched thin with stress. As CEO, he rarely made a point to speak with her—or anyone without a VP in front of his or her title—but Sula avoided him anyway. The other frustrated voice behind the door belonged to Diane Warner, the head of research and development. She was a petite woman with a surprisingly big sound. The two most powerful people in the company were arguing about Nexapra, an antidepressant Prolabs had been working on for years but now everyone was suddenly excited about.

A mention of JB Pharma made Sula step closer to the door. She glanced down the short hallway to see if anyone had noticed her. The door to the human resources department was closed, and the elevator was silent.

Not that it made a difference. She had a right to be here. Rudker and Dr. Warner had agreed to meet her in the conference room to give statements for the press release Sula was working on. JB Pharma, based in Seattle, was acquiring their company, and as a public-relations assistant, it was her job to write up the announcements. She had cranked out quite a few high-impact press releases lately. First, Nexapra's amazing clinical-trial results had set the research and investor communities buzzing. Then the big drug companies had come calling. JB's $2.5 billion offer had won the bidding.

The voice was a little muffled, but Sula was certain she heard Diane Warner say, "We have to tell them about the first set of data. It could change everything."

The declaration sent a tingle up her neck. What could change everything? Was something wrong with the data? She had been sending out glowing press releases about the drug for weeks. Were they all wrong? She needed to know what they were talking about. Sula remembered the conference room opened onto a smoker's balcony on the other side and the exterior door was usually open this time of year. She moved quickly, afraid the argument would be over before she got there.

Serves you right, she heard her mother's voice say in her head.

Sula kept moving. She had a right to hear the conversation. She had created the promotional material that encouraged doctors to enlist their patients in the Nexapra trials. If there was a problem with the drug, she needed to know.

Down the hall and through the executive lunchroom, the steady click of her low-heeled pumps echoed in the empty rooms. Sula slipped out onto the balcony and glanced at her watch. Fifty-two seconds. A weak April sun filtered through the clouds and warmed the rain-soaked cement. Staying close to the building, she moved toward the conference-room doors. She wished she had a cigarette to explain her presence in case anyone came out while she was lurking around, but she had quit smoking six months ago. Mostly.

The argument was still in full swing. From her new position next to the partially open door, Sula caught glimpses of Warner as she paced back and forth in front of the window. Middle-aged with close-cropped silver hair, the doctor gestured with both hands.

"The new owners have a right to know about the deaths in the early trials," Warner insisted. She held out her hands and used her fingers to tick off her points. "The two patients who committed suicide in the Puerto Rico study were cousins, and I think I found a genetic marker that made them susceptible. Two: Developing a screening test can be accomplished in less than two years."

Warner paused, and Sula was grateful. She was still reeling from hearing that people taking Nexapra had killed themselves. Warner seemed to think it was the drug's fault. How could that be? The medication was supposed to help people who were depressed. She thought of the patients' families, the grief they had experienced and were still feeling. The *why?* questions that would never be answered. She knew firsthand what they had gone through. Those questions still haunted her.

Then the guilt hit her. She had helped bring those patients in!

Sula noticed the notepad still in her hand. She reached into her jacket pocket for a pen and instead found the tape recorder she'd brought for her session with the two executives. She pressed the record button as Warner continued, "If we get the three thousand patients we need for the phase III trials, the incident rate could be high enough to cause the FDA to reject our application anyway."

"Horseshit," Rudker thundered.

Sula aimed the microphone toward the open door.

"The percentage of suicides in the Puerto Rico trial was lower than the national average. You cannot conclude that Nexapra caused those deaths."

Warner stopped pacing for a moment and drew in a long breath. "Goddamn it, Karl. They killed themselves within a month of starting on the drug. We have an ethical responsibility to find out why." Under the anger, the doctor sounded tired. Sula wondered if the recorder had picked up her counterargument.

Rudker suddenly moved into view. He had thinning blond hair and sharp Nordic features, and at six-two, he towered over Warner. "JB Pharma might not see it that way," he said, his voice nasty with sarcasm. "As far as they're concerned, Nexapra is a potential blockbuster with a very good side-effect profile. If we tell them differently, they'll withdraw their offer. We don't have the cash to continue on our own. Do you want to bring this company down?"

"But we've only—"

Rudker cut her off. "If we develop a screening test, we're obligated to use it. And that jacks up the cost of R&D, slows down the FDA approval process, complicates marketing and prescribing, and in the end, substantially limits the market. And for what? A statistically insignificant risk for people who are prone to kill themselves anyway."

Sula sucked in her breath, stunned by the man's coldness. The room was silent, and she wondered if Dr. Warner had walked out. Unbelievable. Prolabs' tagline was "Putting Patients First." Sula had bought into that motto. She had felt like she was part of something bigger and better than herself. Clearly, the slogan was just corporate branding, a pretty package wrapped around a pile of deceit and greed. At least for Rudker anyway.

"We're going ahead with phase III clinicals," he said with a dismissive wave of his hand. "You'd better not tell anyone else about your theory."

Warner didn't respond.

"The merged company doesn't need two heads of R&D."

Warner stiffened. "So? I'm good at what I do and I get job offers all the time."

"That could change." Rudker lowered his voice to a mean whisper. "Too much is at stake here. Don't cross me on this."

After a long silence, Warner spun around and headed into the interior hallway.

Sula clicked off the recorder and repocketed it. Anxiety shot through her in waves. She had to get away. Before she could backtrack, Rudker strode toward the opening. She lunged away from the door, dropping her notebook. As she scooped it up, Rudker stepped out to the balcony.

"What are you doing out here?" His pale face had gone pink.

"I was looking for you and Dr. Warner." Sula glanced at her watch. She had been out here three and a half minutes. It felt more like fifteen.

His gray eyes bored into her, and Sula's stomach turned to mush. She began to chatter. "I'm putting together a press release about the acquisition. I was hoping to get a statement from you and Dr. Warner. We had a meeting scheduled."

"You were listening."

"No. I was just hoping to get your attention from here." Heat surfaced in her face, but her armpits had gone clammy.

With lizard-like quickness, he reached out and snatched her notebook.

"Hey." It came out more of a squeak than a protest.

Rudker glanced at the blank page, then stared with expressionless eyes. "Do not fuck with me. You will regret it."

Sula stared back. It was all she could do. She didn't know what to say and her legs trembled too much to walk away.

Finally, the CEO turned and strode back into the conference room. Sula's heart, which had been strangely quiet during the encounter, started to pound. Anxiety churned in her stomach and she fought the urge to empty it. Sula forced herself to move, to walk purposefully back to her office and sit down. It wasn't enough. She lowered her head to her lap and breathed deeply to calm herself. As a child, she had been afraid of many things. As a teenager, all of them had happened to her. Now, she had only one significant fear, and it wasn't her boss. Yet today he had scared her, and she was having a mild panic attack, or as her counselor called it, "a posttraumatic stress episode."

Sula fought for control, and after a few minutes, her journalistic instincts kicked in. She grabbed her pen and notepad, and with a shaky hand recreated the argument from the beginning as best she could. *The two people who had committed suicide in Puerto Rico were cousins.* She hadn't even known they had conducted trials there. *I may have found a genetic marker.* How many people with depression had that marker?

Eleven million people in the United States took antidepressants, including her. If Nexapra became a global blockbuster, hundreds, maybe thousands, of lives could be at stake. How much money was involved for Rudker? she wondered. How many lives was he willing to sacrifice to improve his net worth? Sula knew the drug was potentially worth billions to JB Pharma and its stockholders. She had seen the analysts' forecasts.

Anger pushed away her anxiety. How could Dr. Warner walk away from a problem of this magnitude? Someone had to stop the clinical trials. People with mental-health concerns needed protection. They needed medication that would help them, not send them over the edge. Sula felt powerless to do anything. She wasn't a scientist or a manager. She didn't have access to the data.

Rudker's warning echoed in her thoughts. If she did anything to undermine Nexapra, he would fire her—at least.

Losing her job was unthinkable right now. She could not do anything that would jeopardize her chances of getting Tate back. After years of struggling to pull her life together, she had finally worked up the courage to file a custody petition for her son. The hearing was three weeks away. To prevail against his foster parents, a middle-class couple who seemed to have everything, she not only had to be employed, she had to be perfect.

Sula felt light-headed. It was all too much to think about. She forced herself to take long, slow breaths. The oxygen helped quiet her mind and she decided she would talk to Warner. Maybe the doctor could be persuaded to take the suicide data to the research people at JB Pharma. Or even to the FDA. Sula told herself she did not have to get involved. She glanced at her watch. It was 3:40. Her visitation started in twenty minutes. She would see Dr. Warner first thing in the morning.

Chapter 2

Diane Warner strode toward her office in the research building. Rage propelled her forward and kept her from seeing anything. If people had spoken to her along the way, she hadn't been aware. The anger burned off the bone-deep fatigue she'd been feeling for months. Karl Rudker was an asshole and a social Neanderthal. But if she fought him—after five years of twelve-hour days spent coaxing this amazing little molecule along—she would be cast out and made to scramble for a new position at the age of fifty-five. She had no desire to move again. She liked Eugene and was tired of relocating. Moving back to New Jersey, where most of the pharma industry was headquartered, would be depressing.

She didn't trust Rudker not to screw her either way. Even if she kept quiet about the data, he was likely to dismiss her when the merged company downsized. Nexapra would proceed through development without her. Without a genetic-screening test. The thought made her ill. She was certain the two Hispanic men who had killed themselves shared a gene that produced a protein that interfered with serotonin.

Now that Rudker knew the suicide response was genetic and most likely ethnic, he would try to exclude minorities, particularly Latinos, from the phase III clinicals. That meant once the drug hit the general population, the death toll could be horrendous before the adverse-reaction reports triggered a withdrawal from the market.

If they even triggered a withdrawal. It was almost impossible to prove a cause-and-effect relationship between medication and suicide, especially with depressed patients. Nor did the act of killing oneself leave a physical trail of evidence pointing out what went wrong, the way a liver, for example, would show a buildup of statins.

Diane slumped at her desk. She felt compelled to resolve the situation, but she wasn't sure what move to make. Her soon-to-be new boss, JB's chief executive officer Gerald Akron, was notoriously inaccessible. The competitive-intelligence reports she'd gathered said the company was facing generic-drug competition and desperate to acquire a potential blockbuster. So JB Pharma's board of directors would not be receptive to the idea that Nexapra needed to be put on hold while they partnered with a diagnostics company to develop a screening test. No one would want to hear it. Five years down the road when the lawsuits started pouring in, they would look around for someone to blame.

Diane had no idea what she would do in the long run. But short term, she intended to violate scientific protocol for the first time in her life and make copies of patients' files to take home with her. The patients, Miguel and Luis Rios, no longer needed privacy protection.

If she didn't preserve a record of their Nexapra use and consequent deaths, their files might be permanently erased from the database. First, she would make backups of their DNA testing. Diane logged on to the R&D portal and began to burn files to a compact disk.

* * *

Rudker retreated to his office near the executive lounge and stood in front of the window. His view of a sloped hillside ruined by an abandoned computer-chip manufacturing plant only added to his irritation. First Warner, then that damn PR person, whatever her name was. Why did they insist on challenging him? He was in charge because he had the business skills to make these decisions.

Very soon, he would have an office twice this size. One that looked down on the city of Seattle from the tenth floor of JB Pharma's corporate headquarters. Although only 288 miles north, his new position would be a long way from the sandal-wearing, tree-hugging inhabitants of Eugene. He'd been here too long and it had made him sluggish and dull. He should have moved on after his divorce, but his son had been going through a rough patch then and it hadn't been right to leave. Now the boy was older and they didn't have much to say to each other. It was time to step up and expand his opportunities. His new wife would support an upward move.

Rudker plopped down at his desk, with its familiar piles of papers. His résumé, his life, his power base, was about to change. As part of the merger deal, he had asked for a seat on the board of directors in addition to the executive vice president position. He was confident he would get what he wanted. JB badly needed a blockbuster like Nexapra and he held the cards.

Rudker's skin tingled thinking about the numbers. The global mental-health market was a bottomless pocket, and Nexapra could become the best-selling drug ever. Bigger than Prozac. Bigger than Prilosec. They should give it a brand name that started with *Pr* just for luck. Preva. Precor. Preven. No, Preven sounded too much like prevent. The FDA would never allow it. He made a mental note to check with Prolabs' marketing director to see if they had started testing brand names with focus groups yet.

If they could get the drug approved in the next eighteen months, it could hit peak sales by mid-2013—just in time to prevent a bloodletting from the drop in sales after Altavar went off patent. The merger was happening just in time to keep Prolabs from going under. JB Pharma needed a new blockbuster and Prolabs needed a new source of R&D cash.

In fact, it needed a whole fresh start. Rudker would be glad to see the name Prolabs disappear. The company had been through its share of problems since he came on board in 2003. The manufacturing irregularities, the FDA fines, and the privacy-invasion lawsuits over some foolish marketing tactics—it had been one fiasco after another. To keep the company afloat while they developed Nexapra, Rudker had put in sixty- and seventy-hour weeks for years.

It hadn't been enough. He and Neil Barstow, the company's chief financial officer, had been forced to create two phony holding companies that allowed Prolabs to borrow from itself. They had also given themselves sizeable stock options that had never been declared as a business expense. Without a merger, Prolabs would eventually collapse on itself from the weight of all its debt. Rudker could feel the twinge of a migraine coming on, but he couldn't stop thinking about his situation. Prolabs was on the edge of the abyss, but the white knight was in sight. He just had to hang on for a while longer.

If only he hadn't borrowed so much money for personal projects—especially the llama ranch in Lorane that was intended to keep his new wife happy. It had cost him nearly $2 million. For fucking llamas! Now those loans were overdue and he couldn't shuffle the paperwork to hide the debt much longer.

If Nexapra were FDA approved by the time JB's accountants sorted out the bookkeeping mess, his transgressions wouldn't matter. The new owner would write it all off as a merger expense. If the product was delayed, or the merger fell through, he would be financially devastated. Maybe even unemployable. He could not let anything slow Nexapra down.

Rudker rubbed his temples. He would have to deal with Warner. She could be trouble. He suspected he had not heard the last of her genetic-test idea. Warner was a neurologist who had come over to the pharma industry out of the frustration of not being able to help her patients. She thought like a doctor, not an MBA. He wondered if she had any dirty secrets he could use against her.

Rudker reached for his Imitrex. He washed down two tablets with the bottled water he kept at his desk. And that damn PR person! How much had she heard? He had been so startled to find her standing there. Maybe she would have to go away too. He could not take any chances.

He took another swallow of water, then logged on to the company's enterprise software system and entered the clinical-trial database. Only a certain level of R&D employees could access the information, but as CEO he had right of entry to all the systems—sales, marketing, patient registries, and pipeline progress. He entered 1299, the drug's R&D number, into the search field, then scanned down the page for the Puerto Rico research site.

In a few minutes, he located the files of the patients who had died. They had signed up for a study in San Juan that had ended last year. Actually, that section of the trial had never really got going. Right around the time of the suicides, the clinic's lead investigator had quit because of family problems. The research center had been having a difficult time recruiting patients, so they abandoned that arm of the trial. The suicides had never even been reported, and the results from the parallel studies in Eugene and Portland had provided enough positive data for the FDA to green-light the large phase III that would lead to approval.

Rudker scanned the data. Both subjects had been diagnosed as clinically depressed; they had tried seven medications between the two. Miguel Rios was forty-one. His cousin Luis, thirty-four. An image of the two of them, sitting at a picnic table in a backyard filled with family, food, and noise flashed in his brain.

Rudker deleted the image, then deleted the first file.

Gone. As if Miguel Rios had never been in the study. Before Rudker could trash the second set of data, a pop-up screen notified him that another system user was trying to access the file.

Warner! It had to be. Damn her. What was she doing? Looking at the data again? Rudker waited for the message to disappear, then quickly erased the file. Of course, there was a paper backup somewhere in the R&D building, and there was probably another set of paperwork in the clinic in Puerto Rico. Eventually, he would find and destroy all of it. Now, he had a million things to do before he left for Seattle tomorrow. The first was to prepare for a meeting with JB's board of directors. Rudker buzzed his secretary.

Minutes passed. The wait made him irritable and he began to pace. A voice in his head began to rant about the stupidity and slowness of the average person. It caught him off guard. He usually heard the voice only when he was driving, or sometimes when he worked late. Rudker reminded himself to take his daily dose of Zyprexa as soon as he got off the phone.

He hated the damn stuff. It made him feel sedated. It also kept his paranoia in check and his relationships civil. Most people couldn't handle his natural energy and directness. He'd learned that the hard way in his early twenties. After doing a few months in jail on an assault charge—which wasn't his fault—he'd made himself swallow his meds and keep most of his thoughts in check.

Chapter 3

As Sula hurried toward the employee parking lot, her anxiety dissipated a little. A warm sun peeked through the clouds—perfect for an hour in the park. She climbed into her purple Dakota and sped out Prolabs' long entryway. From Willow Creek, she headed down West Eighteenth Avenue to Westmoreland Community Center.

She got to see Tate for only an hour every other week, but the community center had a lot of activities. Sometimes they played ping-pong or basketball. Today, they would goof around on the swings and the jungle gym and soak up the sun. Walking away from her sweet little boy after only an hour crushed her every time. But it was better than not seeing him at all.

Sula pulled into the parking lot the center shared with Jefferson Middle School and shut off the truck. Knowing she was a little early, she leaned back and closed her eyes. Sound-bites from the conversation she'd overheard at work began to play in her head. Sula tried to block them out, not wanting to think about Rudker right now.

At exactly four o'clock, Tate's foster parents, Emily and John Chapman, pulled up next to her in their shiny silver Toyota Prius. Sula figured it had cost them about a third of the value of the house she lived in. She got out of her truck and waited for Tate, who was getting last-minute instructions from his guardians. They were thirty-something, attractive, and perfectly nice people. Sula tried not to hate them.

In a moment Tate joined her on the grass. The first two minutes of every visit nearly overwhelmed her. Seeing him was such joy...and such longing, all rolled up in one raw explosion. Tate looked like his father. Blond, blue-eyed, and with a smile that could light up the sky. He was good-natured too and rarely complained about anything.

She gave him a big grin. "Hey, Tate. What's new?"

He smiled back and shrugged. "Not much. What are we gonna do today?"

"I thought we'd stay outside, play on the swings and stuff."

"Okay." He held out his hand. Sula's heart melted. She took his little-boy fingers in hers and walked toward the swings. In a moment, he started to pump his arm and make engine noises. She joined him, and they ran for the playground.

For the next hour, she was a kid: climbing, sliding, running, and laughing. At times, Sula even forgot that Emily and John were sitting in the parking lot, watching them. At one point, they rested and Tate talked a little about preschool and T-ball, but mostly they played. She always made sure he had a good time with her. Her greatest fear was that her boy would decide he didn't want to see her anymore.

What would be left in her life then?

Sula had a court-ordered visitation right, but Tate didn't know—didn't remember—that she was his mother. Or maybe he did. Even after a year and a half apart, he had taken right to her. Emily and John referred to her as a "friend of the family," but Tate called her Aunt Sula. She had lost custody of him before his first birthday, and the guilt and shame were never far from her heart.

When he was born, she had been a kid herself, only eighteen and still grieving for her father, mother, and sister. Part of her had believed that a baby would make things right by giving her a new family. After his birth, her depression had deepened and she had no one to turn to. The baby's father, James, had come and gone in her life in the space of one blurry month, and her mother's family had long ago rejected the whole Moreno clan.

The Relief Nursery had helped her with daycare but it wasn't enough. She had been so lonely and so overwhelmed by Tate's constant needs that she tried to medicate herself into a state of numbness. Eventually a combination of pain pills and alcohol landed her in the hospital. She'd woken to the news that the state had taken custody of her little boy.

Losing him had spun her even further into despair until a friend had suggested she try taking antidepressants. Prozac had changed her life. Not overnight, but in time. She began to see that she had a future, that she could find a reason to get up each day. She started seeing a therapist. Eventually she quit drinking, started classes at Lane Community College, and wrote daily in a personal journal. After a year of sobriety, she petitioned the court for visitation and was granted it.

The bimonthly contact with Tate, who was walking and talking by then, had given her hope that she could fully reclaim her life and eventually bring Tate back into it. Yet she knew she couldn't raise him by herself, take journalism classes, and work full-time.

It just wasn't possible. Not for her. Some people seemed to be able to do it all, but she struggled every day just to keep going.

Even if she had been Superwoman, it wouldn't have been fair to the boy. If he had lived with her during college, Tate would have spent all his time in daycare. Sula wasn't selfish enough to do that to him. Not when he had great full-time care from Emily and John. She could have given up her education, but she hadn't trusted a judge to give custody to a single mother with a recent history of substance abuse. She worried that her Native American name and heritage would work against her too. Yet deep in her heart, Sula had also been scared that she wasn't ready and that she would fail as a mother.

She'd earned a degree, landed a great job, and she'd taken parenting classes just for good measure. When she felt confident the state would see she was ready, she'd filed a petition to regain custody. In response, John and Emily had filed their own petition seeking to terminate her visitation. They would all end up in court in a few weeks.

Sula glanced over at them, the perfect couple reading behind the glass of the windshield. Emily taught first grade at McCormick Middle School and John was a chiropractor. They had taken good care of Tate; she could tell by how happy and kind he was. Sula hated to be pitted against them, but what else could she do? He was her son. They were meant to be together.

"Aunt Sula?"

She turned back to Tate. "What, honey?"

"Are you my mother too?"

Sula's heart nearly stopped. None of them, not her or the Chapmans or the social workers, had expected this question until he was older. She smiled and squatted to look him in the eye. "Yes I am. We can't talk about it right now, but we will someday, I promise. I love you. Never forget that."

"I love you too."

The radio blaring an upbeat pop song to keep her from crying, She recited her mantra: *Every moment I have with him is precious, and I will see him again.*

After she made a left turn on Twenty-Fourth, traffic slowed. Sula pressed her brakes. Her purse tumbled off the seat, dumping its contents on the floor. She made a quick grab to retrieve it.

When her eyes came to the road, she saw the car in front of her had stopped. Sula slammed the brakes, sending the purse and her notebook back to the floor. The front end of her Dakota tapped into the bumper of the white Mustang.

Oh hell. This was the last thing she needed. The guy in the Mustang stared at her in his rearview mirror. He seemed oddly familiar. The Mustang pulled into the Healthy Pet parking lot. Sula waited for the light, then followed him in. She parked next to his car, where he stood waiting.

"I'm so sorry," she apologized as she got out. "I took my eyes off the road." She stopped and stared. It was a guy from the parenting class she had recently completed. "I'm Sula Moreno. We had a class together." She held out her hand.

As he shook it, she was reminded of how attractive she found him. Tall, with short dark hair and beautiful white teeth, he was one of those mystery people, like her, with a dark exotic look that refused to betray their heritage. His only flaw was his slightly crooked nose, but his green eyes lit up when he smiled.

"Aaron DeSpain. Nice to meet you, officially. Although I wish it were under different circumstances."

"Me too. With my luck, I'll be taking driving classes next."

He laughed, then paused for a moment. "Do you have insurance?"

"Of course." She had the paperwork in her hand. She copied her insurance information on the back of a business card and handed it to Aaron.

"Thanks." He stared, as if he was going to say something more. "Maybe—"

Sula cut him off. "Sorry for the damage. Let me know if my insurance company gives you any trouble."

She waved, got in her truck, and left the parking lot. If her life had been different, she would have gladly gone out with him. He would be a lovely distraction from all the negative strangeness at work right now. The timing was wrong though. What if the guy had a criminal record? And the Chapmans' lawyer pointed it out to the judge? With the custody hearing only weeks away, she had too much at stake. She had to keep to herself and not take any chances. She had to stop thinking: *If my life had been different…*

By the time she reached the little two-bedroom house on Friendly Street with its warm red/brown paint, the sky was nearly dark. She had rented the cottage a couple of months ago in preparation for Tate coming to live with her. The owners had offered her a sweet deal. If she bought the house within two years, all of her rent would be applied to a down payment. Sula couldn't wait to sign the papers. Now that she had a garage and a backyard, she couldn't imagine living without them again.

At the moment, she was a little shy on furniture, but she could not bring herself to prepare a room for Tate until she knew for sure he was coming home. If she lost the hearing, seeing the room ready but lifeless would be devastating.

Sula opened a can of chili, dumped it in a bowl, and added a healthy dose of green Tabasco sauce. While it heated in the microwave, she dug the newspaper out of the recycling. She was a decent cook when the occasion called for it, she just hadn't had an occasion in a long time.

The *Willamette News* kept her company while she ate. When she'd started at the University of Oregon, she'd had hopes of landing a job at the newspaper someday. Then Craigslist had killed the classified section, and the recession had gutted display advertising. The paper had started laying people off and was now down to a skeleton crew. Sula accepted that she would probably work in public relations for most of her career. She wasn't leaving Eugene. Not as long as Tate was here.

Sula read through the meager help-wanted ads. Switching jobs right now wouldn't be a good custody move, unless the new position paid much better. Yet she didn't know how much longer she could work for Rudker. He had always intimidated her, but now he disgusted her too.

What if Rudker fired her? Where would she work that would pay enough to provide for her and Tate? The judge wouldn't take her seriously if she were unemployed, or even underemployed. The thought of standing in court and hearing him deny her custody made her heart race. Sula's counseling kicked in, and she began to breathe from her stomach. Still, she couldn't stop her mind from playing an image of Tate walking out with Emily and John, never to be seen again.

Unable to calm herself, Sula got up and began to pace. She thought about taking a Xanax, then changed her mind. She tried to save the mild tranquilizers for when she had serious anxiety episodes in public situations.

Sula pulled on a denim work shirt and headed out to the garage for her own brand of therapy. The unfinished room was almost empty except for her metalworking tools. The one she used the most was her cutting torch, which she was still making payments on. In the center of the limited space was her work in progress: a six-foot-tall metal sculpture of a twisted form, part human and part alien. Just seeing it made her feel better.

The frame, which had once been part of a plow, didn't look feminine yet, but she would round it out later with some motorcycle fenders she'd picked up at a yard sale. The next step was to use the MIG welder to attach a piece of metal tubing that fanned out at the end like a hand. First she clamped the tubing in place at the body's shoulder, then set her MIG welder next to the sculpture. Next she attached the ground clamp—which looked like the end of a jumper cable—to the base of the sculpture. She studied the seam for a minute to get a feel for its flow and depth.

Sula took a few long, slow breaths to make sure her hands were steady. When she was in the zone, she buttoned her shirt up to the neck, pulled on her welding helmet, and donned a pair of heavy work gloves. She flipped the welder on and a spark jumped from the end of the welding wand. She held the end near the seam and watched as liquid metal oozed from the wand. With a steady hand she added a bead of molten metal to the two pieces. She loved to see the steel come together. Two seemingly unbendable and unaesthetic objects fused into one superior form.

She'd learned to weld at the Center for Appropriate Transportation, a co-op that designed, repaired, and sold bicycles, as well as tried to teach life skills to teenagers who didn't fit into traditional high school. The center also made metal bike racks for local businesses. Sula had welded dozens of the huge racks in her year at CAT and had loved every fiery seam.

She'd also been encouraged to write a few news stories for its monthly cycling publication, and that had sparked her interest in journalism. It had not been a traditional high-school experience, but in many ways it had been better. The co-op owners were sweet, passionate people, and its few students were misfits, which meant they were more interesting than most kids their age.

The weld took forty minutes and didn't turn out as well as she wanted. She could grind it down to make it look all right, but that wasn't good enough. Two sculptures she'd created in classes at the university had won awards at local art shows, and she hoped to enter this one in a statewide show in Portland this fall.

She would cut the piece off tomorrow after it had cooled and start over. Sula put away her tools, read a few chapters in a book about freelance reporting, then headed for bed. Tired as she felt, her brain kept leaping from one wild thought to another. The talk of suicides that morning had triggered childhood memories that had plagued her all day. She had managed to shut most of them down as they surfaced. But now the scene in which her father played Russian roulette at the kitchen table with a loaded pistol could not be repressed.

His sweaty forehead, the pink flush of skin, the blank stare. For a moment this afternoon, Rudker had reminded Sula of her dad, sitting at the yellow Formica table on that summer evening two days before her tenth birthday. Fate had intervened in the form of a barking dog and her father had survived—to play variations of the suicide game again and again, until one day he lost.

Chapter 4

Tuesday, April 13

Robbie picked six white pill bottles off the conveyor belt, wrapped clear tape around them to create a bundle, then slid them into a box and taped it closed. Then he did it again. And again. For eight hours a day, unless the plant was on overtime. Some days he got so bored in the afternoons he nearly walked out. But so far, he'd resisted the urge. He could not afford to be unemployed again. Before he'd started taking medication, he'd lost a few jobs because he was occasionally too despondent to get up in the morning.

He forced himself to look at the bright side. Clean, easy work for $8.50 an hour was considered a great job these days, and most of the people at Prolabs were quite nice. Keeping that in mind, the morning passed quickly. When the lunch buzzer rang in his ears, relief washed over him. He set down the six-pack and joined the moving wall of people in the corridor. From the back, they all looked the same. White lab-style coats, white booties, and white hair caps. He'd felt silly the first few times he suited up, but even the big bosses in suits and ties put on sanitation gear before entering the factory.

Sometimes the white walls and stainless-steel machinery made him a little snow-blind, but it was still better than the stinking, wet mess of a dishwashing job he'd had before. This job didn't make his father proud, but it was a step in the right direction. Plus, working at a pharmaceutical factory gave him good material for his occasional stint at a local stand-up comedy club. Writing and performing comedy gave him a way to turn his gloom-and-doom personality into a positive, if fleeting, experience.

The group moved silently until they entered the changing room. As booties and hair caps came off, their voices burst forth.

"Want to run over to Taco Time?"

"Did you see Rudker's new wheels? The SOB is driving a Commander."

"No shit. What do they cost? Forty grand?"

Robbie ignored them, changing as quickly as he could. He wanted to get to the lunchroom in time to snag a seat next to Julie the receptionist. Lunch hour was the only time he was able to see her. He shoved his booties and hair cap into the wall slot for disposables and hung the white coat in his locker. He grabbed his lunch sack, hurried out into the exterior walkway, then broke into a jog.

"Hey, Robbie, what's the hurry?" Mark, the mixing-room operator, was going the other direction and mockingly jumped out of his way.

"I heard Santana was playing in the lunchroom and I wanted to get a good seat."

Mark was kind enough to laugh.

Robbie pushed through the double doors only to discover he was too late. Julie's table was full. Melissa and Monica, both secretaries, sat on either side, and three guys from the tablet-press room sat across from her. *Damn.* He wanted to ask her out, but he felt like he had to give her a chance to get to know him. Otherwise, she would probably turn him down. She was pretty and popular and he was just okay. Average looking, acceptable body, taller than most girls, and smarter than most guys. So far he'd only managed to sit with Julie twice in two months.

Robbie looked away so she wouldn't see him staring. Disappointment made his legs heavy and he plopped down at the nearest table. Knowing how quickly he could slide into despair, he focused on his food: two slices of leftover pizza, a banana, and a twin pack of Twinkies. Not bad. It was better than Cup-O-Noodle, which he often ended up with because he'd hit the snooze button one too many times and had to run out the door.

"Hey, Robbie, need some company?" Matt, a thin young man about his age who worked the other end of the packaging line, sat down across the table. He laid his hands out flat, the small triangular tattoos showing. It was obvious he had no lunch.

"What's new?" Robbie tried to be friendly.

"I had to get a new battery for my piece of shit car and now I'm broke."

"Cars are like black holes. You put your money in and it never comes back out." Robbie put a slice of pizza on a napkin and pushed it across the table to Matt. "Here, I'm not that hungry."

"Thanks, man."

A little later he gave him one of the Twinkies too.

On his way out, Robbie stopped by the bulletin board, hoping Julie would walk by on her way to the front office. A company flyer caught his eye. In large purple type it asked: *Do you suffer from depression? If you have three or more of these symptoms, you may benefit from a new medicine. To find out more about a clinical trial for an experimental new drug, contact Adriana at Oregon Research Center.*

Robbie knew the list by heart. He was a poster child for most of the symptoms—a sense of hopelessness, inability to concentrate, insomnia. The trial intrigued him. He'd been taking Zoloft for a year and a half now, and it wasn't working that well for him anymore. Before the Zoloft, he'd been on Paxil for almost a year. That drug had made him feel emotionally numb and he'd hated that more than being depressed. Feeling bad was better than feeling nothing. Eventually, he'd asked his mother's doctor to write him a script for something else.

He'd never been in a clinical trial before. He visited online forums cheerily hosted by pharma companies like Prolabs that were keeping all the depressives medicated. Many of the people he chatted with had been in studies, and overall they reported good experiences. Often the research centers paid a nice fee for time and travel expenses.

As he stood thinking it over, the second lunch buzzer rang. Robbie took a moment to memorize the phone number. He had decided to give the trial center a call. He could help Prolabs test one of its products, pick up a little extra cash, and maybe start feeling better too.

For now he had to get back to the packaging line. The fact that his father was CEO of the company didn't mean he could get away with being late from lunch break. He used his mother's family name, so most of the people he worked with didn't know he was Karl Rudker's son. He didn't want people either sucking up to or avoiding him because of his supposed connections. Hah! He and his father hadn't spoken for months.

The supervisors knew who he was and he tried to be an excellent employee. Even though they hadn't gotten along for years, his father's expectations were buried deep in his DNA.

* * *

Sula walked into Prolabs with a sense of apprehension. She hadn't fallen asleep until after one o'clock, then she'd had a long unsettling dream in which Rudker had chased her through a warehouse and she kept running into stacks of boxes. She was still unnerved by the whole encounter yesterday. Rudker's threat had been intense and personal and she suspected she hadn't heard the last of it.

Sula handed her brown leather backpack to the security man and passed through the metal detector. "Good morning, Cliff."

"Morning, Sula. Looks like it will be a gorgeous spring day."

"Sure does. Have a good one."

She picked up her bag and clicked across the tile foyer. Sunlight through the narrow floor-to-ceiling windows cast bright stripes on the floor. In celebration of spring, Sula had worn a short-sleeve blouse and skirt for the first time since last October, but it failed to cheer her up.

Even though she was only a public-relations flack, up until now she'd felt good about working for Prolabs. The company had its problems, sure, but she had always believed it had a good soul because it developed therapies that were meant to help people. Now she didn't want to be here.

Sula stepped into the elevator and checked her watch: 7:53. She was three minutes off her usual time. Apparently, she was moving a little slow. She got off on the second floor and headed for the employee lounge, where she made herself a cup of coffee from the fresh-ground stuff she kept in the fridge. The room was empty except for a guy in a suit whom she had never seen before. He was reading a report of some kind and didn't look up. Sula remembered that most of the sales and marketing staff had gone to a training session in Seattle.

Coffee in hand, she crossed the hallway into her office, a seven-by-ten room with a window, a desk, and a wall of filing cabinets. She turned on her computer and settled in to open e-mails. A few minutes later, an e-mail request from a PR person at JB Pharma reminded her to go see Dr. Warner. Sula zipped through the rest of the mail, deleting at least half without opening them, then headed back out to the elevator.

The R&D staff was in a separate building across a small courtyard. Sula took a moment to stand in the sun, sip her dark coffee, and appreciate that she worked on the outskirts of town with a tree-covered hillside for a view. The Prolabs complex spread out over ten acres and had three main structures: the corporate office where she worked; the R&D building, similar in design but with only one floor; and the manufacturing plant, lower down the hill. Beyond that were wetlands, owned by Prolabs and soon to be bulldozed to make way for a new manufacturing plant. The company had applied for all the necessary permits and most had been granted. Only a city-council vote and an environmental study were holding up the construction. In Eugene, environmental concerns could mean a serious delay. Or a complete shutdown. The thought reminded her that she needed to craft a memo to the city council.

She headed for the R&D lab. It was only her third time in the building but she knew Dr. Warner had the big office in the corner. The doctor didn't answer her knock. Sula thought she might be in a meeting, so she checked the small conference room. It was empty. She heard voices in the hall so she quickly stepped out.

"Excuse me." Two middle-aged guys in lab coats turned around. She had met both before, but despite rapid brain racking, she could not remember either of their names. The one guy had a Christopher Lloyd, mad-scientist look, but that didn't help her come up with his real name. Sula strode toward them. "Have you seen Dr. Warner this morning?"

"No. In fact, we were just looking for her." The guy with the wild hair eyed her strangely. "She was supposed to meet us at eight."

Sula checked her watch: 8:23. "If she wasn't coming in, who would she call?"

"That would be me." The other man, shorter and older, spoke up. Sula recalled that his name was Steve Peterson and that he worked on the Nexapra project. Now he looked at her curiously too. "Why do you ask?"

"I was supposed to meet with her yesterday for a briefing but that didn't work out, so I thought I'd see her this morning."

They shrugged in unison. The three of them stood for an awkward moment. Then Peterson said, "If she comes in, we'll tell her you're looking for her."

"Thanks." Sula forced a smile and moved on. It struck her as odd that Warner would miss a meeting with her colleagues. Especially the day after a blowout with Rudker. Maybe Warner planned to quit. Sula wouldn't blame her. Still, as the head of R&D, Warner was probably making $250,000 a year. People in that pay bracket didn't miss much work. Even if they were upset.

Sula spent the rest of the day fielding calls from real journalists asking about the merger. She envied them, writing for *Businessweek* and the *Wall Street Journal*. Someday she would have a real reporting job, she promised herself. For now, she had to promote Prolabs, to cushion its announcements, good and bad, in a cotton-candy spin. She tried to craft a memo to the city council but had trouble concentrating. She kept thinking about Diane Warner.

Late in the afternoon she called Steve Peterson and asked him if his boss had ever shown up. He hadn't seen Warner. Sula scanned the personnel database and found Warner's home phone number. She copied it to a yellow sticky note and pressed the note to the top of her computer. She would give it a day. Warner might be offended if Sula invaded her privacy at home without good reason. The doctor might not want to talk about Nexapra either.

At four fifteen, Marcy Jacobson, the head of human resources, stepped into her office. Sula's heart sank. She knew the woman had come to fire her.

Chapter 5

Marcy closed the door behind her, and Sula braced herself. She would plead for her job if she had to. If she explained about the custody hearing, maybe—

"Hi, Sula." Marcy smiled as she took a seat in the visitor's chair. "How have you been? I feel like we've been out of touch lately." Marcy was in her early sixties, but only her sun-weathered face betrayed her age. The rest of her was still working hard at looking forty-something.

Sula's mind raced. What was this about? It didn't sound like a dismissal, but Marcy was known for being evasive. "I'm good." She tried to smile. "How about you?"

"Also good." Marcy paused. "I've got a delicate situation I need to talk to you about."

Sula's heart pounded. *Just say it!*

Marcy launched in. "An employee has filed a sexual-harassment complaint about Sergio. I know for a while there he was rather flirtatious with you. Did he ever cross the line?"

Sula wanted to laugh with relief. Sergio, the creep from marketing, had finally gone too far. "Not really. He bugged me to go out with him, but he never touched me."

"Sexual harassment doesn't have to be physical."

"I realize that."

Some of Sergio's comments had been offensive, but he was so annoying and so over the top that she had laughed at him most of the time. He had lost interest rather quickly. Sula couldn't afford to be involved in the situation. "He was irritating, but not inappropriate. I believe he's capable of sexual harassment, so whoever has complained, you should take her seriously."

"We are." Marcy unexpectedly reached over and patted Sula's hand. Sula fought the urge to pull away. Marcy asked, "Are you happy with the company?"

"Sure." Even small white lies made her uncomfortable.

"Good." Marcy stood to leave. "It will be different when JB takes over, but I'm trying to stay optimistic."

"Will you have to lay people off?"

"Most likely."

"What about my position?"

"I think you're safe. Thanks for being up front with me."

"Sure."

Marcy gave her a small wave and left the room. Sula heaved a sigh of relief, shut down her computer, and followed her out.

* * *

Rudker pulled his short-trip suitcase from the walk-in closet and set it on the bed. Packing had become a precise operation, no more complicated than preparing a familiar meal. Two white, long-sleeved shirts, a light-blue short-sleeved one, the charcoal Brooks Brothers suit, casual black slacks, underclothes, and the bathroom kit that he never unpacked. Cell phone, laptop, and financial reports were already in his shoulder bag. Traveling suited his restless personality, but the timing of this trip annoyed him. He wanted to tie up the loose ends of the Nexapra data as quickly as possible, but he couldn't miss this board meeting. Talking with the other scientists on the Nexapra project and locating the paper files would have to wait until he returned in few days.

"Don't forget your medication," Tara chirped as she came up behind him.

"I won't." Rudker turned and kissed his young, beautiful wife. He never tired of looking at her perfect face. Wide-set cobalt eyes, small upturned nose, full sensuous lips with a scattering of freckles that he wanted to lick every time he saw them. She was a work of art.

They had met at a fundraiser for a local charity called Food for Lane County. She was a hostess and he was a main donor. In essence, that summed up their relationship. Tara was a good-natured soul. In addition to feeding the hungry, she put up with his mood swings and sometimes distant personality without much complaint. Unlike his first wife, Maribel, Tara never said no to sex. She was good for him, and Rudker needed her in a way he had never needed anyone before. The thought made him pull away.

"How long will you be gone?" She looked worried.

"Just a few days. Are you all right?"

"Of course. Call me when you know."

"Always." Rudker kissed her again, picked up his bags, and headed downstairs to wait for the car service.

Entering the Eugene airport always gave him a chuckle. If he were searching for someone, it would take about six minutes to cover the entire building. Checking in also took about that long. It was worlds apart from the San Francisco airport he'd flown in and out of for the ten years he'd worked at Amgen. He'd started at the biotech company as a product manager and worked his way up to vice president. Toward the end, he'd been traveling ten days out of every month.

At eight fifteen in the evening, the airport was practically deserted. One person was in the line in front of him and a young woman paced nearby, talking on a cell phone. The guy at the counter was trying to check his bags and had some malfunction with his ticket. To distract himself, Rudker mentally reviewed his presentation to the board.

While he was checking in, the girl on the phone began to cry, then to beg the person on the other end to come pick her up. Rudker turned and stared. She was young, probably still a teenager, and her jet black hair was short and spiky. She also had silver rings in both eyebrows. Rudker didn't understand how any of that was supposed to be attractive.

"Please," she cried over and over. The clerk handed him his boarding pass, which he tucked into his jacket pocket. He dug out his wallet, walked over to the girl, and handed her thirty dollars. "Call a cab."

Feeling grateful he had not had to raise a daughter, Rudker walked away before she could react. After a few seconds he heard her call out, "Thanks." He passed through the inspection area without having his body searched and considered that an immediate payback.

Two and a half hours later, he moved through the Seattle airport with equal efficiency. At midnight it was also nearly empty. He took a cab downtown to Cavanaugh's on Fifth Avenue and checked in. He had swallowed two melatonin tablets on the way, so five minutes after lying down, he was out and slept like the dead for five hours.

Chapter 6

Wednesday, April 14

The six a.m. call from the concierge jolted him awake. Rudker splashed cold water on his face, then spent thirty minutes on the treadmill in the third-floor gym before showering. Until he'd hit forty, his nervous energy had kept him lean. Now he had to work at it. He dressed in the charcoal suit, choosing a striped silver-and-light-blue tie. Pharma people on the West Coast were slightly more casual than their counterparts in the East Coast corridor. He'd been on a panel at a pharma marketing conference in Edison, New Jersey, and every guy in the room had been wearing campaign colors: dark-blue suit, white shirt, and red tie. The women, fortunately, made some livelier choices.

Nervous excitement kept him from having breakfast, but he downed his usual assortment of supplements: vitamins B, C, and E, zinc, kelp, calcium, and DHEA. Prevention was the key. He'd read the side-effect profile of too many pharmaceuticals to leave his health in the hands of drugs. Except for the Zyprexa and an occasional migraine pill, he steered clear of chemicals.

The company sent a car for him at seven and Rudker arrived at the Stewart Street headquarters with thirty-five minutes to kill. Not wanting to look eager, he circled the entire campus on foot, ignoring the dark sky that threatened rain. With twenty minutes left, he headed up to the executive suite. He stopped at Gerald Akron's office, but the secretary told him the CEO was in a meeting. A meeting before the meeting? That seemed odd, perhaps even ominous. No, it could be anything, he told himself.

He found a reading nook on the west side of the executive suite and tried to concentrate on the two reports he'd prepared, but his mind kept surging forward to the board meeting. He imagined the announcement, saw them reach out, one by one, to shake his hand. A board member! Rudker's heart pulsed in his fingertips. Abruptly, he pushed out of the chair and began to walk the hallway again. After what seemed like an eternity, the clock said 8:20. It was time.

Rudker entered the boardroom at the end of the hall and immediately sensed something was wrong. The group didn't exactly go quiet, but they all glanced up at him as they wrapped up hushed conversations. John Harvick, the chairman, walked over and welcomed him with a handshake. Rudker felt a little better. He had to stop being so paranoid. Right. If he could do that, he wouldn't need the Zyprexa.

He took a seat near the door on the opposite end of the table from where the chairman sat. The room was surprisingly small and had no windows. Meeting rooms were always like that. Architects rarely wasted prime window real estate on anything but offices. He hated the confined feel.

Harvick called the meeting to order. Rudker surveyed the people seated around the long mahogany table. Gerald Akron,

Art Baldwin, Harvey Kohl, Jane Kranston, Richard Mullins, and Jim Estes. The "super seven" had control over a company that pulled in $14 billion a year in revenue. They had control over his future.

"Let's get a quick update on the merger," Harvick said, looking at Akron, JB's chief executive officer.

"Firing on all cylinders," Akron reported. The heavy bald man stood to deliver the rest of his brief: "The SEC wants us to sell two of our cardiovascular products, both with sales under eighty million. Genzar wants the pair. We've identified twelve middle-management positions and five R&D staff that can be eliminated during the merger. And plans are in motion to move Prolabs' R&D operation to Seattle. The only holdup is the final approval to build a new factory in Eugene."

"Anything we can do to push that?" Harvick looked at Rudker.

Rudker was ready. "I've got an insider on the city council and all we need to do is wait for their vote. I have a friend on the environmental committee too. So I expect quick approval of our plan to recreate the wetlands. We should know in a week or two."

Kranston and Kohl laughed. Rudker gave Kranston a look.

"Sorry," she said. "It's the idea of recreating wetlands. It's like promising to put up a new ghetto."

Rudker relaxed a bit. "Eugene is a little odd that way. Nothing but weeds and ducks and a few scrubby trees out there in that acreage, but folks want to preserve it. The town also has ten percent unemployment. This factory will be built."

"Excellent." There was a long pause before Harvick continued. "Karl, I know you're anxious to know our decision and we won't keep you waiting any longer. We think it's premature to offer you a position on the board, but we promise to reconsider the idea after you've had six months under your belt as chief operating officer."

The air left his lungs as if being vacuumed. Rudker fought the panic. Fought the desire to shove his fist into Harvick's face. He clenched and unclenched his hands in his lap several times before responding. "I've got twenty-five years in the business under my belt."

"We know that, Karl. But never at a company that does more than a billion a year. Give it a little time."

Stunned by their decision, he considered withdrawing his company from the merger. He had other offers. Yet he sat there, silent. Time was the problem. Prolabs was too close to financial collapse to start over with a new deal.

Finally Rudker nodded. "It won't take long to show you what I can do."

The voices in the room faded away and all he heard was the one in his head. *Second man and no board seat. Nice lateral move.* Rage and shame burned in his veins.

"Anything to update on Nexapra?" Now Kohl was asking questions.

Rudker pulled in a fresh supply of oxygen through his nose and spoke slowly. "We've started recruiting for phase III clinical trials. The FDA has given us a green light for the protocol. We're projecting a late-2011 approval date." He sounded so calm.

"Excellent." Kohl turned his next question to Akron, and Rudker's mind flipped back to his humiliation. How could he have been so wrong about the board-member decision? Did they know about Prolabs' financial mess? Were they toying with him?

He could feel his power position slipping away. Now it all rested on Nexapra. He had to push it through approval and to the top of the charts. He couldn't let anything get in his way.

Chapter 7

Sula tried calling Dr. Warner in the research building while her computer booted up. After three rings, a recording of Warner's voice asked her to leave a message. The head of R&D did not mention that she would be out of the office. Sula called Steve Peterson and he reported that Dr. Warner had not come in yet.

"She usually comes in by now though, right?"

"By seven thirty, usually."

Sula checked her watch, even though she knew it was 7:55. "She didn't call?"

"Not yet."

"Have you called her cell phone?"

"I tried it once and left her a message."

"I'm going to call her home number."

"Let me know what you find out."

Warner's home voice mail picked up after four rings. Her message was pleasant but brief: *You've reached Diane Warner.*

Leave a message if you like. Distressed, Sula hung up. Where the hell was she? The doctor's absence was starting to scare her. Sula hit redial, waited for the answering machine, then left her name and number and asked Warner to please call.

She dialed Steve Peterson's extension and he picked up right away, as if he'd been waiting. "This is Sula. Dr. Warner doesn't answer her phone at home."

"This is very unusual. Have you talked with anyone in human resources yet?

"No, but I will."

"Keep me posted."

Peterson's concern fueled her own sense of alarm. Worst-case scenarios played in her mind. Warner was lying dead on her kitchen floor, a gaping knife wound in her chest from a home-invasion robbery. Or maybe she was at the morgue, victim of a hit-and-run accident. Or in the hospital in a coma, but with no identification, so the nurses didn't know who to call. Did Warner have a family?

By the time Sula reached the HR department on the third floor, her pulse raced and anxiety clutched at her heart like a bony hand. She forced herself to slow down, to breathe from her stomach before she entered the suite. Marcy's assistant, Serena, was in the outer office behind a curved half wall. The young woman greeted her with cheerful chatter.

Sula could not be distracted. "Sorry to be abrupt, Serena, but I must see Marcy right away."

"She's in a meeting with a lawyer." Serena lowered her voice. "There's something big going on, and I think it involves Sergio."

"I have a greater concern. Diane Warner hasn't shown up for work in two days, and she hasn't notified Steve Peterson either time. Has she called either you or Marcy?

"No." Serena's eyes went wide. "Do you think she quit?"

"Maybe. I need you to look up her home address for me."

"Are you going there?"

"I feel compelled to do something."

Serena rolled her chair in front of her computer and made a few mouse clicks. "It's 2862 Spring Boulevard. Are you going now? Should I tell Marcy when she gets out of her meeting?" The girl, fresh out of high school, sparked with the energy of a new drama.

"Yes and yes. Please call North McKenzie Hospital while I'm gone."

"What do I say?"

"Just ask if they have a patient named Diane Warner. If they do, find out whatever you can."

"I'll do it now."

Sula thanked her and hurried from the building.

Driving up Spring Boulevard, Sula barely noticed the half-million-dollar homes. A dark thought kept circling in her brain. What if Rudker had made Warner disappear? It was such a huge leap that she kept pushing the idea away. Her family's trauma had left her with a tendency to *catastrophize*, and blaming Rudker seemed like a classic example of that response.

First, there was no reason yet to assume Warner had disappeared. She might be home, sick in bed, and not answering the phone. Second, even if Warner was gone—for whatever reason—it didn't mean Rudker had anything *directly* to do with it. He may have driven the woman from her job with intimidation or threats, but that was life in the corporate world. Dr. Warner seemed able to take care of herself.

Sula slowed as she approached the 2800 block. Considering the value of the homes here, Sula figured Warner was doing quite well financially and could afford to miss a few days of work or quit without notice. Now she felt apprehensive about her visit. She was overreacting and butting into someone's personal life. She could get fired.

She parked in front of Warner's home and felt a flash of envy. Set back from the road on a slight rise, the house was four times the size of her little place and beautifully designed with fieldstone inlay. The lush yard was thick with grass, ferns, and hostas. Sula wondered if Dr. Warner hired someone to take care of it. She couldn't imagine the tiny scientist out here mowing the slope on weekends.

The truck still running, Sula sat for a few minutes, paralyzed with indecision. What would she say? *Just checking to see if you're all right.* Would that seem reasonable to Warner?

Sula shut off the engine. Now that she was here, she had to check. No one would criticize her for being too concerned. She started up the driveway, her pumps clicking against the smooth asphalt while rain dampened her clothes. Someone was watching her, she could feel it. Sula paused under the covered front deck to check her watch, 9:07, and take a deep breath before ringing the doorbell.

After a two-minute wait, she rang again. Nobody came to the door or stirred inside the house. What now? Should she leave a note? She'd already left a message on the answering machine. She noticed the green newspaper box was stuffed with several editions. Sula trotted down the steps and along the front sidewalk. She stared at the huge garage door and wondered if Warner's car was inside. A locked gate prevented her from walking around to the side of the garage and peeking through the windows. That was probably a good thing. In this neighborhood, that sort of activity would likely get her arrested.

Sula jogged back to the truck and cranked up the heater. She was wet and cold and worried. She reminded herself it was too soon to jump to conclusions. She would wait to see if Serena's call to the hospital had netted any information.

As Sula entered Prolabs' driveway, she saw a young man on a bicycle. It was Robbie Alvarez and he seemed to be late for work. She slowed and rolled down her window.

"Hi, Robbie."

"Hey, Sula. How's it going?"

"Good. Except that every time I see you on your bike, I feel guilty that I don't get enough exercise."

He laughed. "I don't do it for the exercise. I'm just too broke to drive and the people on the bus scare me."

"Any progress with Julie?" He'd told her about his affections one day when they had lunch together in the cafeteria.

"Not yet. But I keep trying."

"That's all you can do. Have a good day."

"I will."

Sula drove away, thinking Robbie seemed so sweet, so different from his father. She understood why he used a different last name and didn't want people to know they were related.

"Dr. Warner is not in the hospital," Serena blurted out as Sula entered the HR office.

"I don't think she's at home either." Sula called Northwest McKenzie again and asked if they had any unidentified patients. They didn't.

Marcy, the HR director, stepped out of her office and joined their conversation. "I called Dr. Warner's son, Jeff, and left him a message. He's the only family member we have contact information for."

"Should we file a missing-persons report?" Sula asked.

"Let's wait to see what her son says. If he hasn't heard from her, we will."

Sula went back to her office and distracted herself by responding to the e-mails and phone calls that had piled up that morning.

At noon, she bought a Luna bar from a vending machine and took it outside to the bench in the courtyard. The drizzle had stopped but the sky was still dark. The R&D building loomed in front of her and she couldn't stop thinking about Dr. Warner. The knot in her stomach made Sula feel certain the woman was not coming back.

What would happen to her research files? Would Rudker destroy Warner's work on the genetic response to Nexapra? Without Warner, the clinical trials would surely move forward and the screening test would be forgotten. The thought filled her with dismay.

People could not be allowed to kill themselves simply because Rudker was too greedy and too impatient to develop a diagnostic test. Sula had suffered the grief of losing someone to suicide and had experienced the impulse herself more than once. She could not sit back and let those lives be lost. The trials had to be stopped. But how? She couldn't go to the FDA without proof. All she had was a conversation she'd overheard. The recording she'd made was barely audible, and she couldn't do anything that would risk her job right now.

Sula wondered if Peterson or one of the other scientists was aware of Warner's discovery. If they knew about the genetic/suicide link, why hadn't they been at the meeting with Rudker to back Warner up?

The horrible thought came back to her. Rudker made Warner disappear. What if he had not stopped at intimidation? On an intuitive level, Sula knew the man was capable of violence. But would he hurt—possibly kill—someone over money?

The thought made her jump up. She had to stay rational about this. She would be no help to Dr. Warner or future Nexapra patients if people thought she was a flake. Sula tossed her wrapper in the trash and went back into the building.

She tried to write a press release, but she couldn't stop thinking about Warner's files. If the doctor had simply pulled a vanishing act, maybe she'd left behind the data that would point out Nexapra's fatal flaw and put a stop to its development. Somebody had to get to that information before Rudker did. Unless it was already too late.

Chapter 8

Robbie had arranged with his supervisor to take the morning off so he could keep his appointment with the Oregon Research Center. They had asked him a dozen questions over the phone: "What is your blood pressure?" "Have you ever tried to kill yourself?" "Do you use illegal drugs?" He smoked pot every once in a while, but it had been weeks since the last time and they didn't need to know about it. This morning he had another screening.

The research center was on Twentieth Avenue and Willamette, so it was an easy bike ride from his apartment near the University of Oregon campus. It drizzled lightly on the way, but he had rain gear and didn't mind. If the weather got worse while he was in the clinic, he'd strap his bike to the front of a city bus and get to work from there. He liked to ride, but he wasn't a martyr about it the way some people were.

The small two-story building looked new and Robbie didn't recall seeing it before. Gray and uninviting with minimal windows.

He locked his bike to a sturdy metal rack and went inside. The interior looked like a cross between a dentist's office and the unemployment division: plush carpeting and soft tones in the front and counseling cubes in the rear. He approached the receptionist and told her he had an appointment.

"For the depression trial? Excellent. Do you have a referring physician?" She had a friendly smile and didn't sound like she grew up in Eugene. Robbie couldn't place the accent.

"No. I work at Prolabs and saw a flyer in the lunchroom."

"Excellent. One of the company's own." She handed him a clipboard with a thick stack of papers. "I need you to fill out this questionnaire. Then we'll analyze your qualifications and let you know if you're eligible. If you are, Dr. Lucent will give you a complete physical. Also, there's a consent form in the back. Please read through it, but it isn't necessary to sign it yet."

"Okay." Robbie wondered what would make him eligible. Did he have to be despondent? Or too poor to afford medication?

The paperwork took forty-five minutes. After completing a health history, the next section detailed the symptoms of depression: sadness or irritability, low energy, difficulty concentrating, insomnia, low self-esteem, loss of interest in social or physical activities. For each, he had to indicate how often he experienced the symptoms and how long the feelings lasted. Then the questions became more specific: *Have you ever taken medicine for depression?* Yep. He listed the other drug he'd taken and noted that he was using Zoloft now.

Have you ever had thoughts of killing yourself? Didn't everybody? He'd never acted on those feelings, so he hesitated to check yes. He figured this was one of the important questions that would determine eligibility. Were they looking for people with serious depression or were they screening out the extremes? He decided to be honest and checked *Yes*. For frequency, he indicated *Occasionally*. He finally flipped to the consent form, which went on for pages about side effects and liability. Robbie skimmed over it. They wouldn't give people the drug if it weren't safe.

He returned the clipboard to the receptionist. She smiled. "If you'd like to wait, one of our clinicians will review this now to determine your eligibility."

"If you're going to run a credit check, I might as well leave now."

She gave him a hearty laugh, which cheered him up considerably.

While he waited, Robbie stepped outside and smoked a cigarette. He'd picked up the habit in high school, and even though he had come to hate it as much as his parents did, he couldn't quit. Every time he tried, he ended up too depressed to function. So he limited himself to five or so a day most of the time. Nicotine had a direct effect on brain chemicals, and his brain needed all the stimulus it could get.

It began to rain, so he tossed the butt into the wet bark and went back inside to wait. In a few minutes, a pretty woman in a white coat came out and called his name.

"Hi. I'm Dr. Lucent. I believe you're eligible for this trial. Would you like to proceed?" She had nearly black hair, an easy smile, and reminded him a little bit of his mother.

"Sure."

"Great. Let's go back to my office and go over some information."

Robbie followed her back to a small room that looked somewhat like a doctor's examining area. She motioned him to sit and they spent about twenty minutes going over his answers to the depression questions. Dr. Lucent kept asking him to rate his feelings on a scale of one to ten. She jotted down his responses and, at the end, performed a calculation.

After a moment, she said, "The good news is that this is not a placebo trial. The sponsor is testing its investigational therapy, Nexapra, against the currently marketed therapy, Prozac. You will be taking one of the two, but you won't know which one. Did you read the consent form?"

"Yes."

"Do you feel you have a thorough understanding of the possible side effects?"

"I'm familiar with antidepressants."

"Do you have any questions about the medication or the trial?"

"When do I start the new drug?"

"In a few days. First, you need to sign the consent form, then I'll give you a complete physical, including an electrocardiogram to make sure your heart is healthy. I'll also draw some blood. We'll test for illegal drug use, anemia, mineral imbalances, and such."

The doctor crossed her legs and leaned forward. Robbie got a glimpse of cleavage and his blood responded.

"You'll take home a two-week supply of therapy today," she continued. "But you must stop taking your other medication for two days before you start. I'll give you a journal to jot down your experiences every day. Please note your emotional feelings as well as any changes in physical health. Any questions?"

"No." Robbie had barely been listening. Dr. Lucent was quite attractive.

The doctor handed him the clipboard with the final page of the consent form on top. Robbie signed it and handed it back. Dr. Lucent smiled brightly.

The blood pressure and heart rate check took five minutes, and the touch of Dr. Lucent's hands made his heart pound a bit.

The electrocardiogram took longer and made him appreciate how careful the researchers were to ensure the clinical trial didn't harm anyone.

In the end, Dr. Lucent announced he was in fine health and retrieved a pharmacy bottle from a locked cabinet. The plain white container had a bar code and a lot number and nothing else.

"Be sure to come back for a new supply before your current supply runs out. It's important not to miss a day." She peered over her glasses to emphasize her point. "If you experience anything unusual or concerning, please call me right away."

"I live on campus, I experience unusual things every day."

Dr. Lucent smiled. "Seriously. Call me if you experience any mental or physical problems."

"All right. See you in two weeks."

It wasn't raining when he left so Robbie rode his bike out West Eighteenth toward Prolabs. The ride energized him. In fact, he felt pretty damn good. For a moment, he had second thoughts about changing medications. Then he remembered how excited his father had been about this drug when Prolabs' scientists first started to test it. That was years ago, when Robbie still lived at home and his parents were still together. He had never seen his father look so happy, so sure of something. He might as well give the drug a try.

As he was pedaling down Prolabs' driveway, a car came up beside him and slowed. Sula, the company's PR person, stopped and chatted with him for a moment. He'd gotten to know her a little and liked her a lot. She was too old for him as a girlfriend, plus she had a kid. Still, she seemed like someone he could count on as a friend.

* * *

Cricket stood outside the entrance to the city-council meeting holding a big sign that read *No Exceptions!* on one side and *Water Quality First!* on the other. He'd arrived at city hall at six in the evening, and every person entering the special session had seen his message.

The land Prolabs wanted to build a new factory on was within the city limits and was designated wetlands. He knew the state land-use codes, and the property could not be developed by any party other than the city. Even the city was required to apply to the land-use commission for a redesignation. The rules were clear, but as usual, big business was trying to go around them.

Cricket accepted that he and his group might not be able to stop the Prolabs/JB Pharma expansion, but at least they could keep it from being too easy. Sometimes, if they threw up enough roadblocks, the corporate money-suckers backed off and went looking for another opportunity.

Despite the seriousness of the situation, Cricket was enjoying himself. He smiled at everyone who had come out on this bright but cool evening to speak their minds. Groups of college students, middle-aged couples in matching Birkenstocks and sweaters, sweet old couples, who sometimes turned out to be not so sweet when they stood up and started expressing their views. And others like him, with dreadlocks and hemp clothes. He knew most of the natural folks—as he thought of them—from Saturday Market, where he sold his handmade bongo drums and copper jewelry. Only three people from his Love the Earth group were here tonight. The rest had gone to Florence to protest a plan to build a Costco on oceanfront property.

Most people smiled back. Some gave him thumbs-up gestures or peace signs. Ten minutes before the meeting was scheduled to start, Cricket moved down the steps, so he had a better view of passing traffic and they had a better view of him. He hoped to catch the attention of a TV reporter. A little news coverage could rally a lot of support.

Two men coming up the sidewalk caught his eye. They wore denim work shirts sporting political buttons that said: *Jobs first!* Cricket smiled and held out a pamphlet that outlined the environmental impact of chemical factories on wetlands. One man started to reach for it, then caught the words on Cricket's sign. He abruptly pulled back.

"If you drink city water, you should read this." Cricket spoke softly. He never preached and he never raised his voice in nonconfrontational situations.

"No thanks." They looked at him with disgust, then walked past. At least they hadn't sworn or spit at him, which happened sometimes.

A few minutes later, a white KRSL TV van pulled up in front of the wide steps. Trina Waterman, his favorite TV reporter, stepped out, followed by a cameraman. Cricket couldn't believe his luck. He moved into the center of the steps. The young blonde reporter and the camera guy both looked at him, then at each other, then shrugged. Trina, particularly pretty in a pale-blue suit, motioned him to come down.

Cricket practiced what he would say as they set up for the shot. Then Trina asked his name.

"Cricket."

"Just Cricket?"

"Yep. I'm with Love the Earth, a Eugene-based environmental group dedicated to keeping the water supply clean."

Speaking toward the camera, Trina gave a brief background about Prolabs' plans and the special council meeting. Then she gave Cricket's name and affiliation before asking, "Why do you oppose this development?" She held the microphone out to him.

Cricket was ready. "First, it's illegal. The land is zoned for preservation and only the city can change that. Second, Prolabs wants to build a chemical factory. Yes, they call them pharmaceuticals, but they're still chemicals. And those chemicals leech into our water supply during the manufacturing process. They also enter our water supply through human use. In some places, there's so much estrogen and progestin in the water from discarded birth control that the fish and frogs are all becoming one sex and can no longer reproduce. In fact—"

Trina abruptly pulled the microphone away. "Thank you." She and the cameraman picked up their goods, then went around him and up the stairs. Cricket was so happy he would have done a little dance had he not been holding a heavy sign. She would probably edit out half of what he said, but that was fine. People who watched the news at eleven would think about the water supply. That made his day worthwhile.

It was only the beginning though. His group planned to fight Prolabs' development with everything they had. To be effective, they had to act now. They also had to get the attention of the media every time they staged a protest.

Chapter 9

Rudker spent the rest of the day in meetings talking about the merger. The details were overwhelming at times. Especially in regard to drug development. The companies had projects that overlapped and they argued passionately about which to continue and which to drop. Rudker believed Prolabs' cardiovascular lineup was superior, but JB's scientists wanted to throw all their resources into an anti-inflammatory molecule that had shown clinical activity against C-reactive proteins. After his humiliation that morning, Rudker refused to back down and they had left the matter unsettled.

At the end of the day he was mentally exhausted, yet physically charged. He left JB's campus on foot in search of a quiet place to eat. He wanted to be on the next flight back to Eugene, but he had another round of meetings scheduled for the morning. He was anxious to get back to Prolabs so he could confer with the Nexapra scientists and find out if anyone was aware of or supported the genetic-test idea. He also planned to search Warner's office and confiscate any evidence of that vulnerability.

He found a small French restaurant called Maximilien in Pike Place Market. It had a great view of the harbor, but Rudker was there for the food. He ordered Tournedos Rossini, a beef tenderloin seared with foie gras and served with truffle and Armagnac sauce. He nearly moaned with the pleasure of it. For dessert, he had the soufflé au Grand Marnier. It might have been the best meal he'd ever had. Temporarily satiated, he paid with his business card and stepped back out into the night.

The sky had cleared, so Rudker passed on a taxi and set out walking. He'd come to love downtown Seattle during his recent trips to meet with JB executives. The night energy was electric. In Eugene, you could find a little jazz and maybe one restaurant open after nine. In Seattle, you could find just about anything. And in this town, for now, he was still anonymous.

Rudker knew what he needed this evening—an outlet for his pent up frustration—and he knew exactly where to find it. He set off at a brisk pace and twenty minutes later reached the unmarked club. The entrance was located in an alley between Stewart and Powel Streets. There were no signs, no windows, and no outward indication that it was a place of business. In fact, he knew from experience that the door was locked and that there was no point in knocking.

In the dark alley, he pulled out his cell phone and called a confidential number. Last time he'd been to Seattle, one of JB's marketers had given him the number after several hours of drinking at Lucky's. The marketer had insisted Rudker enter the number directly into his phone rather than write it down. The cloak-and-dagger scenario had amused him.

An older man answered after two rings. "Yeah?" Rudker recognized the voice from last time.

"Karl Rudker. I'm at the door."

He turned to face the light fixture to the left of the door frame, where a small camera was hidden in the mounting. He knew the old guy was looking him over as they talked.

The man grunted. "Yep."

Rudker heard the locking mechanism click and reached for the handle. He pushed the door open and quickly stepped inside. The brick-lined hallway was barely lit and smelled of moss and cigarette butts. It led up a flight of stairs, where he encountered another solid metal door. He pushed the buzzer and waited. The old guy with bad teeth and a cell phone opened the door and held out his hand. Rudker pressed four fifties into it. They did not speak.

The old guy went back to his table, and Rudker entered the small dark bar. It reeked of cigarette smoke. He'd wished he'd gone back to the hotel and changed. The smoke smell was tough to get out of suits with standard dry cleaning. He approached the counter, and the bartender, a nearly bald guy in his late fifties, looked up and nodded. Two guys near the end of the bar also gave him a quick glance. Rudker gave them a casual head lift in response.

The dozen or so male customers ranged from twenty to seventy. A few were dressed in suits like him, but most were in some variation of jeans and work jackets. There wasn't much heat in the place.

Rudker stood at the end of the bar and ordered a Jack Daniel's and Coke. He wasn't a big drinker—too much alcohol slowed his mind—but some social situations required a drink in hand. He made obligatory chitchat with the bartender about the Mariners' prospects for a good season, then kept to himself until it was time.

At nine thirty, a door in the back of the bar opened, and the men gathered up their drinks and moved through it. The next room was slightly larger than the bar but equally devoid of windows or features. The brick walls sported a few graffiti scrawls but that was it. A small boxing ring filled the center of the room, and a platform with bench seats surrounded the fight area. Rudker was one of the last to enter, and he took a seat near the door. Memories of his first time in the club flooded him, and his breath became shallow with anticipation.

In a few minutes, the fighters entered and passed within a few feet of him. An intoxicating mix of sweat and shampoo hit his nostrils. The girls were both in their early twenties and reasonably attractive—for fist fighters. The blonde was outfitted in a skintight black workout suit with a white sports bra showing underneath. The other girl, with black spiky hair, wore a red halter top with tight purple shorts. She reminded him of the girl in the airport.

The bartender doubled as the referee and entered the ring. He announced the contenders without much ceremony. "Tonight's match is between Felicia the Fearless," he said, pointing at the blonde, "And Badass Brenda."

The dark-haired girl with black eye makeup pivoted in a full circle and waved. The bartender held up a small cowbell, gave it a ring, then quickly stepped out of the way.

The girls circled each other for a moment, then Felicia lurched forward and smashed her bare fist into the side of Brenda's face. The blow glanced off as Brenda pulled away. Rudker's pulse began to accelerate. After a few wild swings, Brenda connected with Felicia's nose in an audible smack. Blood trickled down onto the girl's pale lips. Rudker felt himself get hard.

Then the girls got with it, raining blows on each other with an unexpected ferocity. Brenda went down, and Felicia jumped on her, pummeling her in the face and chest. Rudker realized he'd been holding his breath and gulped for air.

He wanted to be in there, swinging away, fists crashing into tender flesh. Girls, guys, it didn't matter. It was all about release. But his executive position in a conservative industry didn't allow him to live that close to the edge. Showing up for work with a black eye and a fat lip could derail his career. He had not fought with anyone in years. The other night in the parking lot didn't count. That skirmish had been unexpected and accidental.

The fight had only three rounds, each five minutes long. At the end, the audience voted for a winner with applause, and Felicia was the clear favorite. Brenda gave them all the finger and stormed out. Felicia circled the ring twice, arms raised in victory, blood running from her face, then left the room. Rudker wished it had lasted longer, but still, it was the best seventeen minutes he'd spent in a long time.

Chapter 10

Thursday, April 15

Sula went through the same morning routine she'd carried out the day before, only today she felt more panicked. First she called Warner's extension and got no answer, then she called Steve Peterson, who still had not seen or heard from the doctor. She called Warner's cell and home numbers. No answer and no room left to leave a message. Something was definitely wrong, and it was time to call the police. Still, she hesitated. Once the cops got involved, it might be impossible to search Warner's office for the suicide data.

Sula was angry with herself for not doing it yesterday afternoon. She had thought about it obsessively, even formulating several plans. One had involved stealing the master keys to the R&D building from Bob Wurtzer, the building-maintenance guy. She had immediately rejected the idea as insane. It had occurred to her Marcy had keys to all the offices because she was the one who gave people keys when they were hired. Sula had tried to come up with a workable plan for borrowing Marcy's keys, but both ideas were so out of character for her mode of thinking and acting that she had become paralyzed with fear.

Now it was too late. Her priority had to be about Warner herself. The doctor was clearly missing. Sula took the elevator up one level to the human-resources office on the third floor. She checked her watch: 8:27.

Serena's first words were, "Have you heard anything about Diane Warner?"

"She's not in again today. Is Marcy in her office?"

"Yep. Go on in. I think she's expecting you."

Marcy was on the phone, so Sula waited in the doorway. Marcy signaled her to sit. The HR director was listening intently to someone on the phone. Her legs were crossed and the one on top swung impatiently. Finally she said, "You will try to reach him though?"

A pause.

"Thanks. Give him my number please." Marcy hung up and turned to Sula.

"Diane's son, Jeff, works for Doctors Without Borders. Right now, he's in a remote village in Somalia. That was his answering service. They said they would try to track him down and give him my number. I didn't tell them his mother was missing, because we don't know that for sure yet."

"She isn't here again this morning. I think we should call the police." Sula sounded more confident than she felt.

"Did you try her house?"

"Yes."

"Okay. It's time." Marcy heaved a big sigh. "I'm supposed to fly to Seattle today for meetings with JB's human-resources department."

"I'll help in any way I can." For a second, Sula was tempted to suggest that Marcy let her check out Dr. Warner's office, but she chickened out.

Marcy grabbed a phone book and looked up the non-emergency number for the Eugene Police Department. Sula stood to leave.

"Please stay," Marcy pleaded.

Sula sat back down. While Marcy explained the situation to someone at the police department, Sula casually looked around the office for where the director might keep her set of master keys. A desk drawer was the most likely spot, but maybe a filing cabinet. Sula noticed a set of dark-brown luggage leaned against one wall. Marcy was traveling; she would be gone later today. Sula suddenly realized that the woman was talking to her.

"When you went to her house, did you notice if her car was there?" Marcy held her hand over the phone as she talked.

"I didn't see it, but it could have been in the garage."

Marcy relayed the information, then listened for a minute. "I'll send her in right away."

A wave of panic passed through Sula's chest. Marcy hung up and announced, "They want you to come in and fill out a report."

"Why me?"

"Because you noticed she was missing. You went to her house."

Sula's hands instinctively went to her stomach, so she could feel her breathing at work. She could do this. "Should I go *now*?"

"Yes. Officer Rice is expecting you. Thanks, Sula. I appreciate all your help in this matter." Marcy looked relieved.

"How long will you be gone?"

"Only two days. I'll give you my cell-phone number, and I want you to call me with any updates." The HR director jotted down her number on a yellow sticky and passed it to Sula.

She sucked in her breath for nerve, then blurted out, "What if the police want to search Dr. Warner's office?"

Marcy tapped her desk. "Bob can let them in. He has masters to everything."

"I'll go down to the police station now. Have a good flight." Sula turned to leave.

"Wait. Bob is so hard to track down sometimes. I'd better give you the key." Marcy opened her desk drawer and took out a small key, then used it to open the main filing cabinet behind her desk. Sula held her breath. She kept expecting the woman to change her mind again, but Marcy extracted a gold-colored key from a large ring and handed it to her.

"Keep me posted. Oh, and please let Mr. Rudker know what's going on. He's been in Seattle, but he should be back this evening." Marcy gave a small laugh. "We'll probably pass each other in the air."

"I'll go see him in the morning." Sula squeezed the key in her hand. Not a chance in hell she would walk into Rudker's office voluntarily. She gave Marcy a small wave and left.

She could not believe her luck. She wanted to run directly to the R&D building and begin her search, but she had to talk to the police first. After that, Marcy would be gone, and she would have a perfect opportunity. She stopped in her office for her sweater and her purse, then headed out to the parking lot. As she drove downtown, she felt guilty about how little work she'd accomplished in the past few days. Warner's disappearance had thrown everything out of whack.

The Eugene police shared a building with the city court and city council. The white-brick structure formed an L shape around a large round fountain and took up an entire block. Sula got lucky again and found a parking spot right across the street. She locked the Dakota and headed up the wide stairs. The department's entrance was a small, dark lobby with two chairs. A desk officer sat behind a plexiglass window with a speaker mounted in the middle. Sula stated her name and business and said Officer Rice was expecting her. The desk officer made a call. Sula couldn't hear the conversation, but in a few minutes, a solid metal door to the right opened and a woman with cropped blonde hair stepped out into the lobby. She held the door open with her body.

"I'm Officer Rice." She was so buff, she seemed to burst out of her uniform.

Sula felt puny next to her. She held out her hand anyway. "I'm Sula Moreno." The cop's grip was as firm as expected. Sula vowed to start exercising more.

She followed the buff cop down a short hallway, where she made a left into a small office. It had no windows, and Sula hoped she wouldn't be there long. Step by step, she retraced her thoughts and actions during the past two days concerning Dr. Warner. She didn't mention her wild thoughts about Rudker or the argument she'd overheard. It probably had nothing to do with Warner's absence, and Sula didn't want to seem like a crazy person.

Rice's pale-blue eyes registered a connection and she stopped in the middle of another question to ask, "How old is Diane Warner?"

"Somewhere in her fifties."

"What does she look like?"

"She's small. With shoulder-length grayish-blonde hair. I think she has blue eyes, but they could be gray or green. I'm sorry to say that I don't know for sure."

"That's fine. Does she have family that you know of?"

"A son named Jeff, but he's in Somalia."

"I think I know where she is. Do you have a few minutes?"

Puzzled, Sula said, "Sure," without thinking.

"Come with me." Detective Rice stood and held the door for her. Sula started to head back the way they came, but Rice said, "No, this way."

They exited the building through the basement and headed for a black-and-white squad car. Rice unlocked the passenger side and waited for Sula to get in. She stared at the vehicle, legs trembling with fear.

"You all right?" Rice watched her closely.

"Uh, yes." Sula willed herself to step forward and get into the car. The smell of sweat and fear and vomit wafted out of the seat and triggered a powerful memory of the last time she'd been in a cop car. *Her mother was dead. Her beautiful sister Calix was dead. Sula, covered in blood, wailed and rocked back and forth as they drove to the hospital. She wanted to die. As they crossed the bridge over the Willamette River, she tried to open the door and throw herself out, but it was locked.*

Sula fought to bring herself out of it. She used her stomach muscles to pull in air and recited her mantra: *I'm okay now. Life is good. Everything is fine.*

"Buckle up, please." Rice's voice broke through. They hadn't even left the parking structure. Sula did as she was told and Rice backed the car out. As they pulled into the street, Sula looked around for something to focus on. The sky was gray and all she could see were government buildings. She searched for something that would make her feel peaceful. Nothing came to mind. Out of desperation, she focused on Aaron, the cute guy she'd run into the other day.

Rice cut into her thoughts. "You know we're going to the morgue, right?"

"Oh shit." Sula began to shake. She reached for her purse and dug out a small pill bottle. In it she kept Excedrin for headaches and a few Xanax for emergencies like this. She popped the tiny white pill into her mouth, worked up some spit and swallowed. She could feel it stick in her throat. She worked up another round of spit and kept swallowing.

"What was that?"

"A mild tranquilizer. I have a prescription."

"I'm sorry to spring that on you. I thought you understood when I said I knew where she was."

"I'm all right." It was a lie, but Sula willed herself to be calm. "What do I have to do?"

"Look at a body." Rice glanced over as she drove. "Some kids found her by the river near the Rose Garden a couple of days ago. She was dressed in jogging clothes and didn't have any ID."

"How did she die?"

"Blunt trauma to the head."

Sula felt sick. She rolled down her window for air.

"Were you close to Warner?"

"I didn't really know her. But she was a scientist. She was trying to make the world a better place."

"Let's wait and see if it's her."

Rice pulled into a no-parking area in front of Northwest McKenzie, which was only ten blocks from city hall. They entered through the emergency area and took the elevator to the basement.

"We call this Surgery Ten," Rice said as she pushed open the door. Sula didn't let herself look at the room, registering only stainless steel and the smell of chemicals. It was better not to see the details, less likely to haunt her dreams. The Xanax hadn't had a chance to work, so she tried to think about a long hike in the woods on a warm summer day.

Rice handed her a thick white mask for her nose and mouth, and Sula put it on. She waited with her eyes closed. After a minute, she sensed movement and opened her eyes. A man in a blue scrub suit had pushed a gurney up next to her. The outline of a body was clearly visible under a white sheetlike cloth. The guy in the scrub suit pulled the sheet away from the face.

It was Dr. Warner. Yet it wasn't. Her color was wrong and part of her head was flattened and crusted with dried blood. Sula nodded and fled the room. Out in the hallway, she pulled off her mask and leaned over with her hands on her knees. She took long, slow breaths until she could stand back up. Rice came out and touched her arm. "Thanks for helping us."

"Can we go now?"

"Sure."

On the drive back to city hall, Rice told her they had arrested a homeless man in connection with the murder and were questioning him. She said she would be in touch if she needed more information. She handed Sula a business card and told her to take the afternoon off.

Images of Warner jogging along the river and being attacked by a crazed man swarmed in her head as she drove back to Prolabs. The tranquilizer kicked in about the time she reached the parking lot and she was able to focus her thoughts. Although she felt entitled to take the afternoon off, this was her best opportunity to search Warner's office and she was more determined than ever to do it. Warner's work was too important to let it die with her. Too many lives were at stake.

Chapter 11

Rudker's first meeting Thursday morning didn't wrap up until nearly ten, and his jaws tensed with irritability. JB's marketing people had been unprepared to discuss Nexapra's market position, so they had talked about other products with little growth potential. What a colossal waste of time.

With a growing sense of urgency to get back to Prolabs, he called JB's head of R&D and left him a brief message, canceling their ten thirty meeting. Without notifying anyone that he was leaving, he took a cab to his hotel and asked the driver to wait. Fifteen minutes later, he was back in the taxi, overnight bag in hand. He hoped to make an afternoon flight and be at Prolabs before Peterson and the others went home for the day.

Unlike the quiet of his arrival, Sea-Tac airport was a swarm of people mid-day. Rudker aggressively cut through the crowds with barely an "excuse me." He needed to be first on the standby list.

This time he was pulled out for a personal search. "Remove your socks, please." The giant lesbian looked like a prison warden.

"Why the socks?" Rudker made no attempt to be pleasant.

"It's part of the process, sir. Please just do it."

Goddamn. He hated showing his feet in public. His toenails were hideous. "This is ridiculous."

Rudker pulled off his socks, then stood still while the bitch ran her wand up between his legs and over his shoulders. He barely contained his urge to kidney-punch her.

The fat bitch behind the table took her time too, probing into every pocket and pouch of his bag. He had nothing to hide, but the invasion of privacy galled him anyway.

"Do you have a prescription for this medicine?" The toad spoke loudly and held out his Zyprexa.

"Of course."

"May I see it?"

"You're looking at it. Read the label. That's my name."

"May I see your ID?"

"I just showed it to you."

"Show it to me again."

They were fucking with him. It was clear to anyone. Rudker could hear the air whistling in and out of his nose. He pulled out his driver's license again and held it up to her.

"Let go of it, please."

He bit down on the inside of his cheek, and the taste of blood filled his mouth. He reminded himself of what was important. Nexapra's development. The merger. His career. He let her have the license.

She looked at it closely, comparing the spelling of his name with that on the prescription. He wanted to smash her face. After a long minute, she handed it back. "Have a nice flight."

"Unlikely." Rudker grabbed his bag and bolted before they could humiliate him further.

After a twenty-minute delay on the tarmac, his flight was short and uneventful. Halfway through it, he realized he'd forgotten to take his medication that morning. He pulled his bag down from the overhead compartment, dug out his meds, and popped one. He landed in Eugene just after four, grabbed a cab, and headed for Prolabs.

* * *

Sula entered the R&D building and walked briskly toward Warner's office. Her plan was to be bold, so that no one would question her. If they did, she'd say the police had asked her to look in the office for family contact information. She had planned to do the search right after lunch, but the HR director had called Sula up to her office and spent an hour going over a list of things she wanted done immediately. Sula had completed most of them, while getting up every five minutes to look out the window to see if Marcy's Scion had left the parking lot.

Once she was in the R&D building, her heart hammered with anxiety. Sula unlocked Warner's door, stepped into the office, and closed it behind her. Her watch said 4:11.

The tall windows and incredible view caught her attention, but she did not allow herself to gaze out on the lush green hillside. She sat at Warner's desk and pulled open the top drawers. The neatness was stunning. Right away she spotted a small collection of keys in a special little holder.

The second one she tried opened the drawers of the large, main filing cabinet. Sula riffled quickly through the folders, all labeled with phrases like *Cellular response to tumor necrosis factor*. She wasn't sure what she expected to find, but simple concepts like Nexapra or Nexapra's Clinical Trials would have been helpful. She opened and searched the second drawer. It was also full of specific-science labels.

Sula checked her watch: 4:18.

In the third and fourth drawers there were folders with drug names, but most were products already on the market. Shit. Sula wanted to get into Warner's computer, but that was risky and possibly pointless. Without an access code to the R&D database, she likely wouldn't find much. She opened the smaller filing cabinet.

There it was. A foot-thick Nexapra section, with folder after folder.

The reams of paper almost overwhelmed her. She could spend days looking through this stuff and still not find exactly what she needed. She checked her watch: 4:23. She had eight minutes left. She had promised herself she would be in and out in twenty minutes.

Sula frantically flipped through the files, looking for key words such as *suicide* or *genetic response*. The first half of the stack appeared to be about the preclinical development with many references to mice and rats. The second half looked more like a collection of personal notes and observations. She spotted a section with references to patients.

Sula pulled out a handful and rushed to the copier in the corner. She shoved the papers into the auto loader, and while they copied, went to the large desk drawers and began to search. If Warner's genetic discovery was recent, perhaps her notes about it were kept in an active file around her desk. Sula checked her watch: 4:28. She decided to give herself a little more time.

* * *

Rudker had called a cab from the plane, so he had to wait only a few minutes in front of the airport. The dark-green sedan pulled up and an elderly man with a bin Laden beard got out to greet him. Rudker said "Prolabs" and hopped into the backseat. His butt made contact with something small and flat on the back of the seat. Rudker reached behind him and found a driver's license belonging to Richard Morgenstern. The first thing he noticed was that the man shared his basic characteristics: late forties, blondish-gray, and wide jaw. Impulsively, he pocketed the license. It would come in handy for visiting some of Seattle's private clubs while remaining anonymous.

Just knowing he could pretend to be someone else gave him a warm, sexy vibe. He was already eager to use the ID. It made him impatient with the driver, who took his time jotting down information.

"It's on Willow Creek Road," he offered, hoping to get rolling.

"I know where it is."

Of course he did. Prolabs was the biggest business in Eugene. It had started out twenty years ago as a little company that made drug-discovery equipment. Then the founder, who had a talent for raising venture capital, had developed his own high-throughput screening lab. A couple of early hits, which the company had held on to instead of licensing out, had launched its drug-making business. Rudker had been recruited to lead the company six years ago when the founder retired. Most days, it seemed like a good career move. Now he looked forward to the day that flying into Eugene meant only a quick trip to check on the factories.

The twelve-minute drive took twenty. First they hit blue-collar traffic going home from their factory jobs, then a quick stop for a soda took way longer than it should have.

Finally he was driving down Willow Creek toward the company. He could feel himself starting to relax a little. It would be such a relief to put this genetic-test idea completely to rest.

As soon as they turned onto the lane leading up to corporate headquarters, Rudker knew something was wrong. For starters, a white media van was driving in front of them. Up ahead he saw a group of people with picket signs milling around in front of the main office. Goddamn protestors. What the hell was it this time? Giving drugs to poor little mice? People who complained about using animals to test drugs, then took any kind of pharmaceutical when they were sick or in pain, were hypocrites. How else could they get compounds through development?

Damn. This was annoying. Rudker had no intention of dealing with any of it. He had real business to take care of. His PR person had better be out there handling it. It's what she was paid to do.

They reached the turnoff to the main parking lot. "Keep going," he told the cabbie.

As they passed, Rudker peered out the window. A young man with dreadlocks climbed on top of an old green VW van and stood to address the crowd. Someone passed a sign up to him. He held it over his head. Rudker could barely make out the words, but he thought it said *Chemicals Kill.* The scene faded from his sight as the cab moved down the lane. He snorted at the stupidity of the message.

Chapter 12

Cricket was pleased by the turnout. From the top of the van, he counted at least thirty people. Most were Love the Earth members but there were a few faces he didn't recognize.

"Hey, Cricket, KRSL is here." Troy, his friend and fellow earth protector, pointed at a white van coming down the long paved entry.

"Cool. Hand me my sign."

Troy passed it up to him and Cricket held it high over his head. Sometimes drama was the only way to get people's attention, especially the press. He had called Trina Waterman and spoken to her in person about the protest. She'd wished him luck and hung up. But now here she was. Or at least someone from her network was here. Cricket smiled. Must be another slow news day in Eugene.

He shouted, "No exceptions for polluters," a few times and the small group joined him for another seven or so repetitions. He kept his eye on the van, only to see it stop and back out between the rows of cars. Once on the main entry road, it followed the taxi that had been behind it and was now headed for a back entrance.

Cricket was disappointed. The city council had voted two nights ago to allow Prolabs' development to proceed. The bulldozers would resume immediately, and according to the building plans filed, the company was set to pour concrete in less than two weeks. Love the Earth would need a lot more public support than they currently had to stop it from happening. Otherwise, they would have to resort to sabotage.

* * *

The taxi reached the small auxiliary parking lot near the R&D building. "Let me off near the main door," Rudker said abruptly. He paid the man and gave him a ten-dollar tip. Grabbing his shoulder bag, he'd hauled himself out of the cab. It irritated him that he would have to carry his bag back to his car in the main parking lot later, but it was better than facing the protestors.

Rudker checked his watch: 4:31. Peterson would still be here. A vehicle door slammed behind him. Rudker turned and saw that the media van had followed him back here. *Damn.* A little blonde reporter tried to attract his attention. Rudker jogged for the R&D building.

* * *

When the van door slammed in the parking lot, Sula jumped so hard she smashed her knee on the underside of the desk. Unnerved, she shoved the drawer closed and bolted out of the chair. It was time to go.

Sula moved toward the door. As she reached it, she heard a faint *click* behind her, as if something had shifted or fallen. An odd little sound that she couldn't ignore. She turned back and opened the drawer again. Lying on top of the green file folders—where nothing had been moments ago—was a CD case. Stuck to it were strips of scotch tape. It had been taped to the underside of the upper drawer and had fallen loose when she slammed the bottom drawer.

Heart still pounding, she grabbed the CD. If Warner had hidden it, it must be important. Sula wished like hell she had somewhere to put the disk. But neither her A-line black skirt nor her tailored button-up blouse had a pocket. She untucked her blouse, shoved the case under the waistband of her nylons, and started for the door again. As she grabbed the handle, she remembered the papers in the copier. Swearing under her breath, she turned back.

Moving quickly, Sula pulled the originals from the feeder tray and shoved them into the top drawer of the closest filing cabinet. She knew she should relock the cabinets, but her nerves would not let her stay a moment longer. She couldn't even let herself stop and look at her watch. She snatched up the copies she'd made and bolted for the door.

In the hallway she turned left, intending to head back out the way she'd come in. Then she saw him and her heart missed a beat. Rudker was just inside the entrance and coming her way. For a split second, they made eye contact.

Sula spun around and strode in the other direction.

"Hey!" He called after her, but she kept going. She couldn't be caught with the copied files. If not for the paperwork, she would have faced him. Running from the boss looked pretty bad, but it wasn't necessarily grounds for termination. If she could only make it to the side exit.

A female voice came out of nowhere. "Stop. I want to talk to you."

* * *

The busybody reporter caught up to Rudker and grabbed his arm. "I just want a short statement." He shook her off and kept moving. That damn PR person had been standing in front of Warner's office with a handful of paperwork. Now she was running from him. She had taken the papers from Warner's files; he was sure of it.

"A shot of you running from the press will make great coverage for me and bad publicity for you," the reporter yelled after him. Rudker hesitated. He saw Sula turn right at the end of the hall. *Shit.* There was a side door near the labs. Where would she go once she was outside? Across the courtyard to the corporate building? Through the parking lot? Rudker thought it might be better to head her off once she was outside the building.

He stopped and turned. The little newswoman was right in front of him and he nearly knocked her down. Her cameraman was huffing along right behind her.

"I'll give you one short statement and you'll leave me alone. And you can't air any images of me walking away. Deal?" He didn't know why the protestors were out front, but it didn't matter. He knew what he would say.

"Deal." She turned to the guy with the camera. "Ready?"

"Roll."

She held out the microphone. Rudker smiled and said, "Making life-saving medicines is the greatest business in the world. Protesting against it demonstrates ignorance and a lack of compassion for people who are suffering."

He closed his mouth and waited for the cameraman to get out of his away. When he did, Rudker pushed past both of them and ran out the main door. He didn't see Sula in the courtyard, so he started around the side of the building.

* * *

Once outside, Sula's instinct was to run to the front of the R&D lab, cross the courtyard, and scoot into the main building, where she could hide in the safety of her own office. She resisted the idea and turned right instead, running toward the back of the R&D building. From there, she had two choices: keep going up the hill into the trees or go right again and head for the auxiliary parking lot. Her instincts said *trees.* She loved the forest and always felt safe and happy there. She'd spent half her childhood hiking the hillside behind the family trailer.

Again, she resisted her impulse and sprinted across the narrow lawn that spanned the back of the building. The grass was soggy and her heels squished into the soil underneath, slowing her down. For a fleeting second, she wondered if any of the scientists were looking out the windows as she passed, wondering about the absurdity of her mad dash.

As she neared the corner, she slowed, chest heaving from exertion. It occurred to her that Rudker may have anticipated her moves. The last voice she'd heard behind her had not been his. Someone else, a woman, had spoken to him, perhaps slowing him down. To recoup that time, he had probably gone back out the front to cut her off. He could be right around the corner, waiting to grab her.

Sula stopped and gulped in air. A small cry of anguish rose in her throat. She fought the urge to sob. She had to be smart about this. Tall shrubs adorned the corner of the building, so she squatted between the greenery and the wall and peered around the corner. Her view was partially blocked by another shrub, so she slowly rose until she could see the full length of the building.

Rudker stood at the far corner, staring into the parking lot. Sula pulled back, stumbled through the shrub, and took off running—back the way she'd come, passing the same labs with the huge windows. Terrifying as it seemed, she decided to go back inside the R&D building. She would find a place to hide. Rudker might not think to look for her there. She hoped he would give up and go about his business.

Sula rounded the next corner, swinging wide around the shrubs. She sprinted for the side door, reached it, and turned the knob. It was locked.

The master key Marcy had given her for Diane's office was still in her right hand. Her left hand clutched the papers she'd copied. They were badly crumpled on one edge, but she still had them. A small sob escaped her throat. She had risked so much without even know if they had anything useful.

She remembered the disk and clutched at her stomach. It was still there. She could feel it through the layers of fabric. With trembling fingers, she shoved the key in the doorknob and turned. It clicked. Thank God. She entered the building, found the hallway empty, and headed for the labs in the back.

The research area had glass on the top half of most of its interior walls, but the individual labs were separated by supply rooms with solid walls. In the first lab, Sula saw a young man sitting at a bench and peering into a microscope. She kept moving.

The second lab appeared empty, so she entered it and reached for the door to its supply room. Locked again. She used the master key, stepped inside, and closed the door behind her. Her watch said 4:48. The five-by-eight room was lined with shelves filled with clinical supplies: beakers, petri dishes, and an assortment of things she didn't recognize. Sula got her bearings, turned the light off, and took a seat on the floor. She planned to stay until it was dark enough to sneak out.

She crossed her legs, straightened her back, and turned her palms up on each knee. Meditating would be the only way she could get through the long, claustrophobic wait. It took ten minutes just to get her heart slowed down. Emptying her mind proved to be more difficult. The process was abruptly interrupted by someone entering the lab. The sounds were soft but distinctive, the creak of a door, the click of a light switch, soft footsteps across the floor. Her heart took off again, like a startled bird in flight. Rudker had found her.

She heard whistling. A happy sound, very un-Rudker-like. She let out the breath she'd been holding and hoped whoever it was didn't plan to work late. The possibility that he would enter the closet kept Sula on edge.

She checked her watch, which glowed pale blue in the dark: 5:01. A few minutes later, she heard the lab door swing open again, and a different voice called out, "Peterson. Got a minute to talk?"

"Sure." The scientist's voice was barely audible in comparison.

Rudker's voice boomed again. "I just got back from Seattle and a meeting with JB's board of directors. They want some assurance that Nexapra is on track, that its efficacy is as good as we say it is, and that its side-effect profile is as good as we say it is."

"It's even better. We're always cautious in our assessments just to be on the safe side."

Sula stood and stepped toward the door. Peterson was hard to hear.

"Do you have any concerns about adverse drug reactions once the product hits the general public?"

"None. Of course, there will be some ADRs. You know that. It's part of the business. Why the sudden concern?"

"The board is reacting to the regulators who say people under eighteen shouldn't take SSRIs because of the possibility of suicide." Rudker was clearly dismissive of the idea. "They want assurance—before they spend millions on clinical trials and advertising—that the product won't be recalled or given a black-box warning before it produces an ROI."

Sula sensed that Rudker was probing to see what Peterson knew or thought about a genetic flaw.

"A black-box warning?" Peterson's scorn was unmistakable. "That's ridiculous. SSRIs are one of the safest developments to ever enter the market, and Nexapra is going to be the safest in the class. Is this about Warner's theory?"

"Partially."

"It's conjecture," Peterson responded. "Warner is a brilliant scientist, but she's wrong about this. Yes, there are genetic, metabolic differences in the rate at which patients process chemicals through their systems. But pharmaceuticals never made people kill themselves. The people who commit suicide while taking antidepressants are reacting to their own disease state. The drug just gives them the physical energy to act on their impulses."

Sula slumped in despair. Was Warner wrong? Had she risked her job—and possibly custody hearing—for nothing?

Rudker, on the other hand, was pleased. She could hear the happy tone in his voice when he said, "That settles it. I'll reassure the board that their concerns are unfounded. Thank you."

She heard the outer door open and the room went quiet. Peterson started moving around, but he didn't whistle. She realized he probably didn't know Warner was dead. One of the things Marcy had asked her to do was to write a memo to the staff about the R&D director's death, but Sula hadn't circulated it yet. People in the corporate building probably knew because Serena wouldn't be able to keep quiet about it, but the news had obviously not reached the researchers.

Sula started to sit back down, then hesitated. Peterson's foot-steps were moving toward the door.

Chapter 13

Rudker picked up his travel bag and headed out the front exit. He did not feel as relieved as he should have. For one thing, Sula had been in Warner's office and had taken some of her papers. He may not have caught up with her yet, but he would. More important, Diane Warner had specifically said she found a genetic marker that made the two patients susceptible. After hearing Peterson's views on the subject, it seemed Warner hadn't shared her latest discovery with her partner. Because she knew Peterson was skeptical of the whole concept? Or because she didn't have proof?

It also seemed clear that Sula had overheard Warner's concerns and was trying to investigate. But why? Rudker rarely understood other people's motives. He worried that she would go to the press and the negative publicity would scare JB's board. If the FDA demanded to look at the early data, the agency might request additional clinical trials. The drug could be delayed by a year or more. Investors would dump Prolabs' stock at the first hint of bad news, the share price would plummet, and he would be bankrupt. Rudker did not intend to allow any of that to happen.

The best defense was a good offense, he remembered as he crossed the courtyard into the corporate office. A few sales and marketing people who occupied the offices on the first floor were gathered in the hallway. He hoped to get by them without wasting too much time responding to their compulsive butt-kissing. That particular behavior made them good at their jobs, but it annoyed him, even on his good days. Today did not fall into that category.

"Mr. Rudker." One of the men spoke first.

"How was your flight?" a woman asked.

"It was fine. The merger is moving along efficiently."

They fell silent for a moment. Talk of the merger reminded them that their jobs were on the line.

Alicia, a tall redhead with plenty of cleavage, said, "It's too bad about Diane Warner."

The comment took him by surprise. "What do you mean?"

"You haven't heard?" Alicia looked uncomfortable.

"Heard what?"

The marketer who had spoken first, Kyle, he remembered, said softly, "She's dead, sir. They found her body near the river. They think a homeless man killed her while she was jogging."

Rudker scanned his brain for the right response, choosing, "That's terrible. When did this happen?"

"We don't know for sure." Alicia spoke up again. "Sula identified her body this morning, but apparently she's been dead for a few days."

"This is tragic news." Rudker blinked a few times to convey he was having an emotional reaction. "You'll have to excuse me." He walked away and boarded the elevator. As the doors closed, he saw them lean together to continue the gossip. He thought he'd pulled off the right reaction, but maybe not. Often when he believed his behavior to be perfectly appropriate, it turned out to be characterized as offensive or odd. For a long stretch, that offended person had been his first wife.

On the third floor, he hurried to his big corner office. Eventually, he would have to talk to the HR director about whether to replace Warner. With the merger, it might not be necessary. Marcy would handle the details, the flowers and financials and such. Rudker unlocked his office door, tossed his travel bag on the floor, and plopped in his custom-made Italian-leather chair.

He closed his eyes and tried not to think about anything for a minute. He knew it was important to quiet his mind on occasion. Especially when he had critical decisions to make.

Sula, that PR girl, was a wild card. How had she accessed Warner's office and what had she found? Someone in the hallway group, Alicia maybe, had said Sula had identified the body. Was that why she'd gone into the R&D director's office? Was the girl looking for Warner's genetic data or was she just a busybody?

If she had the nerve to show her face around here again, he would fire her on the spot. She must not be allowed to access any of the buildings or offices. That wasn't enough though. Rudker wanted the paperwork back, whatever it was. It belonged to Prolabs and Sula no longer worked for Prolabs. He would have to talk to Marcy about that too, but first things first.

He buzzed the receptionist in the front office. No one answered. *Damn.* He needed her to find a phone number for him. Since when did everyone go home so early? He dialed 911. A dispatcher asked calmly, "What is your emergency?"

"I don't have an emergency, but I would like to speak to the police chief."

"Please hang up and dial 682-5111."

Rudker dialed the number. A woman's voice answered. "Eugene Police Department. How can I help you?"

"I'd like to report a theft."

Chapter 14

After forty minutes in the dark supply room, Sula finally heard Peterson leave. She waited another ten minutes, then crept out into the nearly dark building. Exhausted and shaky, she passed an office with light showing and knew she wasn't alone in the building. She moved quickly and left by the side exit.

She wanted to go straight home, but her purse and truck keys were in her office. The thought of running into Rudker terrified her, so she considered walking, but she needed her house key too. Sula crossed the courtyard and used the master key to enter the main building. Hallway lights were on, but no one appeared to be in the facility. Despite her fatigue, she skipped the elevator and took the stairs to avoid encountering anyone. Sula had never been in the building this late before, but she knew that some salespeople worked odd hours.

She ran from the stairwell to her office, picked up her things, and ran back. Once on the cement stairs, she moved more slowly, not wanting to slip and fall in her muddy heels. In the parking lot, she discovered Rudker's Jeep was still there. Dear God, he was still in the building. Sula's legs shook so hard she could barely stand.

At home, she was too distressed to think about dinner, so she cleaned her shoes, showered, and put on fresh clothes. Washing away the fear, sweat, and mud of the day failed to give her a sense that everything would turn out all right.

The thought that she might have blown her job, and chance for custody, made her sick with despair. How could she have been so reckless? It was one thing to be concerned about a group of patients, but it was a whole new step to risk everything that was important to her. What if her concern for those patients was pointless? Peterson thought it was. Yet Sula had heard Dr. Warner plead her case, and she had read too many news stories about antidepressants and suicides to dismiss the idea that an ethnic population could be at risk. She still held hope the documents she'd pilfered from Warner's office would reveal something.

Sitting down at her computer desk, Sula turned on a reading light and began to scan through the papers. They were intake files with patient names, medical histories, prescription histories, and the clinicians' assessments. She soon realized none of the patients had any antidepressants in their drug histories and none of the notes said anything about depression.

These subjects were from the phase I trials, when they tested the drug in healthy people just to make sure it was safe. Disappointed, Sula kept reading. No phase II data appeared. No Puerto Rican research center was named in the pages. It was interesting to note that several of the phase I patients complained of headaches and irritability after taking the drug for a few weeks, but it apparently hadn't been cause for concern.

She gave up on the photocopied files and pulled the disk out of its unmarked case. It was plain silver and could have been anything. The fact that Warner had hidden the disk, then died shortly after, gave Sula goose bumps.

She popped it into her computer and crossed her fingers that her CD drive would work well this evening. Everything in her setup was out of date, but saving up for the duplex had kept her from buying the laptop she wanted. She clicked the icon and waited while it loaded.

The list of contents was short: *Miguel Rios, Luis Rios, mr DNA, lr DNA*. Sula's stomach fluttered. These must be the cousins in the Puerto Rican trial who had committed suicide. Warner must have made the disk after her fight with Rudker. She'd copied everything she thought was important and hidden it, clearly worried that Rudker would destroy the files in the database. Sula thought it likely that he already had.

She clicked on the folder labeled *Miguel Rios*. The opening pages resembled the documents she'd photocopied. Personal history, followed by medical history, followed by physical exam. Miguel Rios had not been a happy man. He had been diagnosed with depression at age twenty-three and had taken seven different medications during the next nineteen years. At one point, he'd been on Depakote and Prozac at the same time. Depakote was a powerful antipsychotic that was also used to control epilepsy. Her father had taken it for a while, but he'd hated it. He said it took away his spirit.

According to Miguel's intake interview, he often had thoughts of suicide but in all those years of depression he had never tried it. Yet after three weeks of taking Nexapra, the man had killed himself. No wonder Warner had been concerned.

Luis' file was similar, although he had not become depressed, or at least hadn't been diagnosed that way, until age twenty-nine.

So he'd been taking meds for only five years. He also reported occasional suicide thoughts but, according to his intake notes, he had never attempted it. Five weeks into his Nexapra trial, he had killed himself.

Sula's heart went out to the family who had lost two people in two weeks to self-destruction. The parents would never recover. The kids would never understand. It was such a mystery how the same drug could help one person and kill another. It was true of many medications, not just mental health drugs. Working for Prolabs, Sula had learned a great deal about genomic breakthroughs in medical science. She was convinced pharma companies could do a better job of predicting how people would react to medicines. In the case of Nexapra, Rudker had learned they could predict a patient response and he refused to make it part of the prescription process.

It infuriated her.

Sula couldn't get the DNA files to open. She'd suspected they might be too big for her system. She turned off the computer, lay down on her bed, and tried to figure what her chances were for keeping her job.

It seemed certain Rudker would want to fire her. She'd known since Monday when he threatened her. Yet she clung to the idea that she could salvage her job, that Marcy would fight for her. On the surface, Rudker had no grounds for termination, she told herself.

He hadn't seen her inside Warner's office. The papers in her hand could have been anything. She would say she had been distributing the memo she'd written about Warner's death. Running from Rudker was weird behavior, but so what? It had been a tough day for her, with identifying Warner's body and all. Firing her after she had experienced such a thing on behalf of the company would make Prolabs look bad.

Not that Rudker cared.

Sula got up and watched the eleven o'clock news. She was stunned to see the clips of protesters in Prolabs' parking lot. They had demonstrated in front of the company while she was searching Warner's office. She should have been out there making a statement. That was her job. People had probably looked for her. Dereliction of duty was grounds for termination.

She went to bed at midnight but was unable to sleep. She couldn't stop thinking about Tate. About how badly she wanted him back in her life, and how badly she might have blown her chances. How could she have been so reckless? What made her think she could go up against someone like Karl Rudker? Or actually alter the course of a company as big as JB Pharma?

Sula tossed and turned and mapped out what she would say to people at work the next day. Around two, she got up and took a Xanax, hoping it wouldn't make her sleep through her alarm.

Chapter 15

Friday, April 16

Sula pulled into the Prolabs lot and parked her truck in its usual spot. She was struck by how calm and pretty the campus seemed. A blue sky and morning sun bathed the buildings in postcard-perfect light. Yesterday's events—the trip to the morgue, running from Rudker, protesters in front of the building—seemed surreal now, as if they had all been part of a crazy dream.

It was no dream, and it wasn't over.

Paralyzed with fear, she was unable to get out of the truck. She wanted desperately to walk away and avoid the confrontation she knew was coming. The chance that she could salvage her job was so slim, it hardly seemed worth the humiliation of going back in there. Because the chance existed at all, she had to try. Sula willed herself to open the door and step out. Once she had the momentum going, she kept moving.

Inside the building, Cliff stood at his usual spot next to the metal detector walk-through. Sula braced herself for the possibility that he would hand her a small box containing her personal items and turn her away. Instead, he greeted her cheerfully. Sula smiled and asked about his family. He said everyone was just dandy. She grabbed her backpack and moved on. She shared the elevator with the company's vice president, who made pleasant small talk. So far so good.

She made a cup of fresh-brewed coffee in the break room as usual. Two salespeople came in, greeted her briefly, then went back to their own conversation. Sula couldn't detect anything quirky or standoffish in their behavior. Coffee in hand, she trudged to her office and sat down to open e-mails. Her watch said 7:58. Her computer clock said 8:05, but it gained time like crazy.

She needed to go see Marcy—about so many things—but first she had to send out the e-mail she had prepared about Diane Warner's tragic death. In the correspondence, she promised her coworkers she would follow up with a time and place for the memorial service. Sula hoped Marcy would handle it. The thought of attending a funeral filled her with dread.

With an image of Warner's pale face floating in her brain, Sula was already on edge when Marcy appeared at her door with a police officer.

Because of her experience at the department the day before, Sula assumed, for a moment, that he was there to follow up with Warner's death. But as soon as the good-looking officer opened his mouth and said, "Sula Moreno?" her heart started hammering like she'd just run up a flight of stairs. Her throat was dry and she couldn't speak, so she nodded.

"I'm Officer Hutchison. You're under arrest for theft of company property." The young man looked as if it pained him to say it.

Sula closed her eyes and took a deep breath. This could not be happening. And yet, it was. She locked eyes on the HR director. "Marcy, help me. You know this charge is ludicrous."

Marcy looked as if she would cry. "I know it is, Sula, but Rudker filed a complaint. He wants you arrested, and I couldn't talk him out of it. I tried, believe me, I tried."

Sula turned to the officer. "On what basis?"

"Miss, I have to escort you out of the building now. We can discuss the circumstances at the station."

Sula was too upset to argue. There seemed to be no point. She grabbed her purse and sweater and stood. Her legs buckled and she sat back down.

"Are you all right?" Marcy rushed to comfort her.

"Not really." Sula stood again, legs still trembling. "Marcy, I'm sorry about all this. It really is a misunderstanding."

"I know. But before you go, I have to ask for the key."

Sula pointed to her desktop, where it lay, waiting to be returned. Marcy picked it up and pocketed it. Sula looked at the officer. "You're not going to cuff me." She had meant it as question, but it didn't come out that way.

"Not if you come willingly."

Sula moved toward the door and the officer stepped out of her way. She realized she would probably never set foot in this office again. But she didn't look back. Nor did she cry. It was only a job, she told herself. As they walked toward the elevator, Officer Hutchison recited her rights. Then they boarded the elevator and exited the building in silence.

Inside the police department, she was taken to a small windowless room with pale, dirty, gray walls and a scarred wooden table. A second cop followed her and Officer Hutchison into the small room. She introduced herself as Officer Whitstone, then the two cops sat across from her and began to ask questions. Sula was glad she had prepared what to say in hopes of salvaging her job. Now it might keep her out of jail.

"What were you doing in the"—Hutchison looked down at his notes—"the R&D building?"

"Looking for Steve Peterson. I wanted to tell him about Diane Warner."

"What about Warner?"

"That she was dead. She hadn't come to work in a few days, and he and I had both been concerned. I wanted to let him know what had happened to her."

Whitstone spoke up. "What happened to her?"

"She was killed. Officer Rice said something about a homeless man."

The cops looked at each other. Then Hutchison said, "The body in the park." Sula didn't know if he was asking her a question or not. She waited.

Whitstone put it together. "So the woman whose office you took something from is the same woman who was found dead on the bike path?"

"Her name is Diane Warner, and I didn't take anything from her office." Sula silently apologized to her counselor for lying. She believed Diane Warner would want her to have the disk and to take it to the FDA.

"Your boss says he saw you leave the office with papers in your hand."

"I'm a public-relations person. I always have papers in my hand. Notes, press releases, memos. It's my job."

"He says you ran when he saw you."

"He scares me. And I'd had a bad day. I had to identify Diane's body in the morgue, and I was feeling a little skittish."

The cops gave each other a quick look. Sula didn't think they bought her story, but she would stick with it.

"He says you disappeared after that." Whitstone's voice was monotone.

"It was after four o'clock. I went home."

Whitstone leaned forward. "Why would your boss accuse you of theft?"

"I don't know. People say he's vindictive."

"What were you doing in Warner's office?" Hutchison asked abruptly.

"I wasn't in her office."

"Rudker says he saw you coming out."

"Not true. I was passing by. Perhaps he's reacting to Diane's death in an odd way too."

They were all silent for a moment. Hutchison stood and Whitstone followed suit. "We have to book you into the jail," he said with a trace of regret. "You'll probably be arraigned and released in the morning."

Sula bit her lip to keep from swearing. This was insane. Rudker must be throwing his clout around. Dread filled her stomach. She told herself one night in jail wouldn't kill her. She had survived much worse.

As she followed the officers out, anger replaced the dread. Rudker had made it personal. If he wanted a fight, he would get one. She would send a copy of the disk with Warner's files to the FDA. She would hire a lawyer and sue the company to get her job back. By having her arrested, he'd shown his hand. He obviously had something to hide and she intended to shine a light on it.

The redbrick building on Fifth Avenue had always looked more like a huge public library than a jail. Today Sula noticed its lack of windows for the first time. The cop car drove up to an annex next to the main building and waited. Twin steel doors opened and Officer Whitstone drove in. She parked the car in front of a small steel door to the left. Another set of wide steel doors was set into the opposite wall. It was a drive-through, only no one ran up to change the oil or rotate the tires.

Whitstone got out, removed her weapon, and locked it in the trunk of the squad car. She opened the car door for Sula and helped her out. Her hands were cuffed and she was glad for the assistance. In the next room, three desks with computers and chairs were the only items in the small, windowless space. Whitstone sat down at one station and motioned for Sula to sit as well. For a few minutes the cop said nothing as she filled out paperwork and entered information into the computer.

She abruptly asked, "Do you feel ill or do have any medical conditions, such as diabetes, that we should know about?"

Sula wondered if she should mention the occasional post-traumatic stress, but said, "No."

"Do you feel like you might want to commit suicide?"

"No."

"Are you going to become sick from withdrawals during the next twenty-four hours?"

"No." She was glad to know they asked such questions. Many of the people arrested on a daily basis were homeless, addicted, and/or mentally ill.

Whitstone picked up the phone and called for a female deputy. Moments later, a slender middle-aged woman with a buzz cut and a pretty face entered the small room. Whitstone handed the deputy a plastic bag containing Sula's purse, then uncuffed Sula and turned to face her. "Good luck," she said softly, then moved toward the exterior door.

As the jail deputy escorted Sula out of the room, she felt like a piece of property that had just been transferred to a new and unknown owner. The steel door slammed behind her. Sula shuddered. She was a prisoner.

They moved down a short hall into a similar-sized room and sat on opposite sides of a desk. The deputy asked her the same set of questions Whitstone had: "Are you going to try to commit suicide? Are you sick? Will you experience withdrawals?"

Then the woman, whose name tag said Deputy Crouse, asked her to remove her shoes, her belt, and her sweater. Those were added to the plastic bag. Then Crouse read a list of the items, starting with her purse, followed by all of its contents, including the $7.56 in her wallet. Sula signed the document, in essence agreeing with the inventory of her possessions.

Deputy Crouse pulled a blanket from a shelf and handed it to her. They went back into the hall, down another twenty feet, then entered yet another windowless room. This area was larger, about forty by forty, and housed a dozen unhappy women, most in their twenties and thirties, plus a few older street hags. Scattered around the perimeter of the room on wooden benches, some sitting, others reclining, the women formed a colorful and tragic collection of human lives gone inexplicably wrong. As they looked up at Sula in her black skirt and pink silk blouse, it was clear they had no empathy. She did not belong here.

"There's a pay phone over there," Crouse said, pointing as if she were showing a home for sale. "You can make collect calls only. There's a toilet and sink behind that short wall. You might as well get comfortable. You'll be here until you're arraigned at ten o'clock tomorrow morning. If you were a guy, you'd probably be released before midnight because of overcrowding. But unless a whole sorority house gets arrested this evening for drunk and disorderly, you're in for an overnighter."

Sula wanted to ask, *Where do I sleep*? But it was clear this room was her reality for a while. She looked at her watch: 3:10 p.m. Seventeen hours and twenty minutes to go.

She looked around the room and spotted a place along the wall near the phone. Hugging her blanket like a timid child, she walked across the cold concrete and sat on the bench.

"Welcome to the fishbowl," said a skinny young woman. She had the abused hair and skin of a meth addict.

"Thanks."

Sula closed her eyes as if that would make it all go away. She mediated for about ten minutes, then heard her named called out. She looked up to see the deputy waving her over to the door. A flash of hope surged through her. Maybe she was being released. As she got near, Crouse said, "Time for prints and pictures." Sula's hope plummeted.

She followed the deputy into yet another room, where another deputy took her fingerprints, entering her forever into the system of suspects. It wasn't until she stood next to the wall for a mug shot that she felt like a criminal. In that moment, she couldn't get enough air into her lungs.

Sula thought about her father, who'd been arrested so many times. He had treated the arrests like notches in his belt. To him, people who never landed in jail were "slaves to the system." Mindless sheep with no passion. As a child, she had resented his incarcerations and the stigma attached to them. Now, his rebellion gave her a sense of strength.

It was worth it, she told herself. She had the disk with Warner's discovery. The FDA would see it and stop Nexapra's clinical trials. Lives would be saved. She could only hope hers would not be lost in the process.

Chapter 16

Rudker watched from his third-floor office as the cop escorted Sula across the parking lot to the blue Impala. He was disappointed she was not cuffed. An image of Sula naked and cuffed to a bedpost slid into his thoughts. She was not really his type, with her long silky black hair and cinnamon skin, but her face was striking. She had a decent body too, long and lean, but not enough cleavage. Still, she aroused him. Or was it just her humiliation that made him hard?

He would have liked to pursue the fantasy but he had some search-and-destroy missions to carry out. He strode into his outer office and spoke to his secretary. "I'll be out for the afternoon. If anyone calls, tell them I'll get back to them on Monday."

"You have an appointment at four with Allen Sebring from Anderson and Shire Consulting."

"Cancel it."

"You've already canceled him once."

"He'll get over it."

Rudker kept moving. He was not prepared to deal with the accountant yet. Before he reached the elevator, Marcy Jacobson came running up behind him.

"We need to discuss a few things about closing out Diane Warner's employment."

"Like what?" Rudker slowed and turned to face her. Marcy looked pained and the expression irritated him.

"What happens to the money in her pension fund? Who gets her office? Believe it or not, people have already asked."

"All of that can wait until we discuss it Monday. Meanwhile, I don't want anyone in her office."

Rudker boarded the elevator and quickly closed the doors. Why did people bother him with all this trivial stuff? Couldn't they make decisions on their own? In a moment, Rudker chuckled. They didn't make decisions because they were afraid to. Because he was famous for saying, *Why wasn't I consulted?* He knew he was difficult to work for at times, but he paid people well and his job wasn't any easier.

He crossed the courtyard and entered the R&D building. He briefly considered rounding up Steve Peterson to help him with the task of sorting through Warner's files. Steve would be better able to recognize what was relevant to Warner's DNA research. He rejected the idea. He didn't want to stimulate interest in Warner's work by seeming determined to cast it aside. Scientists were inherently curious, stubborn to a fault, and contrary by nature. Rudker had almost gone that route himself. He'd earned his BS in biology but had gone on to earn a master's in business because laboratories bored him. The degrees had suited him well in the pharma industry.

Rudker stuck his key in the lock only to discover that the door was unlocked. It only confirmed his belief that Sula had been in the office. He'd told the cops he'd seen her coming out, but he hadn't. She'd been standing near the entrance. He pushed in and locked the door behind him.

Warner's filing cabinets were unlocked too. He knew she had not left them that way. Proprietary behavior was also in the blood of researchers. Rudker spent twenty minutes skimming through folders, looking for references to the Puerto Rico patients. The search was so tedious. He wondered how long Sula had been in the office. How far had she gotten?

In the third cabinet, he found three folders of notes about the phase I testing in healthy patients. He put them all through the shredder, nearly filling the wastebasket. He moved quickly through the remaining files, growing impatient with the chore. Next, he searched her desk, finding an odd assortment of felt-tip pens, a collection of half-eaten protein bars, and a prescription bottle of nabumetone, an anti-inflammatory often used by people with arthritis.

In a moment, he located a clear plastic case with about ten CDs. A quick search turned up the key for it. Rudker decided to simply take the entire collection. The woman was dead, and her research belonged to the company.

The only other item of interest was a calendar sporting pictures of half-naked firemen. It was dated 2007. Obviously, Warner had kept it for the photos. It was interesting what you learned about people after they were dead.

With the CD case tucked under his arm, Rudker left Warner's office and locked it behind him. He would have Peterson and Marcy sort through everything else. Company property would be boxed and saved, personal property would be boxed and sent to Warner's heirs. If she had any.

Rudker wanted to feel relieved, but it was too soon. Sula had papers in her hand when he saw her yesterday. He believed those papers had come from Warner's office and he intended to get them back. Why would she risk her job looking for Warner's notes unless she planned to do something with them? What if Sula already had? Rudker refused to believe it. The idiot had come in to work this morning as usual. He suspected that whatever she'd taken from Warner's office was in her home.

He intended to take it back while she spent the night in jail. He'd used his acquaintance with the chief of police to pressure them into keeping her overnight. Rudker had looked Sula up in the human resources files and knew she lived alone on the corner of Friendly and Twenty-Sixth. He'd cruised by her place the night before, and it seemed unlikely that the small 1950s home had a high-tech alarm system installed. Sula was a twenty-five-year-old single woman, making $28,000 a year. She couldn't afford anything of value, including an alarm system. Getting in would be a piece of cake. He just had to wait until the neighborhood was sleeping.

* * *

Robbie sat at Jason's computer and tried to write something funny. He'd gone down to the comedy club the night before, but only as a spectator. It bothered him to be there and not perform, but he hadn't written any new material in a while, and he couldn't keep doing the same old bit.

He had three main subjects he could joke about: depression, working at a drug factory, and not getting along with his father. The woman who ran the club said all humor came from pain and Robbie suspected she was right. The clinical trial also seemed like a good source of material. He tried to come up with a before-and-after joke. *Before I started on this drug, I was seriously depressed. Now I'm like the energizer bunny, only not so...*

His roommate burst into their two-bedroom apartment and shouted, "Party!" just as Robbie took his Hot Pockets out of the microwave. He nearly dropped the plate.

"Shit, Jason. You need an early-warning device." Robbie transferred his food to their garage-sale dining table as Jason danced around the living room in a bizarre show of happiness.

"Guess where?"

"Tell me." Robbie pushed aside a pile of newspapers and sat down.

"Jennifer Krazanski's."

"Hot blonde from history class?" Jason was a student at the UO.

"Yep. She invited me personally." Jason was a good-looking guy who didn't lack for first dates, but his puppy-dog energy turned serious girls off.

"I'm happy for you."

"For us." Jason rushed over and punched Robbie on the arm. "You're going." His roommate grabbed one of the Hot Pockets and bit into it, then let out a garbled yell and spit the mouthful on the table.

"Hot?" Robbie tried not to smile.

"How long did you nuke that for?"

"Couple of minutes." Robbie looked away. "I don't think I'll go."

"Bullshit. You've been moping around here for days. You've got to get out."

Robbie didn't say anything. He had been off his old medication for two days, and now this was his second day on the new stuff. So he was in a low spot. It was too early to tell what would happen with the new drug, but it had been a rough week. He'd missed work yesterday for the first time in months. Even though he felt better today he didn't think he had the energy to party.

"Chug some Mountain Dew if you have to. You're going."

In the long run it was easier to go along than to resist Jason. Around nine thirty, they climbed into his roommate's old Toyota and headed for west Eugene. They picked up a six-pack of Miller on the way, and Robbie agreed to drive home. He never drank much. One beer loosened him up, and two beers made him contemplate the pointlessness of most people's lives, especially his.

Located at Jefferson and Twenty-Sixth, the two-story glass-and-brick home jutted above all its neighbors. They found a parking spot across the street, two houses down.

Robbie could hear the music as soon as he stepped out of the car. He recognized Macy Gray's voice, whom he liked pretty well. As long as they didn't play rap all night. He could only take about twenty minutes of the bass beat before he started thinking he would rather be deaf.

Only about fifteen people were in the house, but they all seemed to be talking about *The Girl with the Dragon Tattoo*, a movie showing at the Bijou. Robbie hadn't seen it. He sipped his beer slowly and wondered why he could never seem to connect to people the way others did.

He tried. He discovered that telling people he worked for Prolabs usually sparked a conversation. The subject of drugs was always popular with young people, and the company was in the news because of its controversial expansion plans. After listening to a girl rant about greedy pharma companies, he had to get away.

"Excuse me, I need some air," he said abruptly and walked toward the sliding-glass door. Once outside, the sudden burst of cool air gave him a rush. Robbie stood at the edge of the balcony overlooking a split-level backyard where two guys tossed a frisbee in the dark. A couple in the corner didn't stop kissing to notice his presence. Their intimacy shot a cold ache through him. He'd slept with only one girl in his life and that had been more than a year ago. He was tired of being alone. He was tired of the episodes of hopelessness.

Robbie looked out at the space below and wondered what it would be like to jump. To feel the ground rushing up at him in one glorious flight, knowing that when he hit, it would be over. He envisioned it for a moment, feeling its pull, then stepped back. This balcony wasn't nearly high enough. Unless he landed on a sprinkler, he might not even get seriously hurt. He made a mental note to use that thought for comedy material.

He turned to go inside. The lights of a big vehicle cruised by on the side street. He watched it pass and realized it was a black Jeep Commander. Was that his dad? It sure looked like him. What the hell was the old man doing cruising Twenty-Ninth Avenue at midnight?

* * *

Rudker parked two blocks from the corner and shut off the engine. He regretted bringing the Commander, which stood out from the smaller cars. Yet the neighborhood was so dark and quiet, he saw no reason to abandon his plan now. He'd passed a party a few blocks back and from here he could see the glow of one TV across the street, but other than that, there were few signs of life. He pulled his wallet out of his jeans and slid it under the seat. Now all he had in his pockets were a small, bright flashlight and an expired credit card with his ex-wife's name on it. From the jockey box, he extracted a pair of thin leather driving gloves and pulled them on.

Rudker eased out of the vehicle and gently closed the door. He suspected he hadn't used enough force to latch it properly, but he was more concerned with drawing someone's attention with the crunch of a car door than with someone stealing the Commander.

He moved down the sidewalk, his black jogging shoes making almost no sound. Rudker had also worn black jeans and a dark-brown sweater Tara had bought him for Christmas two years ago but that he had never worn until now. She thought he was having drinks with a JB sales rep.

He approached the side of the fenced yard and slowed. It was fortuitous that Sula lived on a corner lot, making it that much more accessible. With one easy motion, he reached over the gate, lifted the closing mechanism on the inside, and pushed through. A dog in the backyard of a nearby house let out two loud barks. The noise was jarring, but Rudker had taken a beta blocker earlier for that very reason—to keep his nerves calm during this excursion no matter what happened. Rudker moved briskly toward the attached garage, where moonlight bounced off the glass of a side door. He would try it first.

It wasn't even locked. Even if it had been, a fourteen-dollar dead bolt from Home Depot was no match for someone with a credit card and a light touch. Rudker had been prepared to climb in a back window if necessary, but he was relieved that he didn't have to. He pointed his penlight at the floor, clicked it on, and made his way across the surprisingly spare garage. A large metal object caught his eye. It appeared to be some kind of sculpture representing a human form. He would have liked to see it in better light. Abruptly, he turned away and stepped toward the door leading into the house. It was locked.

It took only forty seconds with the card to pop the slider bolt out of its slot. Rudker turned the knob and entered the kitchen. The scent of chili powder and cantaloupe filled the air. He moved quickly through the galley-style room and turned left into the living area. Moonlight filtered through the curtains and he could see the furnishings were minimal: a couch, a TV, an end table, and a few plants. Sula either hadn't lived here long or was as minimalist as a Buddhist monk.

Moving rapidly, Rudker went left again down a short hallway and opened the first door. Even without illumination, he knew it was a bathroom. The air felt wet and reeked of jasmine-scented shampoo. Rudker moved on to the next door. He flipped on the light to see a small bedroom that was completely empty except for a few boxes in one corner. *Stranger still*, he thought. He shut the light off and turned to the door opposite.

The overhead fixture in this larger bedroom gave out a dim glow, which suited him fine. Rudker headed straight for the computer desk. Only a small notepad and pen sat next to the monitor. Otherwise the desk was devoid of clutter. He pulled open the top drawer: nothing but pens and paper clips and assorted office supplies. The next drawer revealed a stack of crumpled, folded-in-half papers. Rudker examined them closely with his pen light. They contained observations of Nexapra's phase I clinical-trial patients.

Sula had been in Warner's office. The nosy bitch. Spending one night in jail was not enough punishment. He had warned her, but she'd foolishly underestimated him. She would beat the theft charge, of course. He could live with that—as long as he rounded up and destroyed all the files relating to the Puerto Rico patients and their DNA.

He folded the papers in half, stuffed them into a back pocket, and continued to search. The girl may have taken more than what he saw in her hands, and as long as he was here, he would be thorough.

Rudker failed to find any more incriminating paperwork, but he did find a shoebox in the bottom desk drawer that contained an assortment of CDs. He rifled through them, only to discover they were all setup disks: Windows, Photoshop, and such.

Seeing the disks made him think Sula might have copied files from Warner's computer and hidden the CD somewhere in her home. He did a quick search of her nightstand, dresser, and closet. Nothing except a lot of black, pink, and beige clothes in soft fabrics. Rummaging through her bras and panties gave him a little thrill. Rudker would have liked to linger, but he heard a siren in the distance and it made him nervous.

The voice in his head was suddenly there, telling him the police were on their way and he had to get out. Rudker tried to ignore it. Sula was in jail and he doubted if anyone had seen him enter the house. He really wanted to boot up her computer to see what she had downloaded last.

He walked over and stared at her monitor for a moment, trying to decide if it was worth the risk. He noticed the CD sitting on top of the computer tower. He picked it up. At first, the case appeared to be unlabeled, then he saw the letters *PRS* in small print along the spine. *Puerto Rico suicides*?

Rudker clicked on the machine. After twenty seconds, he grew irritated waiting for Windows to load. *Get out, idiot*, the voice nagged. Finally, icons appeared on the screen. He loaded the disk, accessed the CD drive, and a window displayed the contents. Four file names were listed: *Miguel Rios, Luis Rios, mr DNA, lr DNA*. A sharp pain flashed through his chest. *Jesus!* The girl had everything she needed to shut down Nexapra and ruin his career.

The traitor! The bitch!

Rudker popped the CD out of the drive, put it back in its case, and crammed it into his other back pocket. He clicked off the computer, picked up his penlight, and left the room.

He left the same way he'd come in, out through the garage and the side yard onto Twenty-Sixth. Rudker found himself whistling as he hurried to his vehicle. He was in control of his company and career again. Yet he couldn't stop thinking about Sula. If she were trying to destroy someone besides himself, he might have admired her audacity.

Chapter 17

Saturday, April 17

Bruised, exhausted, and in desperate need of a shower, Sula walked out of the jail. She had barely slept. In the middle of the night, a deputy had herded everyone out of the holding area and into a smaller room so the larger area could be cleaned. Then an hour later, they were roused and moved back. The activity seemed bizarre and surreal, almost intended to deprive the inmates of sleep. Earlier this morning, she'd pleaded not guilty in the little makeshift courtroom inside the jail and been given a court date of May 11.

Her truck was still in the parking lot at Prolabs, so she walked eight blocks to the downtown station in a light drizzle, waited forty-five minutes to board a bus, then rode out to Willow Creek. She walked the last mile to the Prolabs campus. It had stopped raining, but she was wet and cold and her feet had never hurt so much. She wished she had gone straight home and changed into sneakers before retrieving her truck, but that would have added an hour to her travel time.

She could have called her friend Paul to help her out, but she wasn't prepared to talk about her ordeal yet. Or even to admit to anyone that she had been fired and arrested on the same day. She had to form a plan first, to feel more in control. She couldn't let anyone see her this vulnerable.

It was Saturday, so the company's parking lot was nearly empty. She was glad not to run into anybody. As soon as Sula climbed in her truck, tears of relief pooled behind her eyes but did not spill over. She drove home in a state of numb exhaustion, peeled off yesterday's clothes, and lay down to sleep.

When Sula woke late that afternoon, she was disoriented for a minute. The bright sky made her think it was noon and that she'd slept late. Then it all came rushing back, the humiliating arrest and sleepless, bone-bruising night on the jail bench. She shook it off and crawled out of bed, determined to move forward.

As she showered, her stomach growled and she realized she was ravenously hungry. She hadn't eaten since her breakfast of scrambled eggs and cantaloupe the day before. She really wanted Chinese food, Mongolian beef, in particular, but now that she no longer had a job, she couldn't justify spending the money. She dressed in comfy black sportswear, then made a turkey sandwich and heated a can of vegetable beef soup.

Reading through the want ads as she wolfed down the sandwich, Sula found two jobs to apply for. A public-relations position with the county and a technical writing position offered by Microprobes, just down the road from Prolabs. The possibilities perked her up a bit.

Halfway through the soup, she got full and pushed it aside. She grabbed a notepad and pen from her purse and started a list of things to do: *1) Write a letter to the FDA explaining what was on the disk and where it came from. 2) Make a copy of the disk.* She needed a computer with a big hard drive and CD burner. Paul could help her with that.

Sula continued her list: *3) Mail the letter and a copy of the CD to her public relations contact at FDA. 4) Send out letters and resumes for both jobs. 5) Apply for unemployment. 6) Call Barbara, her custody lawyer, and let her know about her new situation.*

Sula felt better already. Except for the vile taste in her mouth. On her way back to her computer desk, she stopped in the bathroom and brushed her teeth, which felt fuzzy with neglect. Dark circles showed under her eyes and she thought she looked older than she had yesterday morning.

While waiting for her computer to boot up, she jotted down some ideas for her FDA letter. When Windows was up and running, she decided to check her e-mail. She deleted a promotion from Apple without opening it, then scanned through Paul's note, in which he complained about his boyfriend and invited her to go see Three Dog Night at the McDonald Theater.

Sula hit reply, then wrote Paul a quick note saying she would have to pass on the concert for lack of funds and asked him about burning a CD of some large files. She clicked Send, then glanced up at the top of her computer case.

The disk was gone.

Sula's chest tightened in a painful squeeze. *Someone had come into her home and taken it.* Her breath went shallow and she fought for air. *Be calm*, she told herself. The disk had to be here somewhere. The idea that Rudker had broken into her home with the purpose of stealing the disk seemed…crazy.

What else? She was not the type to misplace things. Yet, maybe she had put it away somewhere. Sula searched frantically through her desk drawers. Not finding it, she took two deep breaths and started again, this time making herself move slowly. Piece by piece, she removed every item from her top drawer: the scissors, the bottle of wite-out, scraps of paper with phone numbers, little cases with paper clips. Each went on the floor until the drawer was empty. The clear, unlabeled CD case was not there.

Sula repeated the same process with the other two drawers. She also inserted all the disks she found into the drive to look at their contents on-screen. As she went through the motions, she knew it was pointless. She had left the disk on top of her hard drive. Now it was gone. She had no roommates, dogs, or ghosts who could have moved it.

Anger and frustration burst from her in a wordless wail.

Halfheartedly, she rummaged through her dresser drawers, nightstand, and closet shelves, then flopped back on the bed and stared at the dingy ceiling. She had lost her job and risked her custody hearing for nothing. She had underestimated Rudker and he had beaten her. How had the bastard gotten in? Sula jumped up and rushed to the kitchen to check the door that opened into the garage. It was unlocked. She never left it unlocked. Never. It was a ritual to check that door in the mornings before she left the house.

She crossed through the garage and checked the door leading into the side yard. It was also unlocked. She couldn't guarantee she hadn't left it that way. So he had come in through the garage and had jimmied the interior lock somehow. She knew it wasn't difficult. Any teenager with a student-body card could get past a cheap lock. She had never worried much about it because she had nothing worth stealing, and that would be obvious to any thief observing the size and value of her rental.

Had he hired someone? It was hard to imagine Rudker breaking into her house, standing here in her kitchen. Had he handled her personal things? Her lingerie? Sula fought the urge to gather up all her clothes and run them through the washer.

She had to sit down. Her body and brain were both exhausted. She told herself to let it go, that it was over, she had done all she could do. She had to stop thinking about Nexapra and focus on finding a job. Focus on her custody hearing and her chance to get her sweet little boy back into her life. Once she was past that she would move, so Rudker wouldn't know where she lived. She crumpled the list of things to do and tossed it in the trash.

If only Calix were here, she thought, sitting on the other side of the table, leaning forward eagerly to hear the rest of this sorry tale. Her sister would laugh in the right places without making Sula feel stupid. She would tell her she had done the right thing and everything would work out fine with Tate. Sula knew she would never have another friend like her big sister. It seemed she was destined to spend her life alone, talking to herself, and making lists of things to do. She felt the cold fingers of the abyss latch on, ready to pull her in.

Time for a distraction.

She tried to read her book about freelancing, then remembered she hadn't taken her Celexa this morning because she'd been in jail. Sula went to the kitchen and swallowed one of her tablets, then went back to her computer and logged on to CompuServe. The *New Mail* icon was lit up in bright yellow. She clicked it and her in-box appeared. Paul had responded to her e-mail about opening and copying a big file. It was unusual for him to be home on a Saturday night, but if he was home, it was not unusual for him to be online. His draft was brief: *No problem. Bring it to EFN Monday afternoon.—P*

Sula decided to tell him everything. She couldn't keep it to herself any longer. Paul was a good friend and would not judge her. They had met at the University of Oregon four years earlier in an economics class. They had been lone liberal voices in a sea of young Republicans and had shared an opposition to the trickle-down theory of economics. They later bonded over coffee and their mutual orphan status. Paul had graduated with a political-science degree the same term she finished with a BA in journalism. In Eugene, his degree was about as worthless as an art-history education, so he worked part-time as a waiter and part-time as a computer tech for Rent a Nerd.

Sula hit reply and began to type: *Hi Paul. I no longer have the disk. It's a long and bizarre story, but here's the short version. I overheard Diane Warner (a scientist at Prolabs) tell Rudker (the CEO) that a drug they're testing makes some people kill themselves. She said she could develop a screening test to prevent it. He told her to shut up and forget about it. Then he came out and saw me standing there, so he knew I heard.*

Then Warner disappeared and eventually turned up dead (more on that later). I got worried that her discovery would disappear too and the drug would get approved and a lot of depressed people would kill themselves. (You know how I feel about that.) So I searched her office and found a hidden disk with the DNA data. Then Rudker saw me outside her office and had me fired and arrested (more on that later).

This is the creepy part. While I was in jail, Rudker (or someone he hired) broke into my house and took the disk. So now I'm unemployed, facing criminal charges, likely to lose my custody hearing (which could send me over the edge), and have no way to help the people who will eventually take the drug.

I keep telling myself to forget about the drug, but I can't. People will die. And Rudker doesn't care. He just wants to make more money. It infuriates me, but I don't know what to do now. Sorry to lay this on you, but it's been a wild week, and I had to tell someone. Thanks for listening.—Sula.

She pressed Send, then used Google to search for the state's employment website. She hoped to dig up more job opportunities and find out what she could about filing for unemployment.

There weren't many jobs and none involved reporting, writing, or communications of any kind. Except one TV-producer position, which, in the salary section said, "guarantees minimum wage." Great. She clicked through the site looking for filing info. Her cell phone rang, startling her. Timidly, Sula picked it up, half expecting it to be Rudker. "Hello."

Paul's voice shrieked at her. "Why didn't you call me? This is the wildest story I've ever heard. It's so unlike you and yet, so like you. I want details. Start at the beginning. Where did you hear the first conversation?"

Sula recounted the events of the past six days, with a dozen interruptions from Paul, who kept repeating in a stunned voice what she had just told him.

"You went to the morgue and looked at a dead body?"

"You ran from your boss and he chased you?"

"You spent a night in jail?"

Paul's hysteria made her downplay her reaction to it all, but she had, in fact, taken more Xanax in the past week than in the past six months.

"Unless he has the judge in his pocket, those charges will be dismissed." Paul sounded sure of himself, even over the phone.

"I hope so. Fortunately, my court date is a week after my custody hearing."

"Does your lawyer know about any of this?"

"Not yet. I plan to tell her though."

"Sula, you did the right thing. Don't doubt that. I wish I had your courage." Paul sounded a little choked up, and it made her feel self-conscious.

"Hey, don't get gushy on me. Bravery and stupidity are sometimes hard to tell apart. If I lose Tate over this, I'll never forgive myself."

"Sula, I know you don't want to hear this, but I don't think you should get your hopes up about the hearing."

She knew Paul felt that way, so she rarely discussed it with him, but now she felt defensive. "You don't think anything I do now will make a difference?" She popped up and began to pace.

"I didn't say that. But—"

She cut him off. "What do you think I should do about Prolabs?"

"You have to expose them. By the way, what was on the disk?"

"Patient records of the two guys in Puerto Rico who killed themselves and two other files I couldn't open but that are labeled DNA."

"Would those files still be in the company's computer system?"

"I don't know. Rudker probably destroyed everything he could find. Why do you ask?"

"I could get into the database."

Chapter 18

She had forgotten Paul was a reformed hacker. If there was such a thing. Being a hacker was a lot like being a gambler. People might stop doing it, but they never really got it out of their system.

"I can't let you do that." She chewed on her lower lip. "It's too risky."

"Not really. Hacking into the Defense Department's system is risky. Prolabs' IT people will never know I was there."

"Really?" She felt a little surge of hope. "It would be worth a look."

"Why don't you come over and keep me company while I peek at their system."

"Sure. When?"

"Right now. It'll be fun. I haven't done any snooping in a long time." Paul laughed. "Hey, before I got your e-mail, I was playing online chess with a smart-ass from Singapore. How boring is that for a Saturday night?"

"You're one up on me. I'll be over in twenty minutes."

Still groggy from two sleepless nights in a row, she stopped for a Diet Pepsi. She would need the caffeine to keep up with Paul's energy. She crossed Ferry Street Bridge and drove out Martin Luther King Boulevard to a large apartment complex.

She shut off the truck and checked her watch: 9:33. A few years back, she'd gone through a phase of hating the habit but hadn't been able to break it. Now it didn't bother her. She took the stairs up to his unit two at a time. Paul greeted her with his usual big hug. Sometimes his affection made her uncomfortable; tonight it made her feel less alone in the world. She hugged him back with a good squeeze.

Physically, she and Paul were enough alike that people often thought they were brother and sister. They both had dark hair and eyes, light-brown skin, and a slender, slightly taller than average build. Paul was Philippine and German, while she was Irish, Spanish, and Indian. People were often fascinated when they heard she belonged to a local Indian tribe, but Sula considered it an honorary membership that required no active participation. Her mother's tales of growing up on the reservation had done the opposite of what she'd intended. Sula wanted no part of it. Some cultures had no place in the modern world.

"You're home on a Saturday night. What's up with James?" Sula peeled off her sweater. Paul had the heat going, and it was warm enough to strip down to shorts.

"He found a job in Portland, but I don't want to move. So he's not talking to me."

"Do you think he'll take the job anyway?"

"Hard to say. James is usually more talk than action, but the job is with an ad agency and he's pretty excited."

They moved into the living room, where Paul kept his computer setup—three hard drives, two monitors, a printer/fax machine, a phone, a sound system, and a tangle of cords that looked like it could power a small city. A love seat and small TV occupied the other half of the room.

"Why don't you go with him?" Sula asked. "What's keeping you here in Eugene? I mean, since you don't have family."

"I'm comfortable here." Paul parked in front of a monitor displaying a three-dimensional chessboard with cartoon rabbits for game pieces. "I hate the thought of starting all over. Friends—people like you—are too important to give up."

"That's sweet, but I would ditch you in a heartbeat for a great job in Portland."

"As you should." Paul sent an instant message to the guy in Singapore to let him know he would be leaving the game room for a while. He rolled his chair in front of the second monitor. "Prolabs, here we come." He typed the company's name into Google and pulled up its website. He turned to Sula and said, "We're going to try an old-fashioned Trojan horse."

"What's that?"

"Pretty much like it sounds." Paul rubbed his hands together and grinned. Sula hadn't seen him look this happy in a long time. "First, we send an e-mail to someone at the company. The e-mail contains an embedded program that copies itself to the company's system when the recipient opens it. The program attaches itself to the guest directory and records users' names and passwords for all the databases. Then we check the guest directory, find the program, and copy the passwords."

She followed the scheme up to a point. "How do we check the guest directory?"

"That's the hacker part. Don't worry, I'll get in." Paul turned back to the computer. "Who do you want to send an e-mail to?"

"Is it a real e-mail with a note from me?" Sula had a little guilt about sending a Trojan horse to a friend at Prolabs.

Paul laughed. "Hell no. Nothing traceable. I'll send it from an anonymous hotmail account. I just need an e-mail address."

Sula considered her options. "Will the IT people at Prolabs detect the embedded file? Will they be able to track its source?"

Paul shrugged. "Maybe. Eventually. I doubt if they get much activity. They're probably pretty complacent."

"Send it to Karl Rudker. That's K-R-U-D-K-E-R at Prolabs.com."

"Perfect. He'll have no one to blame for it."

Sula watched over Paul's shoulder as he created a phony e-mail about a vacation resort. In the subject line, he typed: *For top-level pharma execs only.* Then he accessed a program stored on his hard drive.

"You have such a program on hand?"

"The guys at EFN are compulsive code writers and they like to keep me in the loop. I never, make that rarely, use any of the programs they create."

"They're just snoopers, right? They don't send out worms or viruses over the internet, do they?"

"Oh no. They hate that crap as much as everyone else. Maybe more. Ready?"

"Sure."

Paul pressed Send and Sula felt a shiver of excitement. She wasn't sure if it was the idea of getting into places where she didn't belong or using Rudker to sabotage himself.

Paul turned and grinned at her. "That e-mail is now being routed through hundreds of internet providers, so no one will ever trace it back to me. Now, let's take a look at their mainframe and see if they have any vulnerabilities."

She watched him type in an ftp:// address, then in rapid-fire motion, click through a Prolabs' site she'd never seen. The screen changed rapidly and Sula found it hard to keep her eyes on the monitor. It was like watching a speeded-up online computer class.

"I'll park a port scanner outside the main server to monitor all the VPN activity. Sooner or later, we'll pick up a password." Paul tried to sound casual, but she could tell he was psyched. Sula found it hard to stay tuned-in. She was not a techie. She'd taken website-development classes just to be ready for any workplace, but she used her computer to write, look for information online, read blogs, and send e-mails.

She wandered over to the window. A group of young men gathered in the parking lot behind the apartments. They passed a joint and talked loudly. With their blue jeans, black sweatshirts, and dark hair, only their faces were illuminated under the darkening sky. For a moment, Sula envied their carefree lives. She walked back to where Paul was clicking away.

"Next we try the back door. What other websites or FTPs would Prolabs be linked to?"

"You mean like the FDA? For transferring clinical-trial data?"

"Exactly." Paul snapped his fingers and pointed at her. "Except not the Food and Drug Administration. I think they might be a little tough to get into and a little pissed off if they caught me trying."

Sula gave it some thought. "The company's websites are linked to a lot of disease-management sites and PhRMA of course. But Prolabs doesn't send data to any site that I know of." She stopped, realizing that wasn't true. "Except clinical-trial sites and TrialWatch, which gathers data on all clinical studies."

Paul quickly found the TrialWatch site. The home page was divided into two sides: one for patients looking for trials and one for doctors. "What's the name of the drug again?"

"Nexapra."

Paul typed as Sula spelled it for him. He used a scroll bar to select Oregon as a location. Two clinical-investigator names and locations appeared onscreen, one in Eugene and one in Portland.

"Print that page, please." Sula wasn't sure what she would do with the information, but it pleased her to have it. "Plug in Puerto Rico and see if anything comes up."

The location wasn't on the scroll bar, so Paul typed it into the space. As his GE four-in-one printed out the first page, Dr. David Hernandez and all his contact information came into view.

"I'll be damned." This information pleased her even more. "Print that too."

Paul was already on it.

"What now?"

"I'll play around on this site for a while to see if it has any cracks in its structure. But mostly, we wait. Both of our snoop programs may take a few days to generate a usable password."

"I thought hacking websites was instant, in and out."

"I'm using old-school stuff. I'm not current because I don't do this anymore, remember, except as a favor for a friend." Paul grinned.

"Thanks, Paul."

"No problem. This is the most fun I've had in weeks."

"Do you mind if I get out of here? I'm still exhausted from not sleeping last night."

"I'll call you as soon as I get into the R&D database."

Sula folded the printouts and slipped them into her purse. She was still amazed by the information that could be gathered online in twenty minutes or less. She kissed Paul's forehead, then headed back across town.

At home when she plugged her cell phone into the charger, she realized she'd missed a call. She connected to voice mail and braced herself, thinking Rudker may have left an intimidating message.

Instead, a pleasant male voice said, "Hi, Sula. This is Aaron DeSpain. We had the little fender bender the other day. I'm calling to see if you'd like to get together for coffee or something. If you do, I'm at 686-4597."

Chapter 19

Monday, April 19

Trina's phone rang, breaking her concentration. She wanted to ignore it and keep working on her story, but she could no more ignore a ringing phone than she could go on the air without makeup. She believed in the ripple effect of everything she did or didn't do. The one time she didn't answer the phone, she would miss the hottest story of the year. The one time she didn't look her best, a talent scout would be watching her newscast. She picked up the phone.

"Trina Waterman," she said, with a touch of impatience.

"This is Allen Sebring with the accounting firm of Anderson and Shire. I think I have a story for you. Will you meet me this afternoon?"

"I can't make it today. I'm on deadline. What's the story?" She had no time for this, and yet she was intrigued.

"I can't talk about it over the phone, but I guarantee, you'll like the lead."

"Tomorrow morning at ten thirty. Starbucks on the corner of Seventh and Washington. You know what I look like, right?"

"Of course. But I need to do this now, before I lose my courage."

Trina couldn't resist. He seemed to be suffering from the stress holding it all in, and she loved a ripe story. "All right. Same place, in forty minutes."

"Thanks. See you then."

Trina would have liked to walk the short mile to the coffee shop—any opportunity to exercise—but she didn't have time today. She spent another ten minutes crafting her follow-up report about the murdered woman found near the river, then hurriedly ate the fruit salad she'd brought for lunch.

This better be good, she thought as she headed out.

Allen Sebring didn't look like an accountant. He was tall and thin with a long angular face. Hunched over the small coffee-shop table, Trina thought if he swapped his brown tweed jacket for a black overcoat, he could play Lurch. Out of habit, she visualized him from the lens of a camera. Compelling, in a freak-show sort of way.

After the introductions, he held out his hand and she reluctantly shook it. Hand-to-hand contact was the best way to catch a cold, and she could not afford to get sick. The camera was not kind to virus-infected faces. She excused herself to go order a single-shot Americana and wash her hands in the restroom.

When she returned to the table, Sebring leaned in and spoke in a quiet voice. "Are you familiar with Prolabs?"

Trina felt the little charge of electricity she experienced when stories started to come together. She had just been writing about a murdered woman who worked for Prolabs, and now she was about to hear company secrets. Were the events connected? Even if not, talking about them together would make good coverage.

She kept her face deadpan. "Of course. They're the city's biggest employer and they plan to get bigger."

"You know the city council just voted to change the zoning so the company could expand."

"Yes. I know." Trina sipped her coffee. It was still too hot.

"Did it strike you as odd that Walter Krumble, who has never voted to change anything, sided with the business?"

"That is odd. So?" She wished he would just spit it out.

"Neil Barstow, the company's chief financial officer, withdrew fifteen thousand dollars in company funds and made a notation on the withdrawal slip that said *Walter Krumble*."

Another shot of electricity. "A bribe?"

"What else?"

"Why are you telling me? Are you his accountant?"

"I'm *one* of Prolabs' accountants." Sebring's eyes darted around before he continued. "I'm telling you because their books are a mess—largely illegal—and if the JB Pharma deal doesn't go through, the company will collapse."

Trina sat back and gave herself a moment to digest it. She was excited and distressed at the same time. Prolabs was a local success story. It employed hundreds of people, including her brother. Exposing its seedy side might bring it down. She didn't want to be responsible for that. Yet, what else could she do? She had a responsibility to her viewers, many of whom owned Prolabs stock. Besides, bribery and illegal bookkeeping were the stuff of a scandal. If she exposed it now, she might actually help save the company. "Can you provide any documentation?"

"I made a photocopy of the withdrawal slip." He pulled it out of his jacket pocket and pushed it across the small table. The paper unfolded and revealed itself to be exactly as Sebring had described.

Gotcha! She couldn't hold back a smile. "What about the bogus bookkeeping?"

Sebring squirmed. "I don't know. I could get fired for divulging client information."

"I can't do much with the accounting story without some type of evidence."

"You can contact the Securities and Exchange Commission. Call for an investigation." Sebring started to button his jacket.

"I have to give them something to go on."

"I'll fax you a document. It lists a loan to KJR Inc., which is a specialty enterprise set up as a tax shelter. In reality, it functions as a personal line of credit to Karl Rudker. The first repayment is five months overdue."

"How much did he borrow?"

Sebring stood and silently mouthed, "Two point seven mil."

Trina liked the number. She heard herself saying it on air. She wanted more, but Sebring was leaving. "Thanks for the tip. Can I contact you?"

"Please don't." He started to walk away, then turned back. "Good luck."

Trina nodded. The story would require some serious digging, but it could be well worth it. Especially if the dead woman was connected to Prolabs' accounting scandal. Had she threatened to expose Karl Rudker? Was he prone to violence?

Trina decided to skip the coffee. Her energy level was already pulsating. This kind of story never happened in Eugene. Bankruptcies, identity theft, and an occasional scam on senior citizens were about all the white-collar crime the local folks came up with. She tossed her mostly full cup, exited the warm coffee shop, and headed back to the station. Karl Rudker's life was about to undergo a scrutiny that would make even an honest man blush.

* * *

He was in a foreign country and hordes of people lined the sheer cliffs over a mile-wide river. Without hesitation, they all jumped, splashing into the icy water. Robbie knew he should follow, yet he hesitated. He eased up close to the edge and peered over. The water seemed to be moving slowly but it looked incredibly deep. He filled his lungs with air and prepared to push off.

His leap was cut short by the sound of the alarm. Robbie sat up and slammed off the noise. He swung his legs out of bed and planted his feet on the floor. A moment later, he was up and moving toward the bathroom. Halfway there, he became aware of his actions. He'd never come awake so quickly before. It was the first time in years he'd gotten out of bed without hitting the snooze button at least twice. He could not remember ever getting up to face the day without at least some reservation.

He smiled. The new drug must be working.

Once his brain really kicked in, some downbeat thoughts surfaced. Such as how interminably boring his job was. Robbie tried to find a positive thought. Maybe he'd get a seat next to Julie during lunch hour. They would talk and she would smile at him. Robbie decided to leave it at that. No reason to get his hopes up too much.

His energy level stayed high throughout the morning. After the lunch buzzer rang, Robbie zipped down to the changing room and out into the walkway faster than he had moved in a long time. His energy level surprised him. He wondered if this was what meth or speed felt like to a normal person. If so, he understood the attraction. His confidence increased with every step. There would be a space at Julie's table. She would talk to him. Life was good.

Julie was at a table with only one other person, Melissa from the production office. Robbie hurried straight over, skipping his usual stop at the Coke machine. He sat down next to Julie, placing his lunch bag on the table. The tremor in his hands was obvious, so he put them in his lap. He couldn't remember what he'd brought for lunch and wasn't hungry anyway.

"Hi, Julie."

She was so pretty. Light-brown eyes, pale, perfect skin, and the cutest little mouth.

"Hey, Robbie. How have you been? I haven't seen you around much."

She had noticed that he hadn't sat by her lately. Very cool.

"I'm doing great. I started—" Robbie caught himself. He had almost announced his new medication. "I started working out. It feels good." He promised himself he would do push-ups every day for a week.

"Oh yes, I have to exercise or I get cranky."

"I can't imagine you cranky."

"You should see me when I go too long without eating. Whew!" Julie made a mock horror face. Robbie laughed. Julie smiled then bit into her sandwich.

Robbie opened his lunch bag and discovered a brown banana and a carton of leftover rice from Jason's Chinese takeout dinner last night. He was too embarrassed to haul them out. He decided to have a Coke instead.

"I'm going to get a soda from the machine. Would you like one?"

"No thanks. I brought a Snapple." Another bright smile.

He hated to walk away from her, but his throat was dry, and he didn't want it to sound funny when he asked her out. Which he planned to do the moment he got back.

The vending machine was near the cafeteria door, thirty feet away. He pulled some quarters out of his pocket on the way. Root beer sounded better, so he reached for that button instead. Then he worried it would make his breath weird, so he hesitated, then bought a Coke instead.

Can in hand, he whirled around and started back. From across the room, he watched Julie talk and chew in a delicate balance that few could pull off. Then his heart went cold. To his left, Josh Mitchell, the packaging lead, was coming up the aisle between lunchroom tables. The good-looking bastard slid into his spot next to Julie and shoved Robbie's lunch bag aside in one easy motion.

No!

He wanted to run, but his legs wouldn't cooperate. They felt like lead. It seemed to take an eternity, but they carried him back. Josh was already talking to Julie, making her laugh. Robbie tried to cut in, "Hey, Josh, I was sitting there."

Josh finished his story, then looked up with an easy confidence. "There's a spot right there." He pushed Robbie's bag with the beat-up banana down the table. "You're already up. Don't make me move."

Robbie felt paralyzed. His mind whirled but his legs wouldn't budge. Why had he gotten up? How could he have been that stupid? He had been so close to asking her out. He could not bring himself to sit down and watch Josh flirt with Julie. Robbie glanced at Julie, and she gave him a quick smile with a little shrug. Then she turned back to Josh and asked him if he played racquetball.

Robbie's heart was so crushed it was barely beating. Why did he try? Why did he set himself up for disappointment? He picked up his lunch bag and dragged himself to the door. His intention was to leave work and not come back. He could not bear to be humiliated again. He dropped his bag in the trash, but hesitated to ditch the Coke. He was still thirsty.

"Hey, if you're not going to drink that, I will." A short, pretty redhead he hadn't seen before sauntered up to him.

On impulse he handed her the soda. "Go ahead."

"Thanks." She took the can and smiled. "I'm Savanah. I started work here this morning."

"Robbie Alvarez. Six months and counting."

She wasn't Julie, but she seemed nice. Robbie asked her if she'd like a tour of the factory.

Chapter 20

Sula spent Monday morning at the employment office, filling out paperwork and registering for a work search. Because she'd been fired, they told her she would have to wait a week or two while they investigated her claim. Sula hoped to have a job before any checks arrived. She had no desire to take taxpayers' money.

She had stopped at the post office and mailed several resumes on the way, but she hadn't returned Aaron's call. She played his message several times just for the charge it gave her. She almost called him back. What could it hurt to have coffee? Still, she hesitated. She had to find a job. She had to win her custody hearing. If she could, she had to stop the Nexapra clinical trials. All were high-stakes projects and she could not afford to be distracted.

After a quick taco salad at Mucho Gusto, she headed through the downtown area, rehearsing her introduction on the way. A call that morning had netted her a fifteen-minute appointment with a clinician at the Oregon Research Center. Sula had not expected the doctor to agree to the interview and now she felt unprepared and nervous.

The research center was in an ugly gray building on Willamette Street. Sula pulled in and parked next to a blue Honda Civic, the only car in the lot. She checked her watch: 12:52. Eight minutes early. Sula unzipped her black binder and reviewed her questions. It failed to quell her nervousness. She began to doubt her ability to be a reporter. It was a simple interview that would never make it to print. Chill, she told herself. Unable to sit any longer, she climbed out of the truck, smoothed her black skirt, and headed inside.

Soothing tones of teal, forest green, and adobe enveloped the waiting room. Sula felt calmer already. The receptionist greeted her warmly and asked her to wait a few minutes while she located the clinician. Sula sat on the edge of an armchair, ready to pop up at a moment's notice.

A tall, beautiful woman with near-black hair entered the waiting area. Sula caught herself staring. The woman approached and held out her hand. "Dr. Janine Lucent."

"Sula Moreno. Thanks for taking time to speak with me today." They shook hands.

"Let's go back to my office."

Sula followed her through a series of turns and they ended up in an office that was smaller than her old one at Prolabs. The tiny window had a view of a parking lot. Sula didn't imagine the doctor spent a lot of time here, but still, it seemed like someone who had spent eight years in college deserved better.

"What can I do for you?" Dr. Lucent smiled warmly.

Here we go, Sula thought. "I'm writing an article about clinical trials for mental-health drugs. I understand you participate in such studies."

"That's what we do here."

"Were you involved in a Nexapra study? It's a drug in development by a local company."

"Yes. I'm familiar with the therapy. The first trial concluded several months ago. What would you like to know?"

"Was it a success? Did most of your patients benefit from the drug?"

Dr. Lucent let out an almost imperceptible sigh. Sula wondered if she asked something stupid. The doctor began to explain in the tone of a tired teacher. "Only half the patients in the trial received the drug, the other half received a placebo, a dummy pill. But I can't really talk about the results of the trial, because they haven't been published yet."

"The company is now recruiting for a phase III trial, so the phase II stage must have gone well."

"It did."

"Is there more risk involved in studies for mental-health drugs? I mean compared to other types of drugs?"

The doctor scowled. "Yes, I suppose. But we supervise the patient subjects very closely."

"But still," Sula pressed her point directly, "patients who are depressed sometimes attempt suicide. Have any of your patients ever killed themselves while enrolled in a clinical study?"

"It happens." Lucent met her eyes, unashamed.

"Did it happen during the Nexapra study?"

"No, but I couldn't talk about it with you if it had."

Sula switched tracks. "Were there any minorities in your arm of the trial?"

Lucent frowned again. "I'd have to look back at the records to be sure, but I don't believe there were." She seemed intrigued. "Why do you ask?"

Sula was ready. “One of the things that got me interested in writing this article was something I read about minorities being under-represented in clinical trials. The article said drugs get approved without a full understanding of how they affect certain racial groups. Do you think that’s true?”

Dr. Lucent put on her lecturer’s voice. “The full effect of a drug can’t be known until it’s been in use in a large patient population for an extended period of time.”

Sula jotted it down because it seemed like a good quote.

The doctor shifted uncomfortably. “Just because there weren’t any minorities in the trial here in Eugene, doesn’t mean they weren’t in the trial anywhere.”

“There’s a substantial Latino population here. Why do you think none of them participated?”

“I don’t know. Perhaps we’re not reaching them with our messages about the study.”

“Where else did the Nexapra trial take place?” Sula wondered if Lucent knew about Puerto Rico.

“I believe there was an arm of the trial in Portland.”

“That’s it?”

“I think so.”

“Portland doesn’t have many minorities either. Not compared to the whole country.”

Lucent leaned forward, a bit defensive now. “The drug still has to be tested in large patient populations. That’s what phase III trials are for. I’m sure there will be minorities in those studies.” The doctor stood. “That’s all the time I have.”

Sula stood too. “Will you participate in the next Nexapra trial?”

“I currently am.”

“It’s going on right now?” Sula was startled. She thought it would be weeks or months before the phase III round.

"Yes, it just started. We're still recruiting, but I'm very optimistic about this study and this drug."

"Thanks for your time."

Sula shook her hand and left, troubled by the idea that people were already taking Nexapra again, and so far she'd accomplished nothing, except to lose her job. There was another doctor in Portland who had tested Nexapra, and Sula planned to approach this one differently. First she needed to borrow a cell phone with a blocked caller ID.

* * *

From the parking lot across the street, Jimmy Jorgovitch watched the girl come out of the gray building. He liked the way she moved, with long fluid strokes. He liked her looks too but couldn't place her nationality. Maybe she was part Hawaiian. She had straight dark hair that hung well below her shoulders.

Jimmy followed the purple truck out into traffic on Willamette Street. The bright color stood out nicely in traffic. His subject was both easy to look at and easy to follow. That meant easy money. It was about time. His private-detective business had taken a huge hit when the economy went down, and he'd had to supplement his income with security work that involved way too much time on his feet. At fifty-four, he was too old for eight-hour stand-up shifts, but too broke to retire. His cop's pension covered only the mortgage on his home and his mother's monthly supply of medical marijuana.

Jimmy had been barely able to contain his excitement when the big guy in the suit hired him for a round-the-clock surveillance job. The man had called and arranged to meet him in a bar, then declined to give his name. He'd put a stack of fifties on the table between them and Jimmy had agreed to take the job.

Afterward, he'd watched the guy get into the black Commander and had jotted down the license. He'd given the plate number to one of his buddies on the force to check out. Jimmy knew exactly who he was working for. He figured the girl was Rudker's mistress, and Rudker suspected her of cheating on him. Much of Jimmy's work was about other people's distrust.

Tailing this chick was a plum assignment. Jimmy had watched her through his high-powered binoculars last night as she changed into pajamas. He liked her long legs, small perky breasts, and allover tan. Jimmy understood that flesh spying wasn't cool or legal, but since the girl didn't know and wasn't hurt by it, he couldn't resist. Watching her up close on occasion kept him from going stir crazy, sitting in the car on the side of the street.

Today she was on the move, heading back into the center of town. Her stops at the post office, employment office, Mucho Gusto, and Oregon Research Center had been noted in his journal: time of arrival and time of departure for all. He was under strict instruction not to let her detect his surveillance, so he hadn't followed her into any of the buildings.

Her trip to the post office was the biggest worry. The girl had carried a couple of manila envelopes into the main branch and had come out empty-handed. Rudker would be upset about that. Jimmy's assignment also included checking her curbside mailbox—and confiscating anything addressed to the FDA. Stealing mail was a felony and Jimmy had told Rudker he wouldn't do it. Rudker had then offered a ten-thousand-dollar bonus for any such envelope Jimmy brought to him.

As much as he could use the money, Jimmy hoped he wouldn't be faced with the decision. If the shit hit the fan later, Rudker was the kind of guy who would make sure the fan was pointed at someone else. The girl's mailbox had been empty when he checked this morning, but she'd taken big envelopes into the post office. Rudker would be upset, but what could he have done? Knocked her down in a federal parking lot?

The purple truck made a right on Thirteenth Avenue. Jimmy pulled his '95 Olds into the next lane and followed her. A bright ball of sun burst through the thin layer of clouds. He fumbled through the clutter on his dashboard for his sunglasses. They weren't there. He glanced down at the console and spotted them next to an empty drink cup from Taco Bell. By the time he got the shades on, his eyes were already watering.

He looked up and didn't see the truck. He stayed in the center lane on Thirteenth and glanced down Oak to see if she had turned. He spotted the white canopy crossing Eleventh. The next street, Pearl, was one-way, going the wrong way. Jimmy passed it, then turned left on High. Now he was two streets away and two blocks behind. Predicting what she would do next was a crapshoot. She may have already parked on Broadway for some shoe shopping. Or she could have turned right on Seventh Avenue to head across the Ferry Street Bridge. Or maybe she would stay on Oak and take it all the way to the Fifth Street Market.

Jimmy didn't have to guess. He saw the truck turn right in front of him onto High from Seventh. Now he was only a block behind her. The light changed to yellow and he sped through it. The woman in the minivan next to him honked. Jimmy stayed focused on the purple truck. It passed the Fifth Street Public Market, then parked on the opposite side of the street in front of an old building. Jimmy passed by as the girl got out. In his rearview mirror, he saw her enter the one-story structure. He sped up to Skinner's Butte Park and turned around. He stopped a block away from the truck and parked on the opposite side of the street. He had no idea what business was located in the building but he would find out.

In five minutes, the girl came out, got in her truck, and made a cell-phone call.

* * *

Sula parked in front of the plain, no-signage building where her friend Hannah was a drafter for a group of engineers. Hannah would likely be in her office and have her cell phone with her. Her friend paid for the caller-ID block because she was hiding from an abusive ex-husband and was paranoid about letting her phone number get out.

Sula put a quarter into the meter and trotted into the building. Bright and spacious, the interior smelled of apples because of the daycare downstairs. Sula waved and smiled at the receptionist and kept going. She'd been here a few times.

Hannah was hunched over her computer, drawing air ducts with a CAD program. She was heavyset with spiky blonde hair and fifteen years older than Sula. They had played softball together the summer before and had bonded over their shared survivor mentality.

Hannah jumped up and gave her a tight squeeze. "What's wrong?"

"That obvious?"

"Oh yeah. You look stressed."

Sula remembered seeing herself in the mirror and thinking she had aged. Now she knew it wasn't her imagination. "I lost my job."

"Oh shit. What happened?" Hannah sunk back down.

"It's a long story, and I don't want to take up your work time. I'll tell you over lunch, real soon, I promise. Right now I need to borrow your cell phone."

"Sure." Hannah pulled it from her pocket and handed it over. Her curiosity was evident, but she didn't ask.

"I need to make an anonymous phone call."

"Ahh." Her friend nodded in understanding. "You will give me every juicy detail next time I see you."

"Of course." Sula grinned. "Can I borrow your yellow pages?"

Sula quickly found what she needed and moved toward the exit. "I'll bring it back in a few minutes."

"No rush."

She took the phone out to her truck and checked the name and number she had jotted down at Paul's house. She focused for a moment on what she would say, checked her watch—2:17—then dialed the Portland number. She hoped Hannah had free long distance.

"Riverside Medical Clinic." The young woman who answered the phone was cheerful but in a hurry.

"This is Dr. Susan Giacomo. I need to speak with Dr. Gwartney about a patient." Sula had picked Giacomo from the psychiatric physicians' section of the phone book.

"I'll see if he's available."

After a two-minute-and-thirty-five-second wait, a pleasant male voice came on the line. "This is Dr. Gwartney."

Sula took a deep breath. "Hello. This is Susan Giacomo. I have a small psychiatric practice in Eugene. I hope you'll be able to give me some information."

"I will if I can."

"I have a patient, a young man in his early twenties. He's been taking Paxil, and it keeps his mood stable but causes him insomnia. I'm considering the Nexapra trial as a next step. It's a head-to-head study against Prozac, so I expect him to be fine either way. But I wanted to talk to someone who's had experience with Nexapra."

"I'm very excited about its potential," Gwartney said. "Seventy percent of the patients in our arm of the trial responded favorably, and the side-effect profile seems quite mild. Some loss of appetite. Some orgasm delay, but much less than other SSRIs. What else do you want to know?"

"What about insomnia?" Sula didn't want to hit the suicide question too soon.

"About the same as placebo."

"Excellent." A city bus roared by just as she spoke. She hoped Dr. Gwartney wouldn't hear it and wonder where she was calling from. "What about the thirty percent who didn't respond well?" she plunged ahead. "Any serious consequences?"

"Unfortunately, there was one suicide. A woman in her late twenties."

Sula's heart rate picked up, but she forced herself to sound casual. "What do you know about her? Any history of suicide attempts?"

"None that she reported or she wouldn't have gotten into the trial."

"Of course." He sounded a little defensive and she had to be careful with her last question. "Were there any minorities in the trial? My patient is Hispanic and I worry that he doesn't metabolize medicine well."

"We don't ask participants to identify their race, but I can tell you that we had one forty-year-old black man and," Dr. Gwartney hesitated, "the woman who committed suicide looked Hispanic. Her last name was James, but she was married."

Goose bumps surfaced on her arms. *A suicide who looked Hispanic. A third genetic victim?* Sula had to stay with the charade for another moment. "What do you think? Should I get my patient into this trial?"

"If he's been through several therapy changes and you're trying to get him stable, I would wait until Nexapra is on the market. As you know, there will be a delay between the end of the trial and FDA approval. During that time, the drug will not be available, so you'll have to find something else for him in the meantime." The doctor chuckled softly. "But as a clinical investigator I have to say, we need all the participants we can recruit to get this drug on the market quickly. It's your call."

"I'll give it some serious thought. Thanks for the information, Dr. Gwartney."

"You're welcome." He abruptly clicked off.

Sula hung up too and her mind reeled. The information carried a mixed emotional punch. She felt distressed for the young woman who had died unnecessarily, yet she felt fortified in her conviction that she was doing the right thing in trying to stop these trials.

She returned the phone and promised to meet Hannah at the Steelhead for lunch the next Wednesday, even though she knew there was a good chance she wouldn't be able to keep the date. She was more determined than ever to track down Warner's DNA findings. If Paul's hacking efforts didn't produce anything soon, she might just have to go to Puerto Rico.

Chapter 21

Rudker had arranged to meet Jorgovitch at the Wetlands bar on Chambers. The private investigator had picked the time and the location. Rudker had never left work this early before or set foot in such a place. He'd agreed to the time and place because he was anxious to get the report and preferred to go somewhere no one would notice him.

Now he was running late and hoped the fat little man had the good sense to wait. Considering the money Rudker had paid him, he'd better. A $2,000 retainer had bought him the promise that this job would never be documented or discussed. On some level, Rudker knew it was paranoid to watch the girl to see what she would do, but as long as he kept it in check, suspicion often worked in his favor.

If Sula had gone so far as to steal a disk from Warner's office, it was obvious she was out to get him and would not give up easily. Rudker intended to subvert anything she tried.

He pushed the Jeep past the speed limit, ignoring the pounding rain on his windshield and limited visibility. As long as he kept making the lights, he had no reason to slow down. West Eleventh traffic had started to thin from the rush hour and he made good time. He pulled into the pub's parking lot and drove to a back space. He liked to keep his rig away from the reckless masses.

The bright neon sign announcing the name Wetlands irritated him. What the hell was wrong with the people in this town? Wetlands was synonymous with weed patch. Who the hell would name a restaurant and bar after such a landscape? It was bad enough that the city council was making Prolabs create new wetlands just so they could build on their own damn land. All because a group of kooky environmentalists thought the wetlands should be preserved. He could not wait to get out of this town.

The stink of burnt grease hit him as he stepped inside. Rudker tried to ignore it. The one good thing he could say about Eugene was that it had passed a no-smoking law. At least he wouldn't have to suffer that offense on top of the grease and moldy carpet aromafest. He glanced around at the noisy blue-jeans-and-flannel crowd. People seemed charged up. Rudker figured it was either payday or Powerball time. He wondered if it was too late to buy tickets.

Jimmy waved at him from a booth against the window. Rudker pushed through the crowd and slid into the seat without ever looking directly at the guy. He didn't want anyone to ever connect the two of them. Jimmy greeted him with "Hey."

The PI was halfway through a tall glass of beer. Rudker signaled the waitress and ordered a bottle of Henry's, which he would not finish. He did not want to be noticed, and everyone else had a beer in front of them.

Jimmy started to give his report, but Rudker cut him off. "Wait for the waitress to come back. I don't want to be interrupted."

They sat in silence until his beer appeared. Rudker paid the young woman with cash and tipped her a dollar. Just enough to be fair, but not enough that she would remember him. When she left, he signaled Jimmy to begin.

"I checked her mailbox early this morning while she was in the shower, and it had nothing in it. Then she came out of the house at eight o'clock and drove straight to the post office on Tyinn Street."

Rudker's blood pressure bulged. "What did she do there?"

"She carried in two or three manila envelopes." Jimmy squirmed. "A few minutes later she came out, empty-handed."

"Shit." Rudker said it softly. "Any idea what was in the envelopes? Were they bulky, like they had an object in them? Or flat, like paper only?"

"Flat, like paper only." The PI sounded confident.

"Any idea who they were addressed to?"

"No."

"What else did she do today?"

Jimmy looked down at a notepad on the table. "She went to the state employment office on Coburg Road and spent two hours and forty-five minutes there."

Relief washed over him. Sula was looking for work. The envelopes probably contained resumes and job applications. "By the way, when you're done reading your notes to me, destroy them. Tomorrow, commit her movements to memory, please."

Jimmy squinted at him. "I'll try."

"What next?"

"She stopped at a place called Oregon Research Center. It's on Willamette Street."

"I know where it is. How long was she there?"

"About thirty minutes."

"Anything noteworthy?"

"No, but her next stop was kind of odd."

Rudker raised an eyebrow.

"The building on the corner of Fourth and High. Haven't figured what it is yet." Jimmy tossed back the rest of his beer. "The weird thing is, she went inside for a minute, then came out and sat in her truck to make a cell-phone call. Then she went back inside for a minute, then came back out and left."

Rudker puzzled over the sequence of events. "Maybe she borrowed the cell phone from someone inside?"

Jimmy gave him a surprised/impressed look. "Could be. After that she went home. Spent the afternoon in her garage."

Rudker wondered why Sula would borrow a cell phone. She must have one of her own. The only thing that made sense was she didn't want someone to see her name come up. Who would she make an anonymous call to? His greatest fear was that she had made a copy of the disk before he'd taken it back and maybe already sent it to the FDA. Without data, calling the agency would be a waste of her time. They heard from crackpots every day, people who thought pharmaceuticals were evil and blamed the agency for everything from constipation to global warming.

Had Sula contacted the media? He realized Jimmy was asking him something. "What did you say?"

"Should I stay on her for a few more days?"

"Yes. Let me have those notes."

Jimmy ripped the top page off his notebook and pushed it across the table. Rudker scooped up the page and shoved it in his jacket pocket. He would run it through his shredder at home. Rudker took a long swallow of his beer, then stood to leave. "Tomorrow, same time."

"See you then." Jimmy made no move to leave.

"You're going back out to her house, right?"

"I thought I'd eat first if that's all right."

Rudker was annoyed by the man's sarcasm but didn't let it show. "See you tomorrow."

The rain was still pounding down when he stepped outside, so he decided not to go back to the office. Tara would be pleased to see him home before seven for a change. He backtracked the way he'd come, then headed up Timberline. The mortgage on his home was nearly $3,000 a month, but the location was empowering. Rudker liked being at the top.

He turned left on Meadow View and saw an unfamiliar blue Bronco in his driveway next to Tara's Mercedes. *Damn.* He was in the mood for sex, not small talk with one of her charity ladies. He parked on the street because there wasn't room in the driveway for all three vehicles.

Rudker hurried up the steps, entered the house, and stripped off his wet overcoat. He tossed the coat on the hall table and called out to his wife as he moved through the foyer into the living room. He was surprised to see it empty. Tara and her guest were not in the family room either. Rudker headed upstairs to their bedroom to change his shoes. Tara and her friend were probably in her office, planning some event.

As he reached the top of the stairs, his wife came out of their bedroom, followed by a man Rudker had never seen before. At first, the sight confused him. Who was he and why was he here? Had she called a repairman? Then the man's young age and stunning looks hit him like a chest blow. Dear God, this thirty-year-old Adonis was fucking his wife.

Rudker's throat went dry and he couldn't speak.

"Hi sweetie," Tara gushed. "This is Doug. He's a volunteer fundraiser for the food bank."

Rudker swallowed, finding his voice. "Why were you in the bedroom?"

As his wife struggled to formulate a believable response, Rudker took it all in. Tara's tousled hair and hard nipples pushing through her sweater, unrestrained by a bra. Doug's flushed face and sockless ankles.

"We were looking for a list of donors that I'd made out earlier and—"

"Shut up!" Rudker's heart valves pounded like a herd of thoroughbreds at the racetrack. His muscles tightened until he thought his chest would explode.

Doug stepped forward and started to speak. Rudker rushed him, knocking him to the ground. He landed with his knee in Doug's crotch. The man cried out and Rudker silenced him with a fist to his mouth. The crunch of bone on bone was both painful and rewarding. Rudker pounded the pretty face again.

Behind him, Tara shrieked for him to stop. Rudker ignored her and hammered the guy again and again. He didn't stop until his wife grabbed a handful of his hair and yanked his head back. In a flurry of pain, he swung awkwardly at her, striking her softly in the thigh.

Behind him Doug jumped up and knocked Rudker on his ass. While he lay stunned for a moment, the coward bolted downstairs. Tara stood her ground, biting her lip. The front door slammed as Rudker got to his feet.

"Jesus, Karl. It's not his fault. It's mine. I'm sorry—"

He lashed out and slapped her mouth to stop the flow of words. Tara's hands flew to her face, but she didn't cry out. For a moment, they made eye contact and silently accused each other of a dozen wrongdoings, big and small. Tara conceded first and fled into the bedroom. Rudker slumped on the top step and put his head in his hands. He heard Tara opening and closing drawers, slamming them occasionally to express her anguish. She was packing to leave. He made no move to stop her.

After a few minutes, she dragged a suitcase by him as she pounded down the stairs, crying softly.

"Why?" he called out to her retreating back.

For a moment she kept going, then at the bottom of the steps she stopped and turned back.

"Because I'm lonely. Because you're never here." Her voice gained volume and her face twisted in anguish. "Because you're not really here even when you're home. Because I don't want to move to Seattle."

His wife spun around and stormed out the front door. For a second, he heard the rain beating on the front step, matching the fury of his heart. Rudker wished he hadn't hit Tara; that one slap could cost him dearly. But damn it, she had betrayed him. Totally blindsided him. After several long minutes of waiting for his heart to stop pounding in his ears, he went downstairs and took two Ativan. He thought he might have missed his Zyprexa again that morning, so he took one of those too.

Blood seeped from his knuckles, so he stood at the kitchen sink and ran cold water on his swelling hand. Rudker vowed to get back on track, to stay in control of himself until his external problems were resolved. He knew he should fight for Tara. He could win her back with the right promises—and he would. But it would have to wait. He was juggling too many critical things right now, any of which could blow up on him. The land rezoning and expansion. The fraudulent accounting, which could surface and derail the merger. And that damn PR person's obsession with the Nexapra trials.

Rudker shut off the water and retreated to his study. Sula was his greatest concern and containing her was his top priority. Her visit to the research clinic had unnerved him. He doubted the girl had learned anything significant, but clearly she was not giving up. He wondered what it would take to intimidate her. The idea of assaulting her was certainly attractive. Punishing offenders could be quite satisfying, as he had just experienced. Yet an anonymous attack would be difficult to pull off, and Sula would probably send the police to him even if she didn't actually see her assailant. He could not afford to be questioned. Not with his career on the line and with Warner so recently assaulted.

On the other hand, an accident might be just what Sula needed.

Chapter 22

The time Sula spent working on her sculpture was therapeutic. She'd managed to not think about her custody hearing, her unemployment, the theft charges against her, or the Nexapra trials for nearly two hours.

Of course, as soon as she put down the MIG welder, she'd started brooding about all of it. Her custody lawyer still didn't know she was unemployed, and Sula needed to make that dreaded call. She had decided not to tell Barbara about being arrested. The theft hearing was after the custody hearing, and no one involved in the custody dispute needed to know about it. The only thing she could do to improve her chances of winning custody was to find a job, one that paid more than unemployment. That might take a while. Unemployment in Oregon was over ten percent.

Recovering the DNA data seemed even more difficult. Paul hadn't called yet to report how their Trojan horse was doing. On the positive side, she'd learned the last name of a third Nexapra suicide, but wasn't sure what good it would do her.

She wanted to get out for a walk but it was too wet. She put on shorts and a Beyoncé CD, then worked up a sweat dancing around the living room. Exercise was not a discipline with her. She did it only when she felt like it, and only as long as she enjoyed it.

Sula showered and changed into jeans. Unable to wait any longer, she called Paul. "Hey. How's the hacking coming?"

"Hi. And I'm fine, thanks."

"Good to hear. If you're going to keep me in suspense about it, maybe I should drive over and pick up pizzas on the way."

"Excellent idea. I have nothing here but a moldy tomato, a can of peaches, and some cat food." Paul didn't have a cat.

Sula didn't take the bait. "See you in thirty."

She called in two small pizzas from Papas—a Mt. Bachelor classic for her, with pesto, sausage, artichoke hearts, and wax banana peppers, and a Canadian bacon and pineapple for Paul. They had shared this meal a few times. The pizzas were ready when she arrived, and Sula put them on her UO/Visa card. Intuition told her she needed to keep what little cash she had on hand.

It stopped raining on the drive over. She heard her mother's voice—a sweet, faint memory—calling it an omen for good things to happen during her visit with Paul. As much as she liked to keep her mother's memory close, Sula rejected her spirituality. Gods and chants and superstitions hadn't made her mother happy or kept her safe.

Paul opened the door as she got there and ushered her in with a string of exclamations about food and love. Sula took the boxes to the kitchen table, while Paul dug out a stack of napkins. They each devoured half a pizza before saying much.

"What's happening with our Trojan horse?" Sula asked between napkin wipes.

Paul grinned, mouth full and all. "I have a password."

"Great news. Do you know who the user is?" Sula pushed her pizza aside, too excited to eat now.

"Eric Sobotka."

"He's a scientist. He has access to the clinical-trial database."

"I know." Paul was still grinning. "I've already been in there."

Sula jumped up and went around the table to hug him. "What have you found?"

"Tons of stuff. But I don't have any idea what I'm looking for, so that's why I needed you here."

"We're looking for anything we can find about Miguel and Luis Rios. I should have given you the names."

"You probably did." Paul shrugged. "Let me eat one more piece of this heavenly pie, then we'll get right on it."

After forty minutes of searching, the names did not come up.

"Rudker deleted the files. I knew he would." Sula slumped into a chair. She'd been pacing Paul's living room for the last thirty minutes, checking over his shoulder on occasion. "Warner must have expected him to do that, which was why she made the disk. And I lost it."

Paul turned to her. "You didn't lose it. The bastard had you arrested, then broke into your home while you were in jail and stole it from you. Who would have seen that coming?"

"Certainly not me."

"What now?" Paul did not give up easily either.

"You're not going to believe this, but I'm thinking of going to Puerto Rico."

"Get out." Paul's mouth fell open. "You don't fly."

Sula hadn't let herself think about that part of it. "I have to get that data. A woman in Portland also committed suicide while taking Nexapra during a clinical trial. She was only twenty-eight. Her last name was James, but the clinician said she looked Hispanic."

"Jesus. Clearly not a good drug for Latinos." Paul shook his head. "Can you do it? Get on a plane and fly across an ocean?"

"I hope so. Maybe with enough Xanax in me."

"Can you afford the ticket?"

"No, but I have a credit card."

Paul leaned forward and grabbed her hands. "I have a free flight from years of building up credit-card points. It's good for anywhere on US soil. I'll get you a ticket with it."

"I can't let you do that."

"Of course you can. It's not a gift; it's a loan. Without any interest. You'll pay me back whenever you can."

Sula was overwhelmed by his generosity. She tried to refuse again, but he ignored her and turned back to his computer. In a few minutes, the Chase credit-card site came up and Paul found the number to call for cashing in his travel points. While he was on hold, he asked, "When do you want to go?"

Sula's pulse quickened. It was happening so fast. "Soon, I guess." If she waited, Rudker would have an opportunity to destroy the original files in Puerto Rico. What if he had ordered someone to do it already?

"Wednesday?" Paul was waiting for an answer.

"I don't have a passport."

"You don't need one. It's a US territory."

The only thing she had planned for the next few days was more job searching. "All right. I'll go."

Great gods. Sula could not believe she had just agreed to get on a plane and fly fifteen hundred miles. She'd never done this before and didn't know how to prepare. Her pulse escalated.

"When do you want to come back?"

How long would it take? She planned to visit the research center and maybe the families. "Two days," she finally said. Was that reasonable? She couldn't afford to be gone longer than that.

"Which airport?"

"I don't know. The research clinic is in San Juan."

As Paul talked his way through the ticket purchase, Sula paced the room and tried not to hyperventilate. She could do this. Thousands of people got on planes every day and so could she. She had never left Oregon before. Did they speak English in Puerto Rico? she wondered. She would get online as soon as she got home and find out everything she could.

When Paul got off the phone, he printed out her itinerary while simultaneously reciting it to her. "You'll catch a flight at 5:45 in the morning and fly to Phoenix. From there, you'll fly to Orlando, Florida, then on to San Juan, arriving at 9:36 in the evening, San Juan time. Three flights and twelve hours of travel. Quite an ordeal for your virgin flight."

Sula had to sit again.

"Take your cell phone. Call me as often as you like." Paul hugged her. "You'll be fine."

"You should come with me." She didn't want to do this alone.

"I wish I could, but it's too short notice for me. I have two jobs."

"I know. I'm being selfish. This terrifies me."

"What doesn't kill you will make you stronger."

"Nietzsche didn't have to worry about falling from the sky."

Chapter 23

Wednesday, April 21, 5:58 a.m.

One Xanax was not enough. Sula began to hyperventilate the moment she felt the air rush under the plane and lift it off the ground. To keep from vocalizing her terror, she put her head on her lap, closed her eyes, and recited an old prayer her mother had taught her as a child. She had no faith the gods would keep the plane afloat, but forcing herself to remember the strange Native American words helped distract her.

Once the plane leveled out, she was able to breathe somewhat normally. Everyone around her seemed so calm. The young boy next to the window had been reading before the takeoff and was still reading now. The men and women in suits with their laptops all seemed intent on their work. She glanced out the window—from her seat on the aisle—and had to close her eyes again. This was not natural. The physics made no sense. Taking off in a glider plane would have been less frightening.

Sula stopped the flight attendant, a woman who looked old enough to be her grandmother, and asked for a glass of water. When she came back with it, Sula took a second tranquilizer. Two hours and twenty-one minutes, her itinerary said. An eternity. And only one leg of a three-flight journey. What in the hell was she doing? Sula breathed from her stomach and let her mind go blank. After a while she drifted off.

The second takeoff out of Phoenix was only slightly better. At least she knew what to expect this time. About the time the plane leveled off, they hit turbulence. The first dip made her physically ill. Her head went to her lap. She could not even pray. She begged Tate to forgive her for being so selfish. For running off on a wild goose chase to help people she didn't even know and getting herself killed. Why hadn't she made out a will?

The shaking and dipping seemed to go on forever. Sula looked up occasionally between spells and noticed other people chatted and read as if they were riding a bus across town. She vomited twice during the descent and vowed that when this trip was over, she would never get on another plane.

The Florida airport was considerably more intimidating than the Phoenix layover had been. The crowds were thicker, the languages more diverse. While in the bathroom brushing her teeth, Sula overheard a conversation that sounded like Swahili. She hadn't even left the mainland and she was homesick already.

She had to ask directions three times during the long hike from Southwest to American Airlines, but people were friendly and helpful. Sula hoped that would be true in Puerto Rico as well. She'd read on the visitors' information website that seventy percent of the population spoke English. She was counting on that because she spoke no Spanish. She'd brought a pocket dictionary for emergencies.

Her watch was no longer useful, so she kept checking the time on her cell phone, even though the airport had clocks everywhere. During the two-hour wait to board, her stomach finally settled down so she ate a cheeseburger and watched people come and go.

She could not believe so many of them traveled as part of their job. The whole experience was surreal, like a bizarre dream. Intellectually, she wanted to embrace it, to be adventurous and excited by the unknown. Emotionally, she was on edge and wanted more than anything to be home.

The last leg of the flight was the easiest. She was too tired and too worried about what she would do once she arrived in Puerto Rico to worry about crashing into the ocean. The flight was smooth and her cheeseburger stayed down. She even snoozed for a while.

She arrived at 9:41 local time and reset her watch to match. Her brain felt numb and her body was on autopilot, but she was pleasantly surprised by the airport's small size and American feel. None of the drinking fountains worked though.

Outside, the air hit her with a warm, moist gush. Sula had never experienced anything like it. She peeled off her lightweight jacket and stood for a moment, taking in a sky full of stars. It felt like summer, and she was at ease for the first time in twenty hours. After gulping in a few more deep breaths of warm night air, she approached one of the dark-green cabs that seemed to arrive every few minutes.

The driver, a small, middle-aged man, jumped out, opened the trunk, and tried to take her overnight bag. She realized he meant to be helpful, but Sula refused to let go. "I want to keep it with me." He shrugged and made a "whatever" face.

"Where to?" he asked with a soft Hispanic accent.

"The El Canario Inn." She'd found the hotel online, three miles from the airport, five miles from the Fernández Juncos Clinica, and only eighty dollars a night. There were cheaper places to stay, but they did not have internet connections. It was cowardly, but she wanted to stay near the airport and the tourists. She didn't have the time, money, or courage to experience the culture. She was pleased when the cab fare came to only $4.20.

The hotel was old and beautiful. Its high ceiling was inlaid with dark wood and ornate engravings, and the warm peach-colored walls were lined with lush green plants like she'd never seen before. The surprising chill of air-conditioning set her teeth on edge. The warm air outside had been so much nicer.

A pretty young woman about her age was behind the desk. She spoke perfect English, with an accent Sula didn't recognize. After exchanging a credit-card number for a plastic card that served as a room key, the woman pointed out some of the hotel's features. Sula was barely listening. She was so tired, she couldn't focus and knew she wouldn't have time to enjoy the pool or the casino.

To reach her room, Sula had to go outside, pass by the long pool, and walk down a foliage-lined path. She felt moisture everywhere—in the air, dripping off the plants, oozing from her skin. Once inside her room, she shut off the air conditioner, opened a window, stripped off her clothes, and passed out.

* * *

Robbie pedaled home from the store in a daze. He'd gone out to buy cigarettes after calling in sick and falling back asleep for hours. It surprised him to feel so blah after starting out so great yesterday. He wondered about the new medication. Maybe it was a mistake. He had been taking it for less than a week and that was not enough time to tell.

The roads were wet, the sky was dark, and traffic was heavy, but he barely noticed any of it. He couldn't stop thinking about how badly he'd blown his chance to ask Julie out yesterday. And he was mad at himself for missing work today. Why did he keep making the same mistakes? Because at the end of his day, what did he have to come home to? A crappy apartment, an empty wallet, and a lonely bed. What was the point? The same thoughts kept circling in his brain, round and round with the motion of his tires.

A blaring car horn snapped him out of it. He braked as he looked up to see an old yellow truck making a left-hand turn right in his path. He barely slowed, the wet brakes failing to do their job. The truck swerved as he laid down his bike to avoid the head-on collision. They missed each other by inches. The driver took a moment to stop, roll down his window, and yell, "Fucking idiot."

Robbie picked himself up, unaware that traffic had stopped around him. He climbed back on the bike and continued down the street, his shoulder throbbing. He'd come so close to being killed. Part of him wished he'd let it happen. His struggle would have been over, just like that. He laughed bitterly. With his luck, he would have ended up in a wheelchair, a paraplegic with his mother spoon-feeding him for the rest of his shitty life.

No, if he was going to kill himself, he would do it right. He'd given the subject some previous thought and decided that an overdose of downer meds or a jump off a tall building was the only way to go. At home in his sock drawer was a small collection of tablets: some sleeping pills he'd pinched from his mother, a handful of Vicodin left over from when he'd had his wisdom teeth pulled, and two Oxycontins he'd scored at a party six months ago. Was it enough?

Robbie didn't know, and it wasn't the kind of question you could call "Ask a Nurse" and find out. But in the last five minutes, he'd made a decision.

He reached his campus apartment and carried his bike upstairs. He could have left it on the sidewalk, he realized as he reached the top, because he wouldn't be here tomorrow to care if it had been stolen.

He parked the bike against the wall in the living room and flopped on the couch, feeling exhausted. For hours, he lay there thinking about his own death. About what would happen afterward. Would they do an autopsy on his body? Would they cremate him or seal him up in a casket? Who would come to his funeral? *Not many*, he thought.

His mother would be devastated, but she would get over it. She was a bounce-back queen with a new boyfriend and religion to comfort her. She would pray and think of him in heaven and, in the long run, have one less thing to worry about. Robbie had no idea how his dad would feel. The old man had always been a mystery. Mr. Mood Swing. Robbie liked to believe they had loved each other long ago, but he wasn't sure it was still true.

He pushed himself off the couch and headed for the fridge, where he hoped to find a beer. He needed a little boost of courage. Plus the alcohol would add to the effect of the pills.

A chilled half bottle of vodka was waiting for him instead. Next to it on the top shelf was a package of lunch meat and a half-empty quart of orange juice. Jason must have been making screwdrivers the night before and brought the leftovers home. A stroke of luck, just when he needed it. Robbie poured a liberal dose of each liquid into a green plastic glass, then downed half of it in a few gulps.

The concoction hit his stomach and revolted. Robbie fought to keep from throwing up. He sat at the kitchen table and waited for the nausea to pass. Moments later, he felt light-headed. He hadn't eaten since breakfast, which had consisted of a Pop-Tart and a handful of raisins.

He hurried back to his bedroom and found the pills while he was still sober enough to walk straight. Clutching the container, he went in search of the house phone. He'd lost two cell phones already and couldn't afford a new one yet. But he had to call his mother and say good-bye. He owed her that.

He found the cordless phone in Jason's room on top of a pile of dirty clothes. Jason was such a slob. A funny, best-friend kind of slob. He would miss the guy. Robbie shook his head. No. Jason might miss him, but he would be dead and have no feelings. That was the point.

Next he went to the kitchen for a glass of water. He wanted everything in place for the moment when the courage struck him. Back at the table, he pressed #3 and called his mother. Robbie wished he'd given more thought to what he would say. After three rings, her answering machined picked up. The sound of her voice made him sad, and he was glad she hadn't answered.

"Hey, Mom. Just wanted to say hi. I love you. Good-bye."

It was the last thing he would ever say to his mother.

Should he write Jason a note? It felt wrong to leave the world without speaking to someone or writing a real farewell. He started to get up for a pen and paper but the room lurched and he slid back to his chair. He laid his face on the table and waited for the dizziness to pass. Images of his father flashed though his hazy thoughts. His dad standing in the back of the auditorium during a sixth-grade Christmas concert because he'd come in late. His dad standing at the foot of his bed on a Saturday morning saying, "I don't understand you. Get up. It's a great day."

Robbie struggled to remember his father's cell-phone number. His first guess was wrong and a Chinese woman answered the phone. He mumbled, "Sorry," and hung up. Maybe he had dialed wrong. His fingers felt clumsy. He tried again. The phone rang three times, then he heard his father's impatient "Hello."

"Hi, Dad. It's Robbie."

"Hello, son." Long pause. "It's been a while."

"I know. I was just thinking about you and decided to say hello."

"You sound drunk."

"Maybe a little."

"You should call back when you're sober. Unless you called for a reason. Do you need money?"

Robbie wanted to cry. He needed so much, and yet so little.

"Not money. Sorry to bother you."

He hung up and his head fell to the table, with his heart thumping in his ears. The vodka was overwhelming him. He knew he needed to act fast before he passed out.

Where had he put the pills? He could barely lift his head to look around. Had he taken them already? He must have, he couldn't keep his eyes open.

Chapter 24

Rudker snatched up the buzzing phone and barked, "Yes?"

"Gerald Akron is on line one." His secretary said the CEO's name as if he were God. Her deference for the fat, arrogant SOB soured Rudker's mood even more.

He pressed the top red button. "Hello, Gerald. What can I do for you?"

"What's the word on the expansion, Karl? We need to know if it's a go. We've been offered a sweet deal on some land up here and need to make a decision." Akron sounded a little distant, a little edgy.

Rudker was immediately worried. "The council voted our way. Now we're just waiting for the environmental report, which I guarantee will be favorable. I made sure of that."

"Good. But when will we know?"

"By the end of the week. Monday at the latest."

A grunt, followed by a pause. Rudker knew something unpleasant was coming.

"John and Harvey and I had a meeting yesterday, Karl. We decided that in light of the merger, we needed to reorganize the leadership structure."

Long pause. Rudker's face began to sweat.

"In essence, we're creating a group of vice presidents, each with his own area of responsibility."

A knife to the gut. They were taking his power and giving it away.

"You'll oversee operations."

The knife twisted. A glorified plant manager. He felt ill. Outraged. He could not speak.

"Karl? Are you still there?"

"Yes."

"We think it'll make the company stronger. We expect your cooperation. I'll e-mail you the memo outlining the new structure."

"Who's being promoted?"

"Tibbs, Reilly, and Oberkow. Good people. You'll see the responsibility breakdown on the memo."

Rudker tried to recover, to keep himself in the game. "I'll make a call today about the environmental report and put some pressure on. I'll have it signed, sealed, and delivered by Monday." His voice sounded strange, even to him.

"Excellent. You'll make a great head of operations."

"Talk to you soon."

He set the phone down and began to rub his temples. He had manipulated the company's books, bribed the local government, and neglected his wife to the point that she cheated on him—all so he could relocate to Seattle for a plant-manager's job. Jesus H. fucking Christ.

He slammed the fat side of his fist against the desktop. It wasn't enough. He smashed it again and again, ignoring the pain from the other night's bruising. The action was rhythmic and loud, like a drummer at the end of a hard-rock set. About the time he couldn't take any more, Alice timidly opened the door to his office.

"Sir? Are you all right?"

"Do I seem all right?" Rudker gave her a look that sent her scurrying.

He stopped pounding, lest he start any rumors about his instability. Just what Akron needed to hear. The asshole. His hatred for his new boss felt physical, like a tumor growing in his belly. He hoped he would be able to hide his feelings from the man. At least long enough to put feelers out for a new position.

He checked his e-mail, looking for the management-structure memo, but it wasn't there yet. Probably a good thing. Why feed the fire?

He called Cindy Taylor, his buddy on the county's environmental committee, but she wasn't in. The message he left on her voice mail was briefer and gruffer than he intended, but he had only so much control over his mood.

While the cell phone was still in his hand, Jimmy Jorgovitch called.

"Hey, Karl, it's Jimmy."

Rudker was startled by the man's use of his name. He hadn't given it to the PI. "I don't know how you got my name, but don't say it again. In fact, forget you know it."

"Seems extreme, but I'll go along."

"What's the girl up to?"

"You're not going to like this."

"Ah shit." Rudker couldn't take much more bad news. "What the hell is it now?"

"She took a flight first thing this morning. I just spent five bills of your money on a pimply faced kid to find out where. "

"Just fucking tell me."

"San Juan, Puerto Rico."

The air left his lungs and a wave of heat traveled through his body. Sula was now up there with Akron on the list of people he would gladly murder if he ever decided to let go completely. "When is she coming back?"

"I didn't find out."

"Why the hell not? For five hundred dollars, I expect to know exactly when her return flight hits the runway."

"I'll find out and I'll be there."

"Just call me and let me know." Rudker hung up the phone. "Fucking nosy, pain-in-the-ass bitch!" He was no longer concerned with what Prolabs' employees thought.

His cell phone rang again. Rudker was afraid to answer it.

It was his son, Robbie. The call surprised and pleased him at first. Then he realized the boy was drunk and obviously not at work, where he should have been. Rudker was in no mood for nonsense, so he put him off until later. The boy was clearly having trouble again, and Rudker wished he knew how to help him. He had never understood Robbie's problems, and he certainly did not have the time or patience to deal with them at the moment.

Rudker grabbed his jacket and strode from the office. Alice averted her eyes as he walked by. She was a pain in the ass too. He would fire her as soon as he got back. Right now he needed to think and plan and he couldn't do that in his confining office.

A company saleswoman stepped in the elevator in front of him. She was in her midthirties, with shoulder-length hair, and an attractive face. Rudker recognized her from a recent sales meeting, but couldn't remember her name. He didn't care and didn't return her nod.

Thoughts and images he could not control flooded his mind. He visualized Sula's plane crashing into the ocean and killing her on impact before she ever reached the island. He imagined a pack of indigent thieves coming out of an alley in San Juan and stabbing her to death for the cash in her purse. If only he could get that lucky.

The saleswoman behind him began to whisper. At first he thought she was making a cell-phone call and trying to keep her conversation private. Then he realized she was making comments about him. *Sleazy crook who runs this business can't even keep his wife happy. Now he's after that poor PR girl who used to work here before he fired her.*

Rudker jerked around to face her. "Shut up!"

The woman drew back in shock.

Phony bitch. He turned around without further comment.

She was quiet for a moment, then started up again with her snakelike whisper. *Sula's right, you know, and she may beat you at your own game.*

The elevator jerked to a stop. Rudker turned around again. "You're fired." The door opened and he stepped off.

The saleswoman ran after him, calling, "Why?"

Rudker ignored her, crazy as she was, and strode through the lobby. A few people glanced up, aware that something was going on, but no one looked him in the eye. He stopped long enough to snap at the security man, "Keep that woman away from me."

He stepped out through the glass doors and into the bright sun. The backstabbing saleswoman didn't follow. Rudker took in the blue sky and warm breeze and longed for a day on the golf course. He suspected it would be quite a while before he could relax that much again.

Taking the wheel of his big rig and powering it down the road helped clear his mind and reinstate his confidence. For a few minutes. Soon the voice from the elevator was in his head. It insisted Sula was dangerous. *She went to the clinic in San Juan*, it whispered. *She traveled halfway around the world to gather evidence against you. She is hell-bent on sabotaging Nexapra's development and will stop at nothing to accomplish her mission.*

Rudker could not silence the voice or ignore it. In his gut, he knew it was all true. Sula was a fanatic. By raising the stakes, she had changed the rules of the game. Now anything was fair. Rudker could play at that level too.

* * *

Cricket was in a funk. He couldn't believe the city council had voted to amend the zoning regulations. Now the only thing standing between Prolabs and its new chemical-spewing factory was an environmental-impact report. That report, which was being produced by a county-appointed committee of three, would not have any real *green* input.

He sat on his back deck in a canvas chair and stared into the tall pine trees. He wanted to smoke a joint, but he wouldn't let himself. Not until he had formulated his next step. He was giving some serious thought to quitting pot anyway. A comment he'd heard behind his back yesterday made him realize he had become the very thing he'd run from all his life—a stereotype.

So much weighed on his mind. The council vote had been close: four to three. The big surprise had been Walter Krumble of district four. He was an old conservative—by Eugene standards—who liked the status quo. He rarely sided with any kind of change, progressive or not. As Krumble liked to say: "Yes votes mean spending more of the taxpayers' money."

Why had the old man gone along? Cricket always suspected the worst of big business and this was no exception. Krumble had been pressured, he was sure. But what could he do now? If the environmental report came back with a watered-down analysis that said, "Go right ahead, the birds can move and the frogs don't mind the poison," then the foundation would be poured. They were out there digging it right now "in anticipation" of a green light.

It was time to get serious. Cricket slowly rose to his feet and stretched his legs from their lotus position. He had to mobilize people who could commit to a long-term campout. He needed to arrange a support group to bring in food and water. It would take several days to get it all going, but that would give the bulldozers time to finish digging. His Love the Earth group would slip in after hours between the digging and the pouring and make themselves at home.

* * *

Robbie heard the phone ringing but couldn't wake himself up enough to answer. He felt drugged, unable to think straight. Yet his mind wouldn't shut down into complete unconsciousness either. He drifted, his brain floating from one scrambled memory to another. Next he was falling down the side of a mountain, rolling and smashing into shrubs and rocks.

Jason's voice boomed in his ears. "Robbie! Wake up!" His head was lifted up, but his eyes wouldn't open. Thumbs pulled back his lids. A bright light flooded his eyes and made the muscles in his temples hurt. He fought to close his lids.

"Hey. You're scaring me. Wake up!" Jason pinched his cheeks and dragged him to his feet. Robbie realized he was in their dining room. He felt too weak to stand, but Jason wouldn't let him go. He sensed himself being dragged, then a blast of cold air hit him. The shivers brought his body to attention. His legs became responsive and began to carry some of his own weight. After walking for a while, the oxygen helped bring his brain around. He realized Jason was asking him the same question over and over: "Did you take any of those pills?"

What pills? Robbie shook his head.

"Are you sure?"

He didn't know. Random scenes and thoughts from that afternoon came back to him. He had tried to kill himself. Yet here he was, still alive. Robbie began to cry. He didn't know if it was from relief or frustration.

Chapter 25

Thursday, April 22, 3:12 a.m.

Sula woke in the middle of the night to the loud repetitive calling of what she later learned were coqui tree frogs. Hundreds of the creatures, all belting out "ko-kee," over and over, created a cacophony of overwhelming noise. How did people sleep here? She remembered the open window and got up to close it. She gulped down some water from the sink, worried for a moment that it might not be safe to drink, then went back to bed.

She awoke again at 6:33 a.m. bathed in sweat. With the air-conditioning off and the window closed, her stucco-walled room had heated up. She reopened the window, relieved to hear only the faint sound of the ocean and the familiar hum of traffic. The air was just as warm at six in the morning as it was at midnight. She loved it.

She realized the research clinic would not open for hours, so she decided to wander around and enjoy herself. If she had packed a suit, she would have gone for a swim. Instead, she showered and dressed in the shorts and T-shirt she'd packed after reading that the average year-round temperature in Puerto Rico was seventy-eight degrees.

The breakfast room offered complimentary bananas, muffins, and coffee and she helped herself to all three. A little later, Sula started down the Isle de Verde, a long business strip that ran parallel to the coastline.

Nestled among familiar fast-food restaurants—Burger King, Kentucky Fried Chicken, Taco Bell—were small stucco shops with Spanish names that offered tourist take-homes. Sula checked out a few gift shops, selling mostly T-shirts, towels, and swimsuits. A pair of bright blue nylon shorts with orange dolphins made her think of Tate. She wondered if she and her son would ever take any vacations together. More than anything, she wanted to take him to Disneyland, to see the joy on his face at every ride and every familiar character.

She turned away from the children's clothes and selected a pair of sunglasses. She had not thought to bring hers and the sun was brighter than she'd ever experienced.

Back out on the street, the morning was still quiet and few pedestrians were out and about. As the traffic on the strip picked up, she was surprised by how American the cars seemed. She smiled at the thought. Of course they were American, but were they made here or did they have to be imported? She imagined that many things had to be imported, including food like ice cream. It seemed unlikely that the island had any dairies.

What it had were dozens of drug-manufacturing plants. For decades, US pharma companies had built factories in Puerto Rico to take advantage of its low wages and status as a commonwealth with no federal tax. At one point, half of all the prescriptions consumed in the United States were manufactured in Puerto Rico. Sula wondered what other industries were here. She checked her watch: 7:46. Time to head back. She intended to be at the clinic when it opened.

Sula's taxi pulled up in front of a low-slung stucco building painted a pale creamy yellow. Fernández Juncos Clinica was sandwiched between a Rite Aid and a restaurant offering *carne guisada puertorriqueña* as the house specialty. Sula thought it ironic that a drug studies clinic would be next door to a pharmacy.

She paid the cabdriver and asked him to return in an hour, then sat on a bench across the street. Soon she was sweating. The black skirt and beige suit jacket she'd changed into were too warm for the tropical climate, but fortunately she'd decided to skip the nylons.

A tall middle-aged woman approached the clinic and unlocked the door. Her red skirt and jacket set off her long dark hair. Sula guessed her to be in her midforties, and hoped she looked that good in twenty years. Felisa Quinton was the clinic's director, a psychiatrist who had been born, raised, and educated on the island. Sula had stayed up the night before her flight, searching the internet and learning everything she could about the island, the clinic, and its staff. The person she really wanted to talk to was David Hernandez, the doctor who had supervised the Nexapra trial.

Sula forced herself to be patient, to let the woman get settled in with a cup of coffee before she barged in asking questions. After checking her watch for the third time, ten minutes had finally elapsed. She took a long, deep breath as she stood. She'd tried to prepare herself for the possibility she might come away empty-handed—after borrowing a small fortune and enduring six plane rides. The money would be a setback either way, but the idea that she would fail to find the data she needed to stop the trials was hard to accept.

Sula had gone back and forth a dozen times about how to approach the doctor and had decided to use the journalist scenario she had used with the clinic in Eugene. It was also mostly true. Her career goal was to be an investigative reporter, and this was her first story. She intended to write about her experience, regardless of the outcome, and hoped to get the story published.

She stepped toward the street and waited for a pink convertible with a group of young girls to pass by. A minute later, she entered the air-cooled clinic. Cream-colored walls alternated with sage green, and a plush maroon couch invited visitors to sit. The soothing sound of water rippling over rocks served as background music. The effect was quite calming. Sula imagined a fountain in the courtyard, surrounded by big, brightly painted pots filled with ferns.

"Buenos dias," Felisa greeted her from the reception desk.

"Buenos dias." Sula smiled. "Actually, I don't speak Spanish."

The director smiled back. "That's fine. I like to practice my English with people who don't speak with an accent." She stood and held out her hand. "Felisa Quinton."

"Sula Moreno. From Eugene, Oregon."

"You're a long way from home. What can I do for you?"

"I'd like to speak to Dr. David Hernandez."

Felisa's face closed up. "He no longer works here." Anger flickered in her eyes. "I have no idea where he is or how to contact him. I'm sorry you came so far for nothing."

A silence engulfed them, the director lost in an unpleasant memory while Sula reeled with disappointment and paranoia. Had Rudker paid off Hernandez? Or was it merely coincidence that the two people most familiar with the Nexapra suicides—Warner and Hernandez—were unavailable?

A chill ran up her spine. Did Rudker know she was here? What if he had followed her? For the first time, she realized she might be in over her head. Rudker obviously wasn't taking any chances in letting the suicide data get out, and he undoubtedly considered her a risk.

"Did you know David? You look like you've just seen an *aparición*."

Sula shook her head. "It was very important that I speak to him, but perhaps you can help me instead."

Felisa shrugged. "If I can." She touched Sula's elbow. "Let's go into the conference room."

Sula followed her through an archway into a short hallway, then into the first room on the left. It seemed more like a cozy kitchen with a small dark-wood table and padded straight-back chairs. Sula glanced at the sink and refrigerator in the corner.

"Would you like something to drink?" Felisa moved toward the fridge.

"Please."

The director came back with two bottles of cold Frappuccino. Sula noticed Felisa's eyes were light blue, contrasting with her dark skin. She'd read that Puerto Ricans were a racial melting pot of native Taino, Spanish, African, French, German, and Chinese. Her personal observation was that most of the islanders were attractive.

They sat at the table and opened their drinks. Sula took a long slug before speaking. "I'm a freelance writer, and I'm researching the Nexapra clinical trials. I understand that there were two suicides here."

Felisa gave her an odd look. Sula couldn't read the reaction.

"Where did you get that information? The trial was discontinued and the data was not released to the public." Her impeccable English had picked up an accent.

"Were you involved in that study?"

"I assisted Dr. Hernandez with intake. What do you want to know?"

"Are the men's files still here? I mean, is there a record of their participation and suicides?"

"Of course, but I can't release any information to you. It's very confidential."

"Were you surprised when both Luis and Miguel Rios killed themselves within a month of taking Nexapra?"

Felisa stopped midair with her Frappuccino and set it down. She looked at Sula with a mix of surprise, respect, and fear. Sula decided to tell her everything. She had nothing to lose.

"I used to work for Prolabs. One day I heard Diane Warner and Karl Rudker arguing about Nexapra. Do you know who they are?"

"Of course. Dr. Warner discovered the drug when she worked for the Oregon Health and Science University. Rudker runs Prolabs."

That was more than Sula had known. "Warner told Rudker she'd found evidence that the men who committed suicide shared a genetic mutation that influenced the way they responded to the drug. She asked him to halt the trials and give her two years to develop a screening test. Rudker said no. He also threatened to fire her if she didn't drop the idea."

"You heard all of this firsthand?" Felisa let go of her drink and squeezed her hands together.

"Yes. I was waiting to talk with them about a press release I was writing."

"Go on."

"The next day, Dr. Warner didn't show up for work. She didn't call either. Two days later, we found out she was dead. Murdered while jogging along a riverside path."

Felisa's eyes flashed with speculation. Sula took a sip of the sweet caffeine and thought, wait until you hear the rest of the story.

"I became concerned that Dr. Warner's theory and evidence would die with her and that a lot of people might kill themselves in the large phase III studies."

Felisa made a funny noise in her throat, then signaled Sula to keep going.

"I went into Warner's office and found a disk taped to the bottom of a desk drawer. I took it home. The files were labeled Miguel and Luis Rios."

A young man burst into the room. "Hey, there you are. Sorry I'm late." His dimpled cheeks and curly hair gave him a look of innocence.

"Román, I'm very busy right now. Please go watch the front desk and do not disturb me again."

"Yes, ma'am. I'm sorry." He sheepishly backed out of the room.

Felisa shook her head. "Please continue. I'm intrigued by your story."

Sula hesitated, ashamed of her night in jail. "Rudker had me arrested. While I was in jail, he broke into my home and took Warner's disk."

The director leaned forward, disbelief evident in her expression. "The CEO of a pharmaceutical company broke into your house and stole a disk that you believe contained clinical-trial data for Nexapra?"

"Actually, it had their intake information and some kind of DNA files. I have no proof that it was Rudker, but the CD disappeared, and he is the only one who would have a reason to think I had it. Who else would break into my house and take only a disk with DNA information?"

"Nothing else was stolen?"

"No."

The director pushed her hair back with both hands. "This is *ajeno*."

Sula didn't need a dictionary. "I know. Now I find out Dr. Hernandez is no longer with the clinic."

"That was a personal issue. I don't think it's related."

There was a long silence, both of them mulling over the question: What now?

Sula spoke up. "There was also a suicide in the Portland arm of the trial. The clinician said he thought the girl was Hispanic. A lot of lives could be at stake. Hispanic lives."

Felisa jumped up. "David must have talked with Dr. Warner. If she analyzed the Rios men's DNA, she got the samples from here." Her gorgeous face was deeply troubled. She held out her hand. "Please excuse me. I have to check something."

The director strode out of the room, dark hair swinging. Sula stood and stretched her legs, checking her watch out of habit: 10:07. Would Felisa bring her a copy of Miguel and Luis' files? It seemed too good to be true. Yet, even if she did, having the clinical-trial records would not be enough. She needed a sample of their DNA, so that someone—maybe at the FDA or even a university—could replicate Warner's work.

Sula paced the room, glancing at the art on the walls. The outdoor market scenes were colorful, but not particularly skillful or intriguing. She sat at the table and picked up her pen. She hadn't taken a single note during their conversation. It had gone too quickly and had been too intense. Sula jotted down a few questions she still wanted answers to: 1) Was there any history of suicidal thoughts mentioned during either of the Rios' intakes? 2) Why was the trial discontinued?

Felisa was gone for eleven and a half minutes and came back with only a single piece of paper in her hands. Sula tried not to look disappointed.

The director's voice had the quiet tone of a conspirator. "Both Miguel and Luis Rios' paper files are gone. Their blood samples are gone. I think David must have sent the samples to Warner. I have no idea what happened to the paperwork."

"Why was the trial discontinued?"

"We failed to meet our goal for enrollment. And David was having problems at home and asked to take a leave of absence. So Prolabs shut it down."

"It wasn't about the suicides?"

"I didn't think so at the time, but I'm starting to wonder."

"Did you file adverse-drug-reaction reports with the FDA?"

"We notified our advisory board and Prolabs." Felisa sounded a little defensive, but in a moment she continued. "If data from this arm of the trial was never submitted to the Center for Drug Evaluation, then it probably never made it into the MedWatch database."

"Can you file an ADR now? I want the FDA to know about the suicides."

"Yes, I can and I will. But it's not enough to get their attention. We need to get new DNA samples."

Sula noticed her use of the word *we*. "You believe me?"

"Do I think Rudker took the disk from your home? Maybe." Felisa shook her head. "What I do believe is that David Hernandez and Diane Warner both thought there was a genetic vulnerability to Nexapra. If that's true, as you said, a lot of lives are at stake."

"So what now?"

"Go see their families and ask for a lock of hair or fingernail clippings they might have saved."

It seemed like such a long shot. Before Sula could protest, Felisa cut in.

"Don't worry. They'll have something. When you combine Catholicism with Taino superstitions, you get a culture that never lets go of the dead."

Sula understood this. Their bodies had been cremated, but she still had things that belonged to each member of her family. Her father's pocket watch, a small red-and-yellow blanket her mother had kept over her legs when she watched TV, and her sister's brown wool sweater that still smelled like the lilac-scented shampoo Calix always used.

"How do I find their families if the files are gone?"

Felisa held up the paper in her hand. "Their names and addresses were still in our database of initial call-ins."

"Will you go with me?"

"I can't. And you can't tell them I gave you the information. It's confidential and I could lose my license."

"What if they won't talk to me? What if they don't trust me?"

"If you tell them you're trying to stop Nexapra, they'll help you. Both families have come here to vent their anger about the deaths. They blame the drug."

Sula's stomach knotted up. She knew she had to do this, but it intimidated her. "What if they don't speak English? What if I can't find them?"

Felisa dismissed her fears with a small wave of her hand. "Román will take you. He'll interpret if he has to, but most people here speak some English."

Sula sighed with relief. "Thank you for helping me."

Felisa squeezed her arm. "Thank you for coming all this way to find the truth. There are not many who would get so involved." The director gave her a quizzical look. "Why is this so important to you?"

"My father committed suicide." That simple statement didn't even come close to describing the horror of what really happened that day, but it was all Felisa needed to know. "I couldn't bear to do nothing and let others make that same tragic mistake."

The director escorted her out to the front lobby. Her young assistant chatted happily on the phone. Felisa walked up behind him and touched his shoulder. "Román."

He jumped, mumbled something, and hung up. "Yes?"

"I need you to drive Ms. Moreno to these two addresses." She handed him the paper. "Wait in the car unless she asks you to interpret for her."

Román glanced at the addresses and moaned. "One of these is in Bayamon. It'll take half the day."

Felisa's tone was patient, but firm, like a parent. "I'll give you gas money. You get paid by the hour, so it makes no difference whether you sit on your ass here or in the car." She smiled to take the sting out of her words.

"What about lunch money?"

"You test my patience."

Felisa retreated into a back office and returned with a twenty. "Drive nicely." She turned to Sula. "Good luck."

Román scooted across the waiting area and held the door open. Sula stepped out into the bright sunshine. After the air-conditioned office, it seemed quite warm.

"This way." Román headed toward the corner and turned left. A parking lot behind the building contained his 1985 white Volkswagen bug. He grinned and opened the passenger door for her.

After they were both buckled up, he turned to her and said. "I'm Román Batista."

"Sula Moreno. Thanks for driving me."

"No problem. I like to get out of the office."

"The name Batista, wasn't he a famous artist?"

Román pulled out into the street with a squeal. Sula braced herself.

"He was a sculpturist."

"Are you related to him?"

"I wish. I'd love to be an artist."

Sula liked his accent. It sounded more African than Spanish. "What's stopping you?"

"A wife and two kids."

The island was more mountainous and the vegetation was scrubbier and drier than Sula had expected. She'd thought it would be more lush and tropical, like Hawaii, which she'd never been to but had seen in plenty of photos and movies. Yet the countryside here was green and beautiful in its own way, and the sky was a perfect shade of blue.

Sula tried to forget, for a moment, why she was here and soaked in the scenery like a tourist. Román occasionally played the part of tour guide, pointing out things of interest like two mountain peaks that looked like breasts, which the locals called *Mt. Pechos.*

Many of the homes that dotted the green hillsides were large and new with pink-painted stucco and red-tile roofs. Mixed in were dilapidated shacks surrounded by broken-down washing machines, car parts, and smaller shacks. In one yard, it looked as if the occupants were digging up the grass to bury their garbage. Sula wondered about the water supply. They were clearly outside the city limits. Were those people drinking from a well on their property?

After thirty minutes or so, they turned off the well-maintained four-lane highway onto a narrow two-lane road. They were headed toward Bayamon to see Miguel Rios' widow. Here, the houses were more tightly clustered and many had chickens in the front yard. After a few miles, Román pulled the paper Felisa had given him out of his shirt pocket.

"We're looking for 4940. See if you can spot an address."

She didn't see numerals near any of the front doors so she tried to eyeball the mailboxes, but they were moving too fast.

Suddenly Román slammed his brakes and shouted in Spanish. Sula looked up to see a black-and-white goat in the road. While the car was stopped, she took the opportunity to read a mailbox.

"This is 4752, so we must be close."

Román grunted and took off. "Hard to say."

Two minutes later, he made a sudden turn down a long dirt driveway. They passed the small home near the road and bumped their way back to a larger home, a pale blue two-story with a long balcony wrapping around the second floor. A boy of around five played with a dog in the front yard. He looked up and waved as they stopped in front of the carport.

Román hopped out and spoke to the boy in Spanish. Sula thought she heard the word for *mother*. The boy grinned and ran inside, using both hands to push open the heavy wooden door. Sula reluctantly stepped out of the Volkswagen, her heart suddenly pounding with anxiety. A warm breeze played on her skin and instantly soothed her.

A heavyset woman in her late forties came out into the yard. Her black hair was streaked with gray and pulled back into a short ponytail. She wore cutoff jeans, a man's white T-shirt, and worn-out sandals.

"*Hola*," Román called out cheerfully. He obviously had no intention of sitting in the car as Felisa had directed.

"*Hola.*" The woman glanced at Sula and raised an eyebrow.

"Are you Lucia Rios?" Román asked.

"*Sí.*" Now she looked skeptical.

"We're from the Fernández Juncos Clinica."

Her face closed up. "Why do you come here?"

Román turned to Sula. It was her turn. "I'm Sula Moreno. I used to work for Prolabs. I want to find out what happened to your husband, Miguel."

"He killed himself. You know that already." Her English was quite good.

"I think the drug he was taking in the trial may have helped cause his death, but I can't prove it without your help. Can I ask you some questions?"

Lucia hesitated for a full minute. Finally she shrugged. "Come in." The widow went back through the heavy door and held it open for Sula. She looked back to see if Román was coming. He waved and leaned against the hood of his car. She was on her own.

Lucia led her to the dining room table. Sula found herself staring at the walls, which were painted in varying shades of burnt orange. One wall was lined with family photos, another had a large painting of Jesus on the cross. Through an open window, she could see plantains growing on a tree in the backyard. She vowed to come back to the island some day when she had time to explore.

"Would you like some coffee?"

"Yes. Thank you." She was over her caffeine limit, but Sula wanted to be polite.

She watched Lucia pour from a thermos, then add some kind of syrup and maybe cream. She wasn't fond of sweet coffee, but she would be open-minded. Lucia brought the beverages in heavy white mugs, then sat across from her.

"If you work for Prolabs, why do you want to prove the drug is bad? It's called Nexapra, is that right?"

"Yes. That's right." The way Lucia said it gave the word a whole new sound. "I don't work for the company anymore. I'm here on my own. I don't think Nexapra is bad for everybody, just some people who share a genetic mutation."

"Mutation?" Lucia frowned. "You're saying something was wrong with my Miguel?"

"Oh no. I just mean he had a certain genetic characteristic that made him react badly to the drug." Sula pulled her recorder out of her big shoulder bag. "I would like to tape parts of our interview, as documentation. Is that all right?"

Lucia shrugged. Sula took a sip of the coffee. It was surprisingly good, not too sweet, but with a peculiar flavor she didn't recognize. She turned on the recorder and pushed it to the middle of the table. "Please state your name and your relationship to the deceased, Miguel Rios."

Lucia leaned forward. "I am Lucia Maria Sanchez Rios. Miguel Rios was my husband of twenty-three years."

"Before taking Nexapra, did Miguel ever talk about suicide? Or attempt to commit suicide?"

"Never." Lucia shook her head emphatically. "He loved his family. I know he was depressed and life was hard for him sometimes, but he never wanted to die."

"Did he receive any counseling for his depression?"

"He went to a special doctor." She tapped her head. "What's the word?"

"Psychiatrist."

"Yes. For a while, when the kids were young. The doctor gave him Prozac. It made Miguel feel better, so he stopped going."

"What year was that?"

"It was 1990."

"Was he still taking Prozac before he entered the Nexapra trial?"

"No. He switched drugs many times. I think he was taking Zoloft before joining the study."

"Why did he enter the trial?"

"The Zoloft wasn't so good anymore. Dr. Hernandez said the new drug was very good."

"Was he more depressed than usual?"

"A little, but he had been like that many times before. He always tried to get better. That's why he entered the study. He never talked about suicide." Lucia's eyes started to get watery. Sula felt bad for dwelling on such a painful subject.

"Did you notice a change in his behavior after he started taking the Nexapra?"

"Right away. At first, he had more energy. He was more like his old self." Lucia's dark eyes caught Sula's and held them. She was trying to say something without saying it. Was she talking about sex?

"Then what?"

"Then he got irritable like he does sometimes when he drinks too much coffee." She lifted her cup for emphasis. "He stayed that way for weeks. I asked him what was wrong. He didn't know. I asked him if he thought it was the new drug. He wasn't sure." She paused and took a long slug of coffee.

"Then one Sunday, I came home from the market and he was dead on the floor of our bedroom. Part of his head was blown off." Tears filled her eyes. "It tore my heart in a way that will never heal."

Sula knew. "I'm very sorry for your loss, and I'm sorry to put you through this. I won't take up much more of your time." She took another sip of coffee to be polite. "Do you have something that has Miguel's DNA?"

"What do you mean?"

"A lock of his hair, or a toothbrush. Something like that?"

Lucia gave her an odd look. "This will help you find out if the drug made him kill himself?"

"Yes."

Lucia shrugged again. "I'll get it."

Sula clicked off the recorder as Lucia padded down the hallway. In a minute she came back with a small wooden box inlaid with colored glass. Lucia set the box on the table and opened it. Against red velour padding lay a thick lock of dark curly hair.

"I only need part of it. Do you have a ziplock baggie?"

Miguel's widow rummaged through a kitchen drawer and came back with a good-sized freezer bag with a sealing mechanism. "This is okay?"

"It's fine. How about some masking tape and a pen?"

Another longer trip to the kitchen produced both.

"Please write your husband's name on a piece of tape and stick it on the bag, then transfer some of the hair to the bag and seal it. I'll turn on the recorder, and I want you to say what you're doing as you do it."

Lucia did as she'd been asked and tried not to smile at the silliness of it. Sula shut off the recorder and put the hair package into her shoulder bag. She hoped she didn't get searched on her flights home.

"Would you like me to contact you later and let you know what I found out?"

"Please. It would be nice to know."

Lucia wrote down her phone number and address on Sula's yellow tablet.

"Thank you. Do you know Luis' wife?"

"Si. Are you going to see her?"

"We're going there next. Do you think she'll talk to me?"

"I don't know. She's moody. Marta's at work now and doesn't get off until three. I'll call her and let her know you're coming, so she'll go straight home." Lucia made a face. "Sometimes she stops at the *taberna*."

Sula wandered into the living room while Lucia made her call. The conversation was in Spanish, and although she didn't understand the words, she could tell it became intense at one point. She stared at the patterns in a wall tapestry and worried that Luis' widow didn't want to cooperate. One set of DNA wouldn't do any good. The FDA needed a pattern to show the link between the mutation and the behavior. She hoped the agency's researchers would get samples from the young woman in the Portland trial who killed herself, the one named James who looked Hispanic.

Lucia hung up and joined her near the door. "Marta will meet you at her home at 3:15. Do you have the address? It's in San Juan."

"Is she still at 55 Cristo Street?"

"*Si.*"

"Thanks again. I'll be in touch."

The sun's brightness almost blinded her after the dark interior, and the day was starting to heat up. Sula checked her watch: 12:13. Román chatted with the young boy in the shade of a tree. She thought he must be a grandchild or neighbor. She smiled and waved at the two and climbed in the car. In a moment, her driver joined her. Román had smoked a cigarette and worked up a light sweat while waiting, but the combination of smells was strangely masculine and pleasant. Almost sexy.

"Did you get what you need?"

"Yes. Thanks. Lucia called Marta and we're meeting her at three fifteen."

"Good. We have time to stop for lunch, then."

Román took off with his usual foot to the floor. Sula buckled herself in.

They ate lunch at a little roadside stand just outside of San Juan. The *asopao de pollo* was the best on the island, Román assured her. Sula loved the zesty combination of oregano, garlic, cilantro, and chili peppers. Garden-fresh green peas cooled the fire and kept the dish from being too hot. Despite her hearty breakfast, she ate with gusto, sitting at a picnic table under a tattered sun umbrella. It was the best meal she'd had in a long time, and it had cost only $2.75.

Marta lived on the sixth floor of an apartment building in an area of San Juan called Hato Rey Central. They parked in a garage under the building and took the elevator up. Sula normally avoided both parking garages and elevators, but after surviving the flights to get here, finding Lucia, *and* getting a DNA sample, she felt too optimistic to give either much thought. Although on the way up, it occurred to her that the building was quite old, and she wondered if the elevator was regularly maintained.

No one answered their knock. Sula checked her watch: 3:07.

"We're a little early."

"So we wait." Román took a seat on the floor and leaned back against the wall. Sula joined him.

"I really appreciate your help today. This would have been so much more difficult without you."

"You don't have to keep saying that. It's nothing, really."

Marta didn't show up until 3:47, and when she did, she told them to get lost.

Chapter 26

"But you told Lucia you would talk to me." Sula smelled rum on Marta's breath and felt a little desperate.

"I don't feel like it now."

"It will only take a minute."

"I said, 'get lost.'" Marta was a short sturdy woman with long reddish-blonde hair. She wasn't exactly pretty, but Sula thought men would find her attractive. Maybe not at the moment though.

Still hoping to win her over, she held out her hand. "I'm Sula Moreno, and this is Román from the clinic."

Marta turned away. "And you know who I am." She unlocked her apartment door, stepped through, and slammed it shut. Román made an unpleasant gesture.

Damn. Without the second set of DNA, there was no theory to test. Sula struggled to be optimistic. Maybe Marta would feel differently later this evening. Or tomorrow morning when she was sober. Sula couldn't make herself walk away. She stepped up to the door and knocked timidly.

There was no response. She knocked louder. After a minute, the door jerked open and Marta swore at her in Spanish.

Sula didn't back down. "I know how you feel. My father killed himself, and I was angry for a long time. But if you don't help me, many more people may commit suicide. Nexapra has a genetic flaw that seems to affect Hispanic people."

She had Marta's attention. "Why Hispanic people?"

"I don't know. And we might never know if you don't give me Luis' DNA."

Marta bit her lip and mulled it over. Finally, she said, "I'll give you the stuff Lucia said to, but I don't want to talk."

"That's fine. Thank you."

Marta turned and gestured for Sula to follow.

The small space reeked of stale cigarette smoke and perfume, but the view of the harbor was lovely. Marta didn't invite her to sit.

"Wait here." She stalked out of the room through a tapestry-covered arch. A moment later she came back with a hairbrush and a pipe. "These belonged to Luis." She thrust the items at Sula. "It's all I have left of him." Under the anger, she was still grieving.

"Thank you for making this sacrifice. This is important research."

"Are we done?"

"Do you have a plastic bag?"

"Of course." Marta brought her an empty bread bag. Sula decided it would be fine.

"Would you please write a note, indicating that you gave me these items and who they belonged to?"

Marta rolled her eyes. "I don't have any paper."

"I do." Digging with one hand, Sula pulled the yellow tablet out of her shoulder bag. She found a pen in the side pocket and handed both to Marta.

Marta stepped over to the small table near the window. "What do I write?"

"Just say, 'This pipe and hairbrush belonged to my husband, Luis Rios. I gave them to Sula Moreno to give to the FDA.' Then sign it and date it, please."

Without sitting down, Marta scrawled the first half of the note. "How do you spell your name?"

Sula recited it slowly. Marta finished and signed with a flourish. "Is that it?"

"Yes. Thank you." Sula tucked the note into the bread bag and stuffed the bag and notepad back into her purse. "I'm very sorry for your loss. Thanks again for helping me."

Marta brought her hand to her mouth and looked as if she might cry out. Sula hurried from the apartment.

Román looked relieved to see her. Sula gave him a bright smile. "All set."

As they rode the elevator down, Sula felt like humming. Overall, her day had gone well, starting with Felisa's unexpected cooperation. As they walked toward the car, Román asked, "Where to now?"

Good question. Sula knew she should go back to the clinic and thank Felisa again, but then she would have to take a taxi back to the hotel. Now that she had the DNA samples, she really wanted to get on the next flight home and ship to the FDA as soon as possible. "The El Canario Inn, if you don't mind."

It would take months for the agency to compare the men's DNA for a common mutation, but if Dr. Warner was right, they would find the genetic vulnerability. In the meantime, the regulators would ask to see Prolabs' records for Luis and Miguel—along with the rest of the Puerto Rico participants. When Rudker couldn't produce a paper trail, the agency would shut down the Nexapra trial until the company proved it had established a compliant system for storing data. At least she hoped it would play out something like that.

San Juan rush-hour traffic was as bad as any big city's, and the trip to the hotel took thirty minutes. Román grew impatient and muttered things like "*idiota*" and "*mierda*" under his breath. Sula called Felisa to share the success of her visits and promised to be in touch with her.

When they reached the El Canario, she gave Román a twenty as a thank you. She worried he might be offended by the amount, but he happily took the money and wished her "*buena suerte*." Once inside her room, Sula called American Airlines to check for departing flight times that evening. After eight minutes on hold, she learned there was a flight out to Newark, New Jersey, leaving at 7:05. From there, she could catch a connecting flight to Portland, Oregon, followed by a puddle jumper to Eugene, arriving home at 8:15 in the morning. She checked her watch: 5:37. With only carry-on luggage and a ten-minute ride to the airport, she decided she could make it.

She called the front desk for a cab, then quickly packed up her bathroom stuff and dirty clothes from yesterday. A normal person would have taken a walk on the beach, had a nice dinner, and flown home in the morning. At the moment, Sula didn't feel like a normal person. Her life was so unsettled, she couldn't make herself relax. She had to get back home, get the DNA samples to the FDA, and find a job.

She also had to call her custody lawyer. Sula couldn't believe she hadn't done it yet. She dreaded having to tell Barbara she'd lost her job, but it was only fair that the lawyer knew before they got to court. Now that the Nexapra business was taken care of, Sula could focus and start moving her life forward again. She took a Xanax to brace herself for the first of three back-to-back flights and felt more optimistic than she had in weeks. Sula hurried downstairs and stood outside to wait for the taxi, taking in all the balmy air and sunshine she could while she still had the chance.

Shortly after entering the airport, Sula was selected for a bag search. After digging around, the young black woman pulled out the plastic bag containing the lock of Miguel Rios' hair and Lucia's handwritten label.

"What's this?"

"Hair, for a DNA analysis."

The woman raised one tightly coiffed eyebrow.

"Paternity suit. Trying to make a deadbeat dad pay up."

"Good for you." She stuffed the hair sample back into Sula's cheap black bag and sent her on her way.

Sula was less anxious about flying this time. Darkness made a huge difference. Because she couldn't see that she was a mile in the air, it was easier to forget. The trip would have been uneventful, except for the couple sitting directly in front of her. Young, attractive, and clearly in love, they whispered, kissed, and nuzzled each other constantly.

Sula envied their joy in each other. She'd never had a real relationship before. There was the brief episode with Tate's father and a few dates in college, including one unsatisfying sexual encounter. That was the sum of her experience with men. Sula became painfully aware of how alone she was—and had been since she lost her family. If she didn't get custody of Tate…

It was hard for her to think about how she would feel or what she would do. But she had to *live*, no matter how things turned out. Sula made up her mind to call Aaron DeSpain as soon as she got back to Eugene. It couldn't hurt to have coffee with him.

Chapter 27

Trina Waterman flipped through the white pages of the phone book and failed to find Walter Krumble. She called Cathy Cusenik, another city councillor she was friendly with. Cathy didn't know the old guy's home number, but after Trina told her about the possible bribe, Cathy said she would find out and call right back. Krumble was retired; otherwise, Trina would have called him at work.

Cathy failed to get back to her within the hour, so Trina rounded up her cameraman and they went downtown to Willamette and Broadway to shoot a segment about the remodeling of a cornerstone building that had been empty for years.

After interviewing a few downtown employees—a more articulate crowd than those at the trick-bicycle competition yesterday—they went back to the station. A message from Cathy with Krumble's phone number and address awaited her. Krumble didn't answer when she called and Trina didn't leave a message.

She delivered the evening's news, then grabbed a quick salad at Wendy's on Willamette. She was on her way to Crest Street to drop in on Krumble. Trina mentally outlined her plan of approach. Nailing the city councillor on the bribe would be a major coup in her investigation of Prolabs. Her lawyer, David Sanders, whom she was also dating, was currently looking into KJR Enterprises for her. If she could get proof that Karl Rudker had cashed $2.7 million worth of checks made out to a specialty company, then she would have enough to convince the SEC to launch an investigation.

Trina clicked on her defroster as the fog seeped into her Sportage. She went right when Willamette split in two, then made another right on Crest. Krumble lived near the top of the hill.

His house was an older cottage, smaller than most in the neighborhood. A dim light from somewhere inside indicated he might be home. Trina parked on the street and walked up to the door. Her digital recorder was in her jacket pocket and had fresh batteries.

Knocking did no good, so she pressed the doorbell a few times. Krumble eventually jerked open the door and flipped on the porch light. Rum vapors oozed from his pores. Trina thought the alcohol could work in her favor if she could just get inside. "Walter Krumble?"

"Yep." His gray hair was pulled back into a short ponytail, making his round face seem too big for his frame. Trina knew he was sixty-four, but he looked younger.

"Hi. I'm Trina Waterman with KRSL TV. I'd like to talk to you about your recent votes as a city councillor."

"I'm no longer a city councillor. I resigned yesterday."

"I'm sorry to hear that. You've served this community well for many years."

"Thanks. What do you want?"

"To talk. Can I come in?"

"Sure." He burped and stepped aside to let her in.

Trina looked around for a light switch. The glow from the thirty-six-inch TV was not enough for her. Krumble must have sensed her discomfort because he fumbled around the living room, turning on lamps. Trina sat on the couch and looked around, surprised by how tidy the house was.

"Would you like a drink? Rum and Diet Coke is the house specialty."

"Sounds good." She didn't have to drink it, but alcoholics were always happier when someone joined them.

He served the cocktail in a short fat tumbler with lots of ice. Trina decided to consume a little. Her day was over and she didn't have far to drive. "What made you decide to quit the council?" She reached into her pocket and turned on her tape recorder as Krumble flopped into the recliner across from her. He splashed his drink on himself and didn't seem to notice.

"I couldn't stand the sight of Betty Thompson anymore."

Trina laughed out loud. Thompson was even older than Krumble, and a lot more rigid. "She's quite a character." After a pause. "I'd like to ask about your last vote. The one on Prolabs and its land-use permits."

"What about it?"

"It seemed unusual for you. Were you pressured?"

Krumble closed his eyes. He tried to chuckle, but it came out more like a dry hack. "This is Eugene, Oregon. There's no Mafia here."

"But there is a lot of money to be made in pharmaceuticals." Trina pulled out her ace in the hole. "I have a copy of a withdrawal slip from a Prolabs' bank account for fifteen thousand dollars. Your name is on the notation line." She leaned forward with the slip.

Krumble made no move to take it.

"Why would the company give you fifteen grand?"

He sat very still, eyes closed.

After a very long moment, he said. "I couldn't turn it down. My life has been pretty bleak since my wife died. I'd thought I'd take a trip. Maybe buy a Harley, something I've always wanted but Karen wouldn't let me have." He shook his head. "It was stupid. The money's just sitting there. I couldn't spend it. I couldn't even stay on the council."

"You can still give it back and call for a new vote."

"You know what's sad?" He gave her a pathetic smile. "I was going to vote in favor of amending the law anyway. This town needs those jobs more than it needs a few acres of scrub grass."

"Who approached you and offered the money?"

"Neil Barstow, Prolabs' chief financial officer. He called me at home and was, at first, very circumspect. He talked about an offer of stock in the company. I wasn't impressed. Then he got serious with a cash offer."

"Did he give you the money in person?"

"No. He had it delivered by courier service."

"What day was that?"

"I don't know, middle of March."

"Mr. Krumble, I can't keep this story quiet. Prolabs has some funny bookkeeping going on, and it's all going to come out. I wish I could keep you out of it, but I can't. I'll give you one day to come forward on your own first. If you decide to do so publicly, please call me."

He nodded.

She handed him a business card and stood to leave.

"I'm not a bad guy." Krumble seemed close to tears.

"I know." Trina smiled sadly. She had always enjoyed Walter's cut-through-the-bull opinions at council meetings. "Call me if you want to go on camera." She stood, carefully shut off the recorder, and headed for the door. She felt sorry for the old man and hoped he would do the right thing.

As she drove up Willamette toward her apartment, her cell phone rang. Trina fished it out of her purse. "Hello."

A young male voice said, "This is Cricket. We met at the council meeting the other night."

She remembered the odd name, but not much about the guy attached to it. *How the hell had he got her cell-phone number?* "You're an environmentalist, right?"

"With Love the Earth, founded here in Eugene by my father."

"What can I do for you?"

"Our group is staging a protest at Prolabs' building site. We'd like you to give us some news coverage."

A bolt of excitement shot through her. "When?"

"We plan to set up camp sometime in the next few days. I'm still trying to round up volunteers."

"Call me when you're ready to move, and I'll be there."

Hot damn! If things came together, Prolabs would be her lead story every night for the next week.

* * *

Rudker stared at a competitive-intelligence report on his monitor, but could not concentrate. It was late and he was the only one in the building, but he dreaded going home. Not only would the house be empty, but he would be reminded that Tara had screwed another guy there.

Oh hell. Rudker turned off the computer. He was starving and he had to face the house sooner or later. A stop at Newman's Fish Market for some deep-fried halibut took the edge off his physical discomfort. But as soon as he started up the stairs at home, where he'd seen Tara with her lover, fresh rage surfaced. In the bedroom he discovered his wife had stopped in while he was at work and taken most of her clothes. The finality of it hit home. Until seeing the empty closet, he'd thought she would come back, even ask his forgiveness. He hadn't decided if he would take her. Now he didn't have the option. The bitch.

You'll have to punish her for that, you know, the voice mocked. *You can't let her get away with it.*

Rudker changed out of his suit and fled the bedroom. He heard the voice more often now. Sometimes he could ignore it and keep his own train of thought. Other times, it was so dominant, he couldn't distinguish between its thoughts and his own.

A trip to the kitchen for macadamia-nut ice cream and the new issue of *Pharmaceutical Executive* soothed him for an hour or so. Soon he was agitated again and found himself in the family room throwing Tara's collection of Asian masks into a big plastic bag. He'd always hated the damn things, with their big spying eyes.

After dragging the masks out to the garbage, he drank a glass of wine, hoping it would help him mellow out enough to sleep. It seemed to have the opposite effect. Rudker fired up his laptop and tried to get some work done, but he kept hearing the voice in his head mocking him, saying "vice president of operations" over and over. His resentment mushroomed, and he fired off an e-mail to a headhunter he knew, asking if he knew of any executive openings in the pharma industry.

At midnight he went to bed. An hour later he got back up and slipped into some khakis. The Commander fired up with its usual roar. Rudker backed out of the garage and headed down the hill. The fog was so thick he had to crawl along even though no one else was on the road. He had no idea where he was going, but night driving with no traffic often helped him settle down.

Twenty minutes later he found himself parked across from Sula's little house on Friendly Street. He knew she wasn't there because Jimmy had watched her board a plane for Puerto Rico.

The PI had called back that afternoon to say he couldn't find out when Sula's return flight was scheduled. Rudker had ordered him to stay at the airport until she came back. At first, the little prick refused, then he had demanded double his hourly rate. Rudker was unconcerned with the cost. He didn't think Jimmy would be at the airport that long. For Sula, it was probably a quick and dirty trip, and she would be back in a day or so.

He wasn't very worried about what she would dig up either. Dr. Hernandez was no longer at the clinic, and—if things went according to plan—neither were the Rios files. Rudker had contacted an acquaintance at Mova Pharmaceuticals and called in a favor. Carlos had, in turn, called in a favor and someone would remove the files from the research center. How Carlos accomplished it, Rudker didn't know or care. He suspected a clinic employee would simply be bribed to hand over the paperwork. The only question was, did it happen before Sula arrived at the clinic?

Rudker would have preferred to deal with the situation personally, but that simply wasn't possible. Not only did Sula have a head start in getting to Puerto Rico, Rudker couldn't leave town. Not with the expansion plans and the merger hanging on the city council's approval.

A car pulled into a driveway two houses away. Rudker slumped down in his seat. A long-haired woman got out of a minivan and walked up to the home. He couldn't see her well, but she looked young, probably attractive. He thought about what he would do if someone noticed him. Or if the police stopped and questioned him. Did his breath smell like wine? Rudker popped a piece of cinnamon gum in his mouth. He would leave soon.

He wondered where Tara was tonight. Had she moved in with Doug? The thought heated his blood. He would have to find out who this guy was. *Teach him not to fuck with Karl Rudker.*

Teach him to keep his dick out of married women. Rudker ignored the hostile ranting from the voice in his head. Doug would have to wait his turn.

Rudker knew he should get moving, but still he stayed and watched Sula's house. He'd never lived alone before. In college, he'd had roommates, then he'd met and married Maribel. When she left him, Robbie had stayed and lived with him until Tara came along.

What was going on with Robbie anyway? His phone call had been so unusual. His son had never been much of a drinker. Like other young people, he preferred to smoke pot, but he'd never called while he was high before. Impulsively, Rudker scrolled through his contact list on his cell phone until he found the boy's entry. He pushed call and let it ring four times before he remembered that it was one thirty in the morning. He quickly disconnected. He would try Robbie again in the morning. Maybe they would go to lunch or see a movie this weekend. Rudker suddenly realized he missed his son. He couldn't remember what they'd fought about the last time they were together.

Young people seemed so much more complex now than the students he'd gone to college with. Like Sula. He could not fathom what was driving her to be so intent on getting the PR suicide files. What possibly did she have to gain? Did she see herself as some kind of hero?

He stared at her tiny little house and wondered if she had any idea who she was up against. If not, she was about to find out. As soon as she set foot in the airport, Jimmy would let him know, then Rudker would put a stop to her nonsense once and for all.

Chapter 28

Friday, April 23

Rudker got the call earlier than he expected. "Sula's back and headed for the parking lot at the Eugene airport," Jimmy reported.

"Follow her and call me if she goes anywhere but home."

"When will I get a break?" Jimmy sounded weary.

"Soon. Once she's in her house, call me and I'll relieve you."

"I'll tally up my bill while I wait."

Rudker went back to work on his comments for the company's Q2 report. He had so much energy perking in his body, he could barely stay in his chair. He'd slept only a few hours, yet he felt hyper and charged with confidence. Today, things would go his way. He would take control of his world again.

Rudker channeled his energy into his quarterly statement, which came out more optimistic than he intended. The PR director would undoubtedly edit the hell out of it. Fine with him. Prolabs' stock was at an all-time high of $48.76, as of eight this morning. As long as the merger went through, stockholders would stay happy.

At nine, Cindy Taylor, his friend on the environmental committee, called. "We're submitting our report to the commission this afternoon. Overall, we've given the project a green light. I thought you'd like to know."

"Excellent. Thank you. Let me know when you kick off your run for mayor. I'll be the first to donate to your campaign."

"I'm announcing my candidacy next month at the Cinco de Mayo celebration."

"I'll get a check to you soon after. Good luck."

"Thanks." Cindy was off the line. That was one of the things he liked best about her. She got things done but didn't waste time yapping about it.

Rudker felt his fortune turn. If he'd been a gambler, he would have bought a lottery ticket. Instead, he called his broker and bought a thousand shares of a little nanotech company he'd been investigating. Might as well spread his luck around, give the little guys a boost.

Too excited to wait for Jimmy to call, Rudker buzzed the PI.

"JJ's Investigations."

Rudker hated the name, but Jimmy had come highly recommended as someone who could keep private matters private. "What's the word on the girl?"

"Headed for home. She just turned on Friendly Street."

"What took so long?"

"She stopped at Safeway."

"Stay with her. I'll relieve you later this afternoon."

"Why do I have to stay? She was on an all-night flight from Puerto Rico. She's going to crash as soon as she gets home."

"You don't know that. Don't let her out of your sight."

Rudker hung up before he had to listen to any more whining. Jimmy was probably right, but he wasn't taking any chances.

* * *

She had been gone for just over forty-eight hours, but Sula was deliriously happy to be back on the ground in her little home in Eugene. She was exhausted, but she couldn't rest, not yet.

She ate the Kung Pao chicken she'd picked up at the Safeway deli, then called Paul and left a brief message. "It's Sula. I'm back. And I got DNA samples from both guys. A successful trip."

The next call required courage she didn't think she had. Sula paced the house with her phone in hand for ten minutes before she finally pressed the numbers. He answered on the second ring, sounding a little breathless.

"Aaron?"

"Yes."

"It's Sula Moreno. You called last week and invited me for coffee. If it's not too late, I'd like to accept."

"Sure. I'd like that. Hang on a sec."

She heard a door close, followed by the sound of a faucet. In a moment he was back. "Sorry. I just got back from a run and needed a drink of water."

"It's okay. I just got back from Puerto Rico." Sula laughed. It made her sound like a seasoned traveler.

"Wow. I see why you didn't call until now."

"It's been a crazy week."

There was a pause. "I've got a lot going on over the next few days," Aaron said after a moment. "What about Sunday afternoon, around three o'clock?"

"Great. Where?"

"Full City Coffee?"

"Sounds good. I'll see you then."

When she hung up, she realized she was shaking. It's just coffee, she told herself. No need to be nervous. Or excited. Just coffee with a guy, an acquaintance.

Running on adrenaline, she unpacked her bag, threw a load of clothes in the washer, then took a shower. At noon she lay down. The two plastic bags with the Rios men's hair samples sat on her dresser. She couldn't stop thinking about them. Until they were packaged and in the mail to the FDA, her mission was not accomplished.

Sula got up, turned on her computer, and began a letter to Irene Johnson, an FDA public spokesperson she'd become friendly with while working at Prolabs. She tried to keep the letter simple, but her brain was tired and fuzzy and it took forty minutes to craft. Sula hoped her tone would seem concerned, but rational. In her first draft, she mentioned the disk disappearing from her home. Then she decided to cut that part. It made her sound too much like a wacko with active paranoia.

Finally, she hit Print. Sula held her breath. Her printer was a garage-sale special she'd picked up for five bucks. Sometimes it worked. Often, it did not.

She got lucky and the letter came out on the first try. The ink was more gray than black because she needed to replace the cartridge and was putting off spending the twenty-three dollars. Otherwise, she was pleased with her effort.

Working at the kitchen table, she stuffed the samples—plastic bags and all—into a small padded envelope, then put the letter and the small envelope into a bigger manila envelope. She scooted back to her computer to look up the FDA's mailing address, then added it to the front and sealed the package.

Sula lay down again, but her brain kept buzzing from one thought to another. Scenes from her trip to Puerto Rico kept playing in her head. Marta had been so angry, and Lucia had been so helpful. Everybody reacted differently to death. She could see Lucia's warm face suppressing a smile as she spoke into the tape recorder.

The cassette. Shit. She'd forgotten to put Lucia's taped statement into the FDA package. Sula jumped out of bed and trotted up the hall. The recorder was still in her shoulder bag on the kitchen table. She dug it out and hit rewind. It seemed to take forever. Which struck her as odd, because Lucia's statement had been quite brief.

When the machine finally clicked off, she pressed play to see how the recording sounded. All she could hear were muffled voices in the background. Had she accidentally been recording while the machine was in her purse? Sula let it play for a moment, waiting for Lucia's voice to come on. Instead, she heard Rudker say, "Nonsense. The percentage of suicides in the Puerto Rico trial was lower than the national average."

Sula was stunned. It was the conversation she'd recorded outside the conference room last week. Before, she had only played back the first few minutes, but it had been so bad, she'd written the whole thing off. Rudker's statement about suicides clearly indicated there had been adverse events in the Puerto Rico trial, and now those files were missing. FDA officials would be interested in the discrepancy.

Sula played out the tape. None of what Warner said was decipherable, but Rudker came though a few more times. Eventually, she heard Lucia's voice talking about her husband's lock of hair. While the cassette rewound, Sula wondered if the investigators at the FDA would be curious enough about the tape—and her report of the conversation—to have it analyzed. The FBI, or even the Washington, DC, police, would have the technology to enhance the tape quality and volume. Maybe they'd be able to understand some of what Warner said as well. This tape was all that was left of Warner's personal feelings about her discovery. Someone needed to hear it.

Sula peeled the envelope open and slipped the microcassette in. She resealed it with clear packaging tape, then headed back to the bed. After a minute, she got up for the third time and set her alarm for four o'clock that afternoon. She only wanted to nap for a few hours, so she would sleep that night. Tomorrow was her day with Tate and it was time to get her life back to normal.

* * *

As Rudker left work, his secretary gave him a sidelong glance. It was his second day of leaving early after six years of staying late. *Fuck her, the ugly bitch. Really, you should fire her for that.* The voice was insistent. Maybe he would.

His first stop was at Enterprise Rent-A-Car on Garfield. Rudker parked his vehicle on Ninth Avenue and walked to the rental. The young man behind the counter ignored him for a moment while he finished something on the computer, then greeted him cheerfully.

"I need a car for the next two days." Rudker pulled out his wallet as he spoke.

"Small or midsize?"

"Midsize." Rudker fingered the driver's license he'd found in the taxi.

"How about a Ford Taurus?"

"Fine." Under any other circumstances, he would have said no thanks. But being commonplace would be useful to his plans.

"Would you like to put this on a credit card?"

"No. What's your daily rate?"

"Forty-seven plus taxes, plus mileage."

Rudker pulled out four fifties and handed them to the clerk. "This will cover three days."

The young man hesitated. "I need to see your driver's license."

Rudker gave him Richard Morgenstern's ID. The clerk entered the number into the computer and handed it back without ever looking up to compare images.

"You need to fill it with gas before you return it or we charge for that too." They went out to the lot, and five minutes later Rudker was driving away.

His next stop was the Wetlands tavern. The place was dark and packed with a happy-hour crowd. Perfect. Rudker picked up a beer at the bar counter, then moved around the room, pretending to keep an eye on the basketball game. He was really looking for a cell phone. After a few minutes, he spotted one on a table, where two guys were watching the game. He leaned against a nearby wall and focused on the TV, while keeping an eye on the cell phone three feet away.

He hated sports, such a colossal bore. After ten minutes, the guy closest to the phone got up and headed for the bathroom. Moments later, a player scored a three-pointer and tied the game. The second guy at the table jumped up, along with a dozen other guys, and began to cheer. In a flash, Rudker grabbed the phone, spun around, and plowed toward the front door. He half expected to hear one of the guys run up behind him, but they didn't.

Out in his car, he used the stolen phone to call in a couple of pizzas for pickup. Rudker got a charge out of being anonymous. It made him feel invisible, as if he could do anything and get away with it.

His next stop was Papa Murphy's, where he picked up two sausage-and-mushroom pies. From there he headed up to Friendly Street. Jimmy's blue sedan was parked three houses from Sula's.

Rudker eased in across the street from the sedan and walked over with the pizzas. He caught Jimmy snoozing and rapped loudly on the window. Jimmy bolted upright, grabbing for the gun under his jacket. Rudker laughed. He'd forgotten Jimmy carried a weapon.

"Jesus. Don't ever fucking do that." Jimmy yelled as he rolled down the window.

"Don't sleep on the fucking job."

"I wasn't. Yeah, I close my eyes every once in a while. But only for a minute or two a time. I'm trained at this. I don't sleep on stakeouts."

"Hungry?" Rudker pushed one of the red-and-white boxes at him.

Jimmy set it on the seat beside him. "Am I done here?"

"I need you back at midnight. I have some things to do this evening, but I'll be back before daylight, before she makes any moves tomorrow."

"Okay." Jimmy sighed. "I'm still on double pay."

"Of course." Rudker returned to his piece-of-shit rental, watched Jimmy drive off, then dug into his pizza.

The last light in Sula's house went off at 11:06 p.m. She hadn't shown her face outside even once. Rudker looked around the neighborhood for a place to urinate, but nothing looked promising. Jimmy would be back in less than an hour, but he didn't know if he could hold out that long.

Sitting in the car for five hours had been its own special brand of hell. He didn't know how cops and government agents did it. Rudker had gotten out and walked around twice. He'd kept one eye on Sula's house and worn a baseball cap to block his face from view. The second time, he'd seen a woman watching him from her front window, so he'd gotten back in the Taurus and driven off, only to circle the block and park out of her line of sight.

The hour passed slowly, and Rudker grew more anxious by the minute. It occurred to him he hadn't taken his Zyprexa in days. He loved the unbridled energy he was experiencing even though it was dangerous. He would have to settle himself back down eventually, but for now he wasn't ready. He wanted to stay sharp. And aggressive.

He had important things to accomplish. This morning, after dozing for only an hour or so, he'd woken up to a terrifying realization. Even though he'd arranged to have the files removed from the Puerto Rico clinic, he'd forgotten to track down and destroy the Rios cousins' paperwork that was still filed somewhere in the bowels of Prolabs. The thought that the paperwork was still there, just waiting to be discovered, freaked him out. That was the reason he was sitting here now. If Sula would steal from Warner's office and fly to Puerto Rico for her crusade, then she might also try to enter Prolabs in search of the files. She could have a key and might have done it already, before he started watching her.

Stupid, stupid, stupid. You are your own worst enemy. Rudker agreed with his internal critic this time. Tara's slutty treachery had temporarily weakened him, and it was difficult to do battle with a bruised heart and ego. Now he was determined to ignore his emotions and put an end to Sula's campaign to ruin him. She was a self-involved reactionary, a do-gooder who had no idea of the scientific expertise and dedication that had gone into developing Nexapra. It was a miracle drug that would help thousands more people than it would harm.

Jimmy pulled up behind him at 12:07. Rudker took off without getting out of the car and speaking to the PI. People were paranoid about strangers these days. There was no point in attracting attention.

Chapter 29

Saturday, April 24

"I've got your stash, if that's what you're looking for." Jason yawned as he passed by on his way to the kitchen. His roommate had bed hair and was wearing yesterday's clothes. Robbie abandoned his search under the table.

"I need to know how many I took."

"There's about five pills left in the bottle."

"That means I only took about half."

"Only?" Jason gave him angry glance.

"Hey, I'm sorry to put you through that. Thanks for taking care of me."

Jason stopped rummaging through the cupboards and turned to face him. "I want you to get some help. Go see a counselor."

"I will."

"I mean it. Make an appointment today."

"Shrinks aren't open on weekends."

"So call the UO hotline."

"Okay." Robbie moved into the kitchen and helped himself to a tall glass of water and two aspirin. Physically, he had never felt worse in his life, but emotionally he was recovering. "Hey, I'm all right. I have a plan."

"What's that?" Jason's voice was thick with skepticism.

"Monday, I'm going back to Prolabs with the hope I still have a job. Then I'll contact Food for Lane County and start volunteering."

"Doing what?"

"I don't know. Serving meals. Calling donors. Whatever they need me to do. I think it will be good for me to help others, to have a purpose."

"Hmm. I guess it couldn't hurt." Jason poured himself a bowl of Cap'n Crunch. "But call the university's crisis hotline today anyway."

"Chill. I will."

Jason offered him the box of cereal.

"No thanks. I'm not hungry."

Robbie poured himself a cup of coffee, took one of his trial meds, then went out to the deck. He dug through the junk box until he found a partial pack of cigarettes he'd stashed a few weeks back. They were stale and slightly crushed, but he didn't care. He needed the nicotine to stimulate his brain. His life was still shit but he wasn't ready to give it up.

* * *

Sula woke up feeling better than she had in weeks. She would see Tate this morning—that always made her world seem right again. Then she would put the envelope in the mail and be done with the Nexapra business. She had no regrets about her involvement. She would sleep better at night knowing she had done everything she could to ensure the drug was brought to market in a responsible way. It was also a huge relief to have it behind her. Rudker gave her the creeps, and she was eager to move forward with her life and away from any involvement with him. She would take the first steps tomorrow: apply for jobs in the morning, followed by coffee with Aaron.

She scooted into the kitchen, made a small pot of coffee, then stepped out to get the paper. A bright blue sky boosted her spirits even more. She and Tate could play in the park again today. May was coming, followed soon by June and July. If she got custody, they could go camping this summer. And to the water park in Springfield. And to baseball games. Sula couldn't wait.

As she turned to go back in, a tall male figure across the street caught her attention. The guy wore a black baseball cap, which didn't seem to go with his khakis and leather jacket. But this was Eugene; there were no dress codes. The man disappeared from view behind a van, and Sula entered the house.

She cruised though the paper in twenty minutes. Normally she devoured every word of the political stories and commentaries, but not today. The oil was still pouring into the gulf, the wars were still raging in the Middle East, and she couldn't change any of it. She wouldn't let it get her down.

Sula checked her watch: 7:42. She still had two and a half hours before meeting Tate. She put on Quad City DJs, danced for forty minutes, then showered and made eggs and toast.

It was still only 8:45 and she didn't need to be at Westmoreland Center until ten. Saturday morning before nine o'clock was not the best time to call one's lawyer, but at the moment, she had the time and the nerve.

Barbara picked up on second ring and spoke in a bright voice. "Good morning, Sula." Her lawyer was wide awake and checking caller ID.

"I've been meaning to call you."

"What's on your mind?"

"I lost my job. I thought you should know before the hearing."

"Oh no. What happened?" She could hear a chair scoot in the background. Barbara was sitting down for the bad news.

"It's a strange story." Sula decided to give her the short version. Barbara didn't need to be distracted with all the Nexapra stuff. "A scientist at Prolabs didn't come to work for a few days. I got worried about her, so I went to her office." Sula began to pace. "The company's CEO—who's a little crazy, by the way—saw me outside Dr. Warner's office with some papers in my hand. He yelled my name and started running at me. It freaked me out, so I ran from him. Then he accused me of stealing and fired me."

"That's bizarre." Barbara hesitated. "Running from him was a little weird too. Why do you think that happened?" Her voice was gentle. She knew Sula's history.

"I was having a stressful day. You know the scientist who was missing? She was murdered. I had to identify her body at the morgue that morning. I was feeling a little jumpy."

"I can see why."

"How bad do you think this will hurt my custody case?"

"I don't know." Barbara hesitated again. Sula's stomach knotted up. Finally, her lawyer spoke. "Last week, I wouldn't have been worried. But on Friday, I got a call from Adam Bianchi, the attorney who represents Emily and John Chapman. He offered a settlement deal."

"What deal? What are you talking about?"

"The Chapmans plan to bring up your family history at the hearing. Bianchi already prepared the brief. They argue that a history of mental illness could and should be a deciding factor in who raises Tate."

"Oh God." Sula collapsed on the couch. "That's so unfair."

"They've offered a deal. If you'll drop your custody petition and terminate your parental rights, they'll agree to biweekly, unsupervised visitation."

Sula sucked in a sharp breath. She'd been pushing for more frequent visitation for a year. Now they were offering it to her, but she had to give up—forever—her dream of having Tate live with her. "You think I should take the deal, don't you?"

"Not necessarily. The courts traditionally like to return children to their biological parents whenever they can. And you are a fit parent by any court standard. Even if we lose the custody hearing, we can still petition for more visitation."

Stress flooded her system. To get Tate back, she would have to listen to lawyers discuss that tragic day when her father, mother, and sister all died. She might even have to talk about it. "They're trying to scare me off."

"Exactly."

"No deal."

"Good for you. By the way, are you all right for money? Can you collect unemployment?"

"I filed for it. They have to review the circumstances of my termination and make a decision. I haven't heard yet."

"Do you need some money in the meantime?"

Barbara's generosity made Sula's eyes tear up. "I'm fine for now. But thanks for asking. You've been great to me."

"So make my job easier. Get out there and find a new job." Barbara laughed, but Sula knew she was serious.

"I will."

"See you in court."

Sula ignored the anxious, negative thoughts that kept popping into her head. She couldn't let fear paralyze her. She grabbed the classified section of the paper, went through it systematically, and made a list of places to apply. Suddenly it was 9:42 and she was running late. She grabbed her purse and the envelope addressed to the FDA and headed out to her truck.

* * *

Rudker watched Sula leave the house. He liked the way her jeans showed off her ass when she climbed into the truck. She seemed to be in a hurry, throwing the truck into reverse and backing out of the driveway before it had warmed up. That wasn't good for a vehicle.

Then it registered. She'd had a manila envelope in her hands. It looked thick, like it had something more than paper. Rudker's heart quickened. Did it have anything to do with her trip to Puerto Rico? Had she got to the research center before his contact made the files disappear? Were the files about to be mailed to the FDA?

He couldn't let that happen. If she stopped in front of a big blue mailbox, he would ram into her car. That was along the lines of what he had planned anyway, but a little less subtle, and ultimately, less dangerous for her. He followed the purple truck down Friendly Street toward Eighteenth Avenue, staying a full block behind her.

The morning was quiet, no cars shared the road, and no pedestrians were on the sidewalk. Rudker considered making his move now. Slam her car, grab the envelope, and speed away. No, not yet. The risk for him was too great, and the scare factor for her, not nearly high enough. He would stick to the plan.

Sula turned left on Eighteenth. Rudker followed two cars back. He removed the stolen cell phone from his jacket pocket, but the traffic was too thick and unpredictable for him to take his eyes off the road long enough to call. A few minutes later, the girl turned left on Chambers. Very nice. Maybe she was heading out of town without any encouragement from him.

Left again at the first feeder street. Where in the hell was she going?

The truck pulled into the Westmoreland Community Center parking lot. Rudker cruised past the entrance and took the next driveway into the adjacent middle school. He circled back and parked by the street about two hundred yards from Sula's truck. She was already out of her vehicle and walking toward a blue minivan.

Rudker watched with curiosity as a little blond boy, who looked about four, got out of the van and ran up to Sula. The boy gave her a quick hug around the legs, then grabbed her hand and pulled her toward the playground. Perplexed, Rudker wondered whose kid he was. He'd checked Sula's HR file to find her address and cell-phone number—then had read her whole file just for sport—but he hadn't seen anything about a kid. Who were the people in the minivan?

Rudker found the development amusing. Even if the boy wasn't hers, she was clearly attached to him, and that meant he represented leverage. It was just a matter of figuring out how best to use the information.

He played out a scenario, vocalizing his end of the conversation, but the script needed work. He modified the dialogue and altered his tone. A cold, calm delivery could be more effective than an aggressive threat. When he was confident he had it right, Rudker dialed Sula's number. It rang three times and went to her voice mail. He quickly hung up. *Damn.* She must have left the phone in her truck.

He waited. This round of sitting didn't bother him as much as the last two stretches. Knowing he was close to making his move and scaring her off her mission gave him some peace of mind.

Watching her on the swing set with the little boy made Rudker think of his son at that age. Robbie had not been very robust. His son had preferred to play indoors and was always moody. Sweet one minute and distant and sad the next. He'd loved the boy anyway and tried to engage him whenever he could. He still loved Robbie dearly and would make a point to call him when this was over.

After an hour, the woman in the minivan got out and called out. Sula and the boy both looked up. Sula walked the child back toward the van, stopping about ten feet away from the woman. From Rudker's vantage point, it looked like they didn't speak to each other. Once the boy was with the other woman, Sula turned away and returned to her truck. The people in the van quickly left the parking lot, but Sula sat for a minute. Rudker suspected she might be feeling emotional at the moment—making it exactly the right moment to strike.

Chapter 30

Sula breathed deeply and repeated her mantra. *Every moment I have with him is precious, and I will see him again.* As she pulled out into the street, her cell phone rang, startling her. She received so few calls. She fumbled it out of her purse and finally managed to get it next to her ear. "Hello."

"Was that your son?"

Rudker's voice was in her ear, asking about Tate. Sula's heart stopped for a moment, then raced like a frightened rabbit. She was too stunned to respond.

"I'll take that as a yes." His voice was calm, quiet, and terrifying. "You want him to be safe, correct?"

She pulled off the street and parked, unable to think straight. How did he know about Tate? Was the bastard watching her? She looked around, but didn't see his Jeep. "What do you want?"

"The envelope sitting on the seat next to you. And any other files or evidence relating to Nexapra's clinical trials."

Sula pulled the phone away from her face. How did he know about the envelope? Had he been watching her house? She cursed herself for not stopping at the post office on her way to the center. She had been running late and didn't want to give the Chapmans an excuse to leave.

She stared at the small silver phone and noticed the name on the caller ID said *Dan Parker*. Who was he? A tiny version of Rudker's voice was coming from the phone in her lap. Sula put it back to her ear. "What did you say?"

"The boy has nothing to worry about if you give me the files you took from the Puerto Rico clinic. Is that what's in the envelope?"

Dear God. Would he actually harm Tate? How could she have endangered him like this? The game was over. The stakes were too high. "You can have it."

"Great. Meet me at the fire station at the top of McBeth, where it intersects with Fox Hollow."

"Why so far?"

"It's a nice drive. Don't bother calling the police. You've already been arrested for stealing from Prolabs, and my high-ranking friend in the department has a reason to believe you're a little crazy. In addition, your boy might just vanish some day in the future. I'm following the minivan now, just to see where it goes."

Sula wanted to scream obscenities, but instead she tried reason. "Sooner or later, the truth about Nexapra will come out. You can't run from it forever."

"You must let it go. It's healthier for the mind. Now get moving."

Sula hung up. Tears of rage swelled in her eyes. The bastard. It was one thing to exploit a group of depressed patients for profit, but to threaten her child…Rudker was evil.

She would rather set fire to her evidence than give it to him, but the outcome would be the same. Was there any way out of this? Could she get the DNA evidence out, leaving only the cassette, and reseal the envelope without him knowing? If she was at home, maybe. But not here, not without scissors or tape. *Shit.* Another thought hit her. What if the FDA investigated the Puerto Rico trial someday on its own? Would Rudker blame her? And take revenge by hurting Tate?

Sula pulled a U-turn on Chambers and headed up the steep grade. She cursed out loud at the slow-moving van in front of her. She was not in a hurry to confront Rudker—he scared the hell out of her—but she was anxious to get the evidence that could hurt Tate out of her hands.

The road curved at the top then dropped sharply down to Lorane Highway. Sula turned right. On this side of the hill, city gave way to country. Houses were farther apart, vastly different in size, style, and age, and set back from the road. Under different circumstances, she would have taken her time to enjoy the scenery. Instead, she pushed the truck and took the curves faster than the posted sign allowed. The road sloped gently downward, then the grange appeared on the left. Sula pressed her brakes and took the turn in a wild swing. For a second, she felt as if the truck were out of her control. It straightened out and she vowed to keep her speed down.

McBeth Road wandered past a shooting range, then headed sharply up into the south hills. Sula spotted a group of cyclists in bright yellow-and-black jerseys pumping their skinny asses up the steep curves. She slowed and gave them a wide berth.

At the top of the hill, she turned on Fox Hollow, then made a quick left into the parking lot of the volunteer-staffed fire station. No firefighters lived or worked there, only engines occupied the building. She left the truck running. It seemed important to be able to leave in a hurry.

As Sula sat and waited, a cloud drifted in front of the sun. Her skin cooled and she shuddered. She couldn't believe it had come to this. Rudker had actually threatened her son. He was clearly more desperate and unstable than she'd imagined. For the first time, she realized Rudker might be planning to harm her. *Dear God.* Would he?

Sula turned on the heater, then looked behind the seat of her truck for a possible weapon. A tire iron stuck out from under a plastic Fred Meyer bag. She grabbed the iron and laid it on the seat next to her envelope. After another minute, her cell phone rang. Her hand shook as she answered it. "Yes?"

"Put the envelope on the concrete near the doors and drive away." He sounded so serene, almost cheerful. Sula wondered about his sanity. "Then forget about all this. It's the safest thing you can do."

She hung up on him. She would comply with his demand because Tate's life was at stake, but she would not forget. Sula grabbed the FDA package and the tire iron, just for security, and scooted out of the truck. She crossed the gravel and stood on the concrete pad in front of the big overhead doors. Her hands held tightly to the envelope, creasing the edge. Letting go of the evidence she had worked so hard to obtain was not easy.

Sula tried to think of an alternative. A way to beat Rudker at his own game. But the risk to Tate was always there. She set the package down and hurried to her truck. Before getting in, she looked around to see if she could spot his car parked somewhere, but the road curved in both directions and the pine trees were thick on either side of it.

Small sobs bubbled up in her throat as she drove back down McBeth. She vowed to write it all down when she got home, every detail from the very first conversation she'd overheard to her last exchange with Rudker, including his threats to her and Tate. Next she would give two copies of the document to her lawyer, with instructions to turn one over to the FDA and one to the police, should anything ever happen to her.

She would also track Nexapra's development and approval. When the first wave of suicides hit the press, she would send a copy of her testimony to the media. By then, Rudker would be too busy fending off bad publicity and lawsuits to come after her.

Sula suddenly realized she was moving too fast for the next curve. As she lifted her foot to hit the brake, something slammed into the back of her truck. She flew forward into the steering wheel. Her nose smashed against it, blinding her with pain. She bounced back and her foot slipped off the brake. Sula struggled to orient herself, only to realize she was headed straight, while the road curved sharply left. She found the brake again but it was too late.

The truck was airborne.

Chapter 31

Rudker saw Sula's truck leave the road—heading straight out into a space between two tall fir trees—but he missed what happened next. First, he had to yank his own steering wheel to keep from careening over the edge and following her down the mountain. He pressed the brake to get control. The Taurus fishtailed and nearly took out a group of cyclists coming up the hill on the opposite side of the road. Several of them deliberately ran their bikes off the asphalt and into the drainage ditch to avoid a collision. He could hear the bikers shouting obscenities at him as he sped away. He hoped none had gotten a good look at him or noted the license plate.

If not for the bikers, he might have gone back to see where the truck landed. He hadn't intended to slam her so hard. He only meant to run her off the road and scare her, so she'd realize how serious he was about stopping this nonsense. But the *other* had grown excited by the pursuit. The voice egged him on with aggressive taunts: *Show her who she's dealing with. Smash her now! You know she won't give up.*

Rudker had no regrets though. He had warned her and she had brought this on herself. On some level, he knew he would be relieved to read in the paper tomorrow that Sula had died. The little boy obviously had other parents, responsible people, unlike Sula. So the boy would be all right without her. Sula's file at Prolabs indicated she had no immediate family, so there was no one to feel her loss or get worked up about her accident.

She may not be dead. You may have to try again. The voice would not give him any peace.

* * *

For a long moment, Sula was suspended in air, wrapped in a vacuum of silence and disconnected from reality. Her one thought was: *Tate has good parents. He'll be fine without me.* Then gravity took over, sucking her down. Sula's stomach heaved.

The truck landed on a small pine tree that snapped like a pencil, then it bounced hard on the ground. Sula flew up, but her seatbelt held. She clung to the steering wheel as if it would save her. The truck's second contact with the ground was not as smooth. It hit something big and hard and flipped upside down. Her head smashed into the roof as the truck landed and rolled.

It kept rolling, knocking her head and torso around the interior—smashing her against the door, the steering wheel, the windshield. She closed her eyes against the flying glass shards and thought, this is it.

The truck lost some momentum, and the rolling took on a surreal slow motion. With one last jolt, accompanied by a loud whack, it abruptly stopped. Sula opened her eyes to discover the truck was on its side, the driver's side door smashed against the ground. She did not move except to take several long, deep breaths. She could not believe she was still alive.

A moment later, she became aware of the pain. In her head, her shoulder, her left arm. She had to get out, to seek treatment, but how? She seemed to be up against a giant fir tree, with a trunk big enough to nearly cover the windshield, which was no longer there.

Before she could give it serious thought, a trickle of warm blood rolled into her left eye. Sula wiped it away and refused to think about its source. She knew she had cuts, scrapes, and bruises, but nothing felt broken. She hurt everywhere, but not in a way that made her think she might die. Her fingers went to her seat belt. It had saved her life.

Cautiously, she unbuckled it and her body slumped against the door. A sharp pain in her shoulder made her re-evaluate her condition. Still, she had to crawl out of the truck and get up to the road, where she could get help. The truck's front seat was standing straight up from the ground. She reached up and grabbed the edge of it with her left hand and the passenger's seat belt with the other. Twisting out from under the steering wheel, she pulled herself upright until she was standing against the door.

Once she was up, Sula realized the tree didn't entirely cover the windshield and there was room to squeeze out. She noticed her keys in the ignition and pocketed them. Her purse and cell phone were nowhere to be found. Careful to avoid the chunks of glass still clinging to the perimeter of the windshield, she stepped over the steering wheel and brought one leg in contact with the ground. The truck shifted with the redistribution of weight. Sula froze, waiting to make sure it was stable. With a hopping motion, she pulled her other leg through and landed facedown on the ground.

A bed of pine needles cushioned her fall, but her shoulder screamed in pain. For a minute, all she could do was take deep breaths to keep from crying out. Heart still hammering, Sula struggled first to her knees, then to her feet. She turned back to the truck. The roof of the cab and the canopy were both crushed, but the front end was largely unscathed. She stared up the hill to see how far she had rolled. It was impossible to tell. The hillside was dotted with trees and shrubs that blocked her view of the road.

Sula shook her head. She could have so easily crashed into a giant tree with a three-foot-wide trunk. This area had been selectively logged and the vegetation was not as thick as it might have been. That had probably saved her. The sound of a car climbing the hill sent a wave of relief through her. It couldn't be that far to the road.

With a deep breath, on wobbly legs, she started to climb.

* * *

Rudker headed straight for where his jeep was parked on Eighth Avenue. His body hummed with adrenaline. He had to breathe deeply to keep his foot off the gas and his driving civil. Fortunately, traffic was light. Attracting the attention of a cop while still in the rental car would be tragic.

He left the Taurus sitting at the corner of Eighth and Garfield. He would come back later, after the Enterprise office had closed, and drive the car into the lot. Or not. *If* the cyclists coming up McBeth had seen his plate number and turned it in, and *if* the cops spotted the car, they might watch it to see who surfaced. It might be best to just leave it.

While traveling out West Eleventh, Rudker called Enterprise—still using the stolen phone and stolen ID—and explained that he'd caught an early flight that morning before the rental office opened and the gate opened, so he'd left the car across the street.

He reminded the young man that he'd paid for three days and reassured him the keys were in the mail. The clerk seemed to take it well. At least, he didn't ask too many questions.

Rudker was too keyed up to go home. Instead of relieving the pressure building inside him, running Sula off the road tweaked his tension even higher. He needed an aggressive game of racquetball to settle him down, but he didn't want to face anyone just yet. Making idle, social conversation would be impossible right now. Other people's lives and problems seemed so trivial in comparison to what he was going through.

The best thing he could do with his energy was work. First, he had to eat. He stopped at Padres, a new classy bar on Commercial Street. There was a dearth of decent restaurants in west Eugene, and Padres served excellent sandwiches without all the background chatter of a family restaurant.

Rudker sat at the end of the bar near the television. An attractive female bartender took his order for a club sandwich and a Miller Lite. He had to take the edge off, somehow. She brought the beer with a seductive smile. On another day, he would have flirted with her, but today he didn't trust his social instincts.

While waiting for his sandwich, he watched television. In a minute, KRSL's noon news report came on with Trina Waterman and her fruity sidekick, Martin Tau. After a brief rundown on a local bank robbery, Trina reported: "Today's breaking news involves a city councillor, a hefty bribe, and a local company on the brink of disaster. We'll have that story for you when we come back."

Rudker almost sprayed beer out his of mouth. *Jesus*. Did she mean Prolabs? He looked around. The bar was nearly empty. A young couple sat in a corner booth, intent on each other, and an older man sat at the other end of the bar. No one seemed to have heard the news—or cared. Rudker took another long swallow of beer. Neil Barstow, his chief financial officer, had offered to handle the Walter Krumble situation. Had he fucked it up?

Rudker willed himself to relax, to wait until he heard the broadcast. *Why?* the voice taunted. *You know you're screwed. You have been since the day you moved to this inane little town.*

Rudker watched the bartender make his sandwich just to keep his mind busy for a moment. She had a nice ass, but she didn't wear gloves when she handled his food. That bothered him. Then he heard Trina's voice again and his eyes cut back to the TV. The young, blonde reporter had a glint in her eye he hadn't seen before. She charged right into her story: "Walter Krumble, Eugene's longest serving city council member, came forward today and admitted taking a bribe for his yes vote on Prolabs' building plans."

Ah shit. This was the last fucking thing he needed right now.

The camera cut to Krumble, sitting at a small table in a room Rudker didn't recognize. The old man looked as if he'd spent the last two days in an airport terminal. Where was he now? In the police station? Would the DA file charges against Barstow? Would Barstow implicate him?

Shut up and listen!

On the screen, Krumble started talking: "A Prolabs' executive, Neil Barstow, approached me late last month and offered me fifteen thousand dollars to vote yes on the zoning change." The old man's voice was unsteady. He stopped and cleared his throat. "I didn't want it at first, but I've been broke and depressed since my wife got sick. So I called him back and said okay. I had intended to vote for the permit anyway. Now I regret taking the money, and I plan to give it back."

The camera cut back to the newscaster. "Police brought Barstow, Prolabs' chief financial officer, in for questioning this afternoon. As yet, no official charges have been filed, but a police department spokesperson said the case was still being investigated and that charges would be filed soon."

The camera cut away to a riverside scene.

What the hell had gone wrong? Krumble had contacted them. He had seemed so stoic, the last guy on earth who would ever go public with dirty laundry. Rudker did not believe the old man had come forward on his own.

Next, the newswoman started talking about Diane Warner's death, as if the two stories were somehow connected. The bitch. She had probably gone after the story, dug up the information somewhere, somehow. Trying to fill some holes on yet another slow news day in Eugene. Christ, this would be a setback. The building permit would be revoked, the expansion plans would be put on hold, and JB Pharma would blame Rudker.

Maybe you should teach Trina a lesson too.

He let that thought go. One bitch at a time. For a moment, his career, his life as he knew it, seemed to be slipping away from him. The voice mocked him. *Don't be such a pussy. It's not over until you say it's over. Goddamn it, take charge.*

He reached for his cell phone to call Barstow. Rudker intended to let his partner know he would make it worth his while to keep quiet. Barstow was likely to lose his job when the merger went through anyway. Rudker planned to offer him a nice retirement package and find him an excellent white-collar defense lawyer. This was minor, he told himself. As long as Nexapra stayed on track and the merger went through, his career would soon soar.

* * *

On the ride to the hospital, Sula floated in and out of consciousness. The climb to the road and the wait for the ambulance had used up all her reserves. The cyclists had called for help, and once she knew she was being taken care of, her mind and body let go.

By the time she reached the emergency room, she was alert enough to be semi-aware of the proceedings. First, she was wheeled into a small room separated from other small rooms by only a retractable curtain. The space consisted of a bed, medical supplies, and two feet of walkway.

There, a nurse assessed her injuries. He was a soft-spoken middle-aged man who introduced himself as Ron. Blond and boyish, he reminded Sula of a math teacher she'd had. Ron gave her an icepack for her head and told her he'd be back. Long after, a doctor, also in his forties but Ron's physical opposite, came in to stitch her head.

"I'm Mike Rathburn," he said with a quick smile. "I'm going to get you numb, then cut a little of the hair around this wound so I can stitch it."

Sula didn't relish having a bald spot, but she was feeling pretty lucky to be alive. It took almost forty minutes for the doctor to finish his sewing job and Sula was glad she was lying down. The doctor stepped back and announced with a touch of pride. "Ten stitches. You'll probably have a bit of scar, but your hair will cover most of it."

Sula reached up and felt the gash. It ran along her temple, away from her face. She knew it could have been much worse. Most of the glass in her truck cab had broken out.

The doctor left and she was alone for about ten minutes, then Ron came back and said he was taking her to X-ray. He smiled sweetly, his boyish face contrasting with his gray hair and serious nature. "The doctor said you could have pain medication. Would you like some?"

"Please." She hurt all over, and her shoulder felt like it had taken a few blows with a baseball bat.

Ron handed her a white pill and a paper cup with water. "It's Vicodin."

"Thanks."

Sula woke with a start when the doctor came in with her X-rays. She had been moved to a regular room with another patient, a middle-aged woman who slept.

"You have a broken collarbone, two cracked ribs, a skull contusion, and some abdominal bruising." Mike tapped the folder containing the slides. "Your abdomen will probably hurt much more tomorrow than it does now. You can thank the seat belt that saved your life for that bellyache."

"What happens with the broken bones?"

"For the ribs, nothing. They'll hurt for a while and you'll just have to take it easy. For the collarbone, we'll put you in a brace that will keep the bones in place while they heal. You'll need to wear it for a month or so."

"When can I go home?"

"The head injury gives me the most concern. We're keeping you overnight for observation."

Sula sighed. She was ready to go now. The crowded room with the white walls made her claustrophobic. She hated being pushed around in a wheelchair, hated having decisions made for her, but she couldn't work up the energy to protest. She hurt all over, despite the Vicodin. She felt weak, as though her body were operating under extra gravity. Every movement was a slow struggle.

After another hour, Ron came back with a padded-strap harness-like thing. "We need to get your shirt off. Would you like me to get a female nurse?"

"No, it's okay." Sula unbuttoned her short-sleeved denim shirt, which now had a small tear in the sleeve. She got her right arm out but Ron had to help her with the left side, which was attached to the broken collar bone.

Ron stood behind her and looped the brace into place. As he tightened it, her shoulders pulled back into a good-posture position, and Sula cried out with the pain.

"Sorry. I know that hurt." Ron came around to help her get her shirt back on. "You're lucky those cyclists saw, or actually heard, your accident." He shook his head. "Cell phones. I thought they were the end of civilization when they first got popular, but they have saved so many lives."

A brief memory of the yellow-clad bikers standing around as she was loaded into the ambulance came back to her. Followed by another image of the emergency technician touching her forehead. She didn't remember much else between crawling out of the truck and arriving in the emergency room.

Apparently, she had managed to hike back up to the road, but she didn't remember doing it.

"How are you doing? Do you need another pain pill?"

"Yes, please." Not only was her shoulder throbbing, she wanted to stay a little fuzzy. It would keep her from thinking too much about Rudker. About the fact that he had tried to kill her and had threatened her son. If he would kill her, he would kill Tate if she reported him. Even if they arrested Rudker, he would be released on bail. She had no proof he was the one who'd forced her off the road. She'd been too preoccupied to even notice his Jeep behind her. Rudker was rich and he had "a friend in the department"—as he had bragged. She was charged with stealing from Prolabs, and the police might think she was blaming Rudker as a payback.

"Here you go, honey." Ron was back with another Vicodin. Sula sat up and reached for it. "Do you have any kids, Ron? You seem like you'd be a good dad."

"A daughter, but she's in college now." He looked sad, and Sula was sorry she'd asked. He seemed so nurturing, she wanted to pour her heart out to him. The thought surprised her. It usually took her a while to get comfortable with people. Even then, she didn't talk about herself much.

"Let me know if you need anything else." He patted her hand.

"Find out when I can go home."

Ron left and Sula lay down and closed her eyes to wait.

Chapter 32

Late that afternoon, Rudker drove up McBeth and passed by the scene of Sula's accident. There was nothing to indicate anything out of the ordinary had taken place. He wanted to call the hospital to find out what had happened to her, yet he hesitated and he didn't know why. He didn't like having ambiguous feelings. Or being afraid of anything. As he headed back into town, his cell phone rang. "Rudker here."

"It's Pete Zamanski."

Rudker was immediately alarmed. Zamanski was Prolabs' head IT guy, and he had never called him outside the office.

"Why are you calling me on a Saturday night?"

"I'm in the building installing an upgrade. I have to do this when no one's using the server."

"What's going on?"

"We have a security problem."

Rudker's panic escalated. "I'm on my way in. I'll see you in a few minutes."

That's what you get for getting cocky, the voice taunted.

"Shut up!"

Rudker entered the building, rode up to the second floor, and strode to the large office space housing the IT offices and computer servers.

Zamanski was twenty-nine, prematurely bald, and borderline genius. He was also excitable as a puppy and his enthusiasm made Rudker twitchy. Just sharing the same room with the geek—and all his monitors and servers and cable lines snaking across the floor—made Rudker uncomfortable. Yet a possible security breach demanded his attention.

"What's the problem?" Rudker stood near the door.

"A hacker has been into our database."

"And did what?"

"He accessed clinical-trial records." Zamanski's eyes never left the main monitor.

"Which ones?"

"He searched the entire database but only opened files relating to Nexapra studies."

Rudker's blood pressure spiked, making his ears ring. "What files?" He thought he'd erased the Rios entries immediately after Warner approached him with the genetic data. Has something gone wrong?

"Research sites, clinician names, and contact information."

Sula, that little bitch. Why wouldn't she stop? "Anything else?"

"I believe he also took a look at our payroll data but nothing was tampered with. It was spying pure and simple. No worms or viruses left behind."

"Any patient files?"

"Not that I've determined." Zamanski looked perplexed. "He didn't look at any R&D data either, so I don't think it was a competitive-intelligence mission. I'm stumped about who or why. It's not the work of your typical hacker."

"How did he, or she, get in?"

"A Trojan horse." The IT guy blushed a little. "Through an e-mail to you."

"Me?"

"Yes. I told you to let us run a full filter on your e-mail, but you said no."

"Fix the problem, whatever it is. I don't want this to happen again."

Rudker left the IT department and walked out of the building with a clear sense of purpose. Using the stolen cell phone, he called information and got the number for North McKenzie. He dialed the hospital.

"A friend of mine was in an accident this morning and I'm trying to find out if she's all right."

"What's her name?"

"Sula Moreno."

It was a good five minutes before the woman came back on. "She's been admitted for overnight observation but she's fine. A few broken bones and some bruising. She should be going home tomorrow.

Rudker was disappointed but undeterred. Sula had thwarted him for the last time. He would not walk away from her until she had taken her last breath.

Chapter 33

Sula was drifting off to sleep when her nurse came into room. "Sula. This is Detective Jackson, with the violent-crimes division. He wants to ask you about the accident."

The cop stepped up to the foot of her bed. His dark eyes and rugged features were intimidating and she wished she'd bolted from the hospital an hour ago. He smiled and said, "How are you feeling, miss?"

Sula relaxed a little, thinking he was attractive for someone his age. "I'm fine, all things considered."

"Tell me what happened this morning."

"I really don't remember." Sula reflexively touched the gash above her left temple.

"You don't know what made you run off the road over an embankment?"

"The last thing I remember is turning down McBeth." She hated lying to this man. She hated protecting Rudker, but she couldn't risk his retaliation against Tate.

"From Fox Hollow?"

"Yes."

"What were you doing on Fox Hollow? Do you live up there?"

"No." Sula hesitated. Nothing she said would sound right. "I was just taking a drive. It was gorgeous yesterday and the view is incredible."

He nodded. "You're lucky to be alive."

"That's what they tell me."

"Had you been drinking?"

"No. The doctors took blood samples that will verify that."

Jackson shifted his weight. "The bicyclists who called 911 and reported the accident said a gray sedan nearly ran them off the road right after they heard your crash. Did you see that car?" His tone was gentle, and Sula sensed he wanted to help her.

"Not that I remember." That, at least, was the truth.

Detective Jackson gave her a penetrating look. "Did someone run you off the road?"

"Why would they?"

"That's what I'm trying to find out. Who would want to harm you?"

"Nobody. That seems crazy."

"Your truck has a sizable dent in the tailgate, as though it were rammed from behind."

"It rolled several times after I landed on the tree."

"Have you been depressed lately?"

Sula shook her head.

"Are you on any kind of medication?"

"I take Celexa. It's an antidepressant."

"But you're not depressed?"

"I didn't try to kill myself, if that's what you're getting at."

"Yet you nearly had a fatal accident."

"Maybe I swerved to miss a deer. I wish I could remember. I think you're making too much of this."

"And I think you're protecting someone. What I can't figure out is why."

Sula was silent. She bit her lip to keep from blurting out the truth.

For a moment, he just stared at her with his intense black eyes. Then he handed her a business card. "If your memory comes back, give me a call."

"Sure."

After the cop left, Sula wished she could call him back and tell him everything, but Rudker's influence in the department had already landed her in jail. She couldn't go through that again.

* * *

Rudker left Prolabs and headed straight for Fred Meyer, which was open until eleven. He picked up a package of duct tape, a black knit cap, a shovel, and a bottle of Pepsi. At the checkout, he asked for two rolls of quarters and they sent him to customer service. He wished he had more time to plan, and purchase some chloroform. But this had to be done now. He hated waiting for Sula to come home, but it seemed like the best option. He had to get through this one last ordeal. Everything else was minor and would eventually straighten itself out. He filled up his tank, thinking he would drive around for a while to kill some time.

* * *

In was nearly midnight and Cricket was in a state of agitation. What an evening of highs and lows. On the six o'clock news, Walter Krumble had admitted to taking a bribe for his vote on Prolabs' building plans. Cricket had been so ecstatic, he'd e-mailed everyone in his address book.

Later, during the eleven o'clock broadcast, Martin Tau had announced that the city council had convened for a special meeting and voted to go ahead with the zoning change and allow the development to continue. Cricket was stunned. It seemed like political suicide for the councillors. Such a decision, made in hasty, secret proceedings, would outrage the public.

Cricket jumped up from the worn couch. He had to move now. His squatters needed to be on-site before they poured the foundation. His group had to strike while the public was still angered by Prolabs' bribe and the council's decision to ignore it. With the help of Trina Waterman, this could be a rare opportunity to win public support and put a stop to local chemical manufacturing.

Cricket started dialing numbers. It was late, but he didn't care and neither would his comrades. They often did their best work in the middle of the night.

Chapter 34

Sunday, April 25

Once again, Rudker was back on the corner of Twenty-Sixth and Friendly in the middle of the night. A full moon cast strange shadows around the neighborhood. For luck, he pulled into the spot where he had parked that first night when he took the disk.

He felt strangely serene. This unpleasant chapter in his life was about to be over. He was poised to move to Seattle—away from Prolabs, away from Tara the betrayer, away from Eugene and all its bad memories. He would call a real-estate agent first thing in the morning and get his house on the market.

For now, he prepared to go in.

He pulled the knit cap over his head—to keep from losing any hair in the house—and took off one of his black socks. He put his shoes back on, and his bare ankle reminded him of Doug, standing in the bedroom door wearing shoes but no socks, after fucking his wife. Rudker would deal with him later.

The rolls of quarters went into the sock, knotted tightly in the toe. Rudker slipped his ex-wife's expired credit card out of his wallet and moved it to his jacket pocket, along with the now-lethal sock. He took his driving gloves and penlight out of the jockey box. The pen light and duct tape went into his other pocket. He had always loved the big pockets in his leather jacket, but they had never been more useful. Rudker pulled on his gloves and slid out of the Commander.

Moving quickly up the sidewalk to the now-familiar gate, he reached over and let himself in. A few strides and he was across the yard and standing next to the garage's side door. A sudden shout near the street startled him, and Rudker dropped his credit card. A second male voice called back, "Freak that," or something equally absurd. Rudker didn't let himself look up. He slowly bent down and groped around for the card, which he located near his foot.

He stayed on one knee until he heard the car start up and pull away. As it raced down the street—the only sound on an otherwise quiet night—Rudker seized the opportunity to pop the lock on the garage door using the credit card. The latch was so old and out of alignment, it might as well have been unlocked. Easy as pie, just like last time. It surprised him Sula had not changed or reinforced her locks after his last intrusion. Apparently, she'd been too busy trying to fuck with him. She was such a fool.

Rudker moved slowly across the dark garage without flipping a switch or using his penlight. He remembered the tall sculpture and steered clear of it. In doing so, he smashed his sockless foot against a lawnmower. Rudker kept himself from cursing out loud, but the voice in his head swore at him. *Clumsy bastard. Can't you do anything right?*

He paused for a moment while the pain subsided, then moved on. The door between the garage and the kitchen was locked, but after a few minutes of jiggling, he was able to slide the bolt out of its compartment. It popped back with a satisfying click.

Rudker stepped inside. No cooking aromas greeted him. The house smelled stale, as if the windows hadn't been opened in a while. Rudker held still and let his eyes adjust to the barely visible outlines in the dark kitchen. After a minute, he walked down the galley between the countertops and into the dining area.

Where should he hide? It had to be a concealed space, yet not confined. He needed to be able to wait comfortably for as long as it took for Sula to come home, yet he had to be able to move quickly at a moment's notice. He would have only one chance to do this right, without a struggle. The messier it went down, the more likely he would leave evidence. He did not intend to give the cops any reason to associate him with her disappearance.

* * *

Sula woke suddenly and sat up. A bright moon lit up the outlines of the monitors and IV stands and she remembered she was in the hospital. She checked her watch: 2:07 in the morning. A woman began moaning across the way. Soon the sound of footsteps clomped in the hall, and later carts were wheeled in and out.

Sula decided it was time to go. She had slept off and on all afternoon, then slept again from nine o'clock till now. Wide awake, she stepped gently out of the bed, testing her strength. She was bruised but fine. She found her clothes on the visitor chair and dressed by the light of the moon.

Out into the hall and down past the nurses' station. A tired-looking woman in blue called out, "Where are you going?"

"Home."

"Can't you wait until morning?"

"Nope."

"You need to check out."

Sula kept going. "I just did."

On the first floor as she reached the reception area, Sula stopped in her tracks. She had no purse, no cell phone, no car, no money to make a call, and no money to pay a taxi. How in hell would she get home? She felt unexpectedly vulnerable.

Sula worked through it. The hospital would let her use their phone. She would call Paul for a ride. The police would find her purse and return it to her. She even had insurance for her cell phone. Everything was okay. No need for anxiety. She was fine. Tate was safe.

She asked the receptionist if she could use a phone, and the woman pointed to one on the wall near the waiting area. Sula hesitated. Would Paul be home? Was it selfish to call him at this hour? He was a night owl and was often up late on weekends.

Paul didn't answer. She left a message to call her at North McKenzie if he got home in the next fifteen minutes. Sula went back to the receptionist.

"Can you page Ron, the nurse who attended me?"

"He may have gone home. Unless he pulled a double, which he often does." The young heavyset woman made a call. She asked about Ron, then looked up.

"He's in the ICU."

The receptionist made another call. After ten minutes, Ron stepped off the elevator, looking as tired as everyone else on duty.

"Hey. What's up? Are you going home?"

"I'm trying to." Sula hated to ask, but she was desperate. "I don't have a ride, and I don't have any money on me for a taxi. Will you loan me ten dollars? I'll pay you back tomorrow, I promise."

Ron hesitated and Sula cringed. Before she could feel bad, he said, "My wallet's in my locker. I'll be right back."

"Thank you." He was already walking away.

While Ron was gone, she called a taxi. She hoped ten bucks would be enough to get her home. If not, she'd tell the driver to stop when the meter hit the ten-dollar mark and walk the rest of the way.

She thanked Ron for his kindness and asked him to thank Dr. Mike for her too. Her heart felt like skipping out of the building, but her body moved slowly, limping on her left leg.

The cool fresh air jolted her senses and made her feel grateful to be alive. She'd find a job, get custody of her son, then move somewhere Rudker couldn't find her. The Nexapra trials would continue and she could do nothing about it. In time, Rudker would get rich and forget about her. She had to do the same.

* * *

Rudker decided the bedroom offered the best possibility for surprise with the least amount of risk. In the living room, if things didn't go well, she would have an opportunity to run from the house. That would be a worst-case scenario. From the bedroom, she would have a much longer run for her freedom. Rudker knew he could take her. He was quite quick on his feet, despite his size. He would simply stand behind the partially open door and strike her at the first opportunity.

Rudker practiced his moves. One quick step to the side as the door opened, then swing the weighted sock back, then a giant step forward, bringing his arm all the way over and down—whack! After a few run-throughs, the movements felt smooth and natural.

He took the duct tape from his pocket and tore off a series of strips. A short four-inch piece to go across her mouth and two twelve-inch strips for her hands and feet. The ripping sounds penetrated the silence like screams. Rudker knew no one had heard, but it unnerved him anyway. He hung the strips against the back of the bedroom door and put the roll of tape back in his pocket.

The wait was interminable. He went through every mental calming exercise he'd learned in his years of therapy—visualizing a happy place, making lists of things to do, counting backward from one hundred. It was all bullshit, every irritating task. He had gone to the therapist early in his first marriage to make Maribel happy, but of course, he'd never made Maribel happy.

His legs got tired of standing so he stretched out on Sula's bed. Her pillow smelled of jasmine. It felt strange to be off guard, but he knew he would hear her drive up and open the front door, giving him plenty of time to reposition himself. The other didn't like any of it.

Idiot! Reckless fool! Get up and be ready, goddamn it!

Rudker checked his watch: 2:28. He'd been here for only an hour and half. Sula most likely would not be home for another five or six hours. He pulled the stolen cell phone out of his shirt pocket and hit Redial.

"North McKenzie Hospital. How can I help you?"

"When is Sula Moreno leaving tomorrow? I was thinking of coming to visit, but I don't want to miss her." Rudker had tried to keep his voice quiet without actually whispering. Instead, he'd sounded like a pervert.

"Just a moment, I'll check. Did you say Sula?"

"Yes. With a U."

While he waited, he listened for sounds outside. He heard a car on nearby Twenty-Fourth Avenue, but otherwise, the night was quiet.

"Sir? She seems to be gone."

"What does that mean?"

"Her doctor didn't sign her out, but a nurse on the second floor says she left. That's all the information I have."

"Thanks."

Sula had left the hospital. Rudker took his position behind the door. After a moment, he had a worrisome thought. Considering what she had just been through, she might go stay somewhere else.

* * *

Ron's ten dollars barely covered the taxi fare, and Sula apologized to the driver for not leaving a tip. Weary but happy to see her house, she stepped out onto the sidewalk. She wished she'd left her porch light on, but she had not known at nine forty this morning she would be gone this long. At least she had her keys.

As she approached her front door, Sula thought about the night Rudker had broken into her house and stolen Warner's disk. A shiver ran up her spine. She had to stop thinking about him. It was over. He'd scared the hell out of her and she'd given him all the evidence. She was no longer a threat to him. He would leave her alone now, wouldn't he? As long as she left him alone? Wasn't that the deal?

After the custody hearing, she and Tate would move. Maybe even leave Eugene.

Sula stood for a long moment with her house key in hand. An image of Diane Warner, lifeless and colorless in the basement of the hospital, floated into her brain. She shook it off. She was *catastrophizing* again. She didn't know for sure Rudker was responsible for her accident up on the hill. A bitter laugh escaped her throat. The bastard had done it.

Sula unlocked the door and stepped in. A trickle of moonlight filtered into the living room through the tree in the front yard. She passed the table lamp and flipped on the light switch in the dining room. She wasn't sleepy, so she headed for the TV.

She didn't turn it on. Her house no longer felt like home. Her safe haven was gone, and Sula realized she would never relax here again. She couldn't even stay until morning. Sula decided to pack an overnight bag and get the hell out.

* * *

Rudker heard a car pull up outside, then drive away after a few minutes. Someone must have given Sula a ride. Of course. Her truck was probably totaled. What if she had brought someone home to stay with her? *Oh shit.* Why hadn't he thought of that? *Stupid, stupid, stupid.* He looked around for a window. If he heard another voice besides Sula's, he would exit immediately. He was not prepared to take on two people. If he'd had more time, or maybe bought some chloroform. *Shut up.*

The bedroom window faced the backyard and looked large enough to crawl through. Rudker turned back to the door, which he'd left partially open, listening intently. He heard a single person moving around, then the water in the kitchen came on, but no conversation. Rudker let out his breath in relief. Sula was alone.

Rudker tensed as he heard her coming toward him down the hallway. He tightened his grip on the makeshift sap. He hoped she would turn on a light. He needed to see her clearly so he could nail her either on the temple or right behind the ear. It was important she go down with one blow. Even if he didn't knock her unconscious, he needed her on the floor and vulnerable.

Her footsteps stopped right outside the bedroom door. Rudker smelled the jasmine shampoo in her hair. Sula made a funny noise in her throat, then walked into the bathroom.

Chapter 35

Sula grabbed her toothbrush, makeup, and shampoo and threw them into a little travel kit. She caught sight of her bruised face and leaned into the mirror to examine the gash on her temple. The skin was puckered together to close the stitches and she knew she would have a scar. It was minor, she reminded herself. She could have been horribly disfigured.

Had Rudker meant to kill her? Instead of fading as she thought it would, her fear intensified. Would he try again? Sula cursed herself for leading the bastard to Tate. If he hadn't threatened her son, she would have told that detective everything.

A scoffing sound escaped her throat as she reached for her moisturizer. What good would that have done? Would he have believed her? It all sounded so crazy. The police certainly had no power to protect her. They only acted after the fact. Women were murdered every day by ex-husbands and boyfriends who had already threatened and assaulted them. Until Rudker was convicted in court and incarcerated, he would be free to harass her. She was on her own, and for the first time in her life, Sula considered buying a gun.

She clicked off the bathroom light, stepped into the hall, and moved toward her bedroom. She noticed the door was open about a foot. Had she left it that way? She always closed doors, cabinets, and drawers. But she had bolted out of here in such a hurry that morning, thinking she was late for her visitation, that she had probably left it like that. That sort of paranoid thinking was why she had to grab her clothes and get out the house for a while. She pushed open the door, stepped in, and flipped on the light.

The smell of cinnamon tickled the air. Before Sula had a chance to process what that meant, the back of her head exploded in pain. For a moment, her world went dark, then her legs buckled. She landed on her knees, sending another jolt to her brain. The room came back into partial focus as she fell forward against the edge of the bed.

She brought her arms up to push back from the mattress, but a massive weight fell against her back, pinning her down. As she cried out, a thick, sweaty hand pressed against her mouth.

Rudker!

His cinnamon breath was hot against her neck. Sula tried to jerk her head free, but stabbing pains from both sides of her skull weakened her. The pressure of his hand lifted for a split second, then he pressed a wide piece of tape across her mouth and cheeks.

Bile rose in her throat as panic overtook her. She snapped her head back as hard as she could, hoping to make contact with bone. Instead, she hit his chest with a soft thump. He grunted and continued his assault. He grabbed both of her arms at the elbows and jerked them behind her back. Her broken collarbone shrieked in agony. Sula thought she might vomit.

Suddenly the pressure of his weight eased as he leaned away from her. Sula seized the moment and threw herself sideways, pulling free of his grip. Blind from the raging pain in her head, she crawled frantically toward the corner of the room.

Rudker grabbed her ankles and dragged her back. He pressed his knee against her lower spine, trapping her against the floor. His thick hands encircled her forearms and pulled them together behind her back. Pain engulfed her and Sula blacked out for a second. As she came to, Rudker was taping her wrists together.

For a moment, there was calm. Sula pulled air in through her nose trying to get enough oxygen, while Rudker made wet, noisy breathing sounds. His weight lifted again as he moved down to her feet. With a heave, she flipped over on her back. Before Rudker could grab her ankles, Sula kicked up and landed a blow to his chin.

"Bitch!" Rudker cupped his chin with both hands. Sula tried to scoot away, but with her hands pinned under her, it was impossible. She saw him reach in his pocket and draw his arm back. Something came down on her forehead with the force and feel of a hammer.

The room swirled and Sula blacked out.

* * *

Rudker quickly wrapped a strip of tape around Sula's ankles. She had fought more than he'd expected, but the struggle had given him an adrenaline rush that was making him giddy. When she'd crawled away and he had to drag her back by the feet, Rudker had flashed back to the girl fights in Seattle. Now he was turned on, but not exactly in a sexual way. It was a rush unlike anything he'd experienced before.

He considered leaving her for a few minutes while be brought the Jeep around and parked in the driveway, then decided not to. It could be devastating if a neighbor saw his vehicle—and license number—in Sula's driveway on the night of her disappearance.

He would carry her out through the side yard, hidden behind a good-sized fence. The only time the two of them would be visible was for less than half a block on the side street. If he kept her upright at his side and moved quickly, the risk of exposure would be minimal. Rudker hoped the girl would stay unconscious for the trip to the vehicle. He didn't doubt his ability to carry her that far, but if she struggled, it would be cumbersome, to say the least.

He glanced around the bedroom to see if he had lost anything out of his pockets during the struggle. Nothing seemed out of place, but he got on his knees and checked under the bed just in case. There wasn't even much dust.

Satisfied that he'd left no evidence, Rudker squatted next to Sula and scooped her up and over his shoulder. He was surprised at how heavy she seemed for such a thin girl. Breathing harder than he liked, he left the house the way he'd come in, through the kitchen and garage, then out the side door into the fenced yard.

Adrenaline rushed through his torso as he stepped into the night with an unconscious woman over his shoulder. It was a shame he would never be able to tell this story to anyone. He closed the door behind him and set off across the wet grass. Furious barking suddenly filled the air. The back fence popped and shuddered as a massive, unseen dog threw itself against the barrier. Rudker began to run.

Near the gate, he stumbled and pitched forward. With Sula's added weight, he almost went down. Rudker grunted as he caught himself. The dog continued to bark.

Go back in the house. Kill her here.

Rudker hesitated. Maybe he should. Why risk taking her in the Commander and maybe being seen? Because he wanted to hide the body. That was the safest move.

He opened the gate, then slid Sula down to his side and gripped her tightly with both arms. Her face fell against his as he started down the sidewalk. Silky jasmine-scented hair fluttered into his mouth. If not for the barking dog, Rudker would have been aroused by her proximity. Walking with her hugged against him was strenuous and awkward. He had to take short steps and hold her weight with his arms. After a moment, his lungs hurt from the exertion.

As he reached his vehicle, a woman's voice called to the dog. "Quiet, Maxie." The woman's presence was worse than the dog's. Would she step out to see who was lurking?

Rudker stopped next to the car door and wondered how he would take his keys out of his pocket without setting Sula down. At that moment, her body stiffened and she began to squirm. *Oh shit.* She was conscious. The neighbor called to the dog again, sounding closer this time.

Rudker let go of Sula with one arm and grabbed for his keys. She twisted away from him and dropped to the sidewalk. Instinctively, he pushed a foot into her stomach to keep her from rolling away. He pressed his electronic lock and grabbed the back door handle. The car alarm wailed.

Jesus H. Christ. Rudker jerked open the rear door, then grabbed his squirming cargo. With an adrenaline-powered thrust, he heaved Sula into the backseat and slammed the door. As he turned, the neighbor woman opened her gate and peeked out to see who was making the horrible commotion.

Rudker quickly jumped into the driver's seat. Shoving his key into the ignition, he silenced the alarm.

Idiot. Idiot. Idiot. I told you to kill her in the house.

"Shut up!"

Behind him, Sula moaned.

Rudker locked the doors and cranked the engine. He couldn't believe he'd set off the car alarm. Everything had gone smoothly up to that point. It must have been the barking dog, working on his nerves. Fucking dog. He hoped it choked to death on its own abundant drool. He drove away without looking back.

His nerves felt like a bowl of snap, crackle, and pop. He hadn't felt this charged since his college days, before he started taking meds. After a moment, he caught sight of the speedometer and realized he was doing forty in a residential area. He slowed and hung a left. If the neighbor had called the police about stranger danger, it was in his best interest to stay off the main thoroughfares and alter his course frequently. Rudker turned left again and began to hum.

* * *

Sula couldn't get enough air into her lungs through just her nose. The lack of oxygen cut into her brain and made it hard to think. Still, she had to stay alert, to plan. She had to figure a way out of this. She couldn't let the son of a bitch kill her and dump her body like trash. He was insane. How could she not have seen it?

The rig made a wild swing and Sula nearly rolled onto the floor. Her feet went over, but she managed to keep her torso on the seat. From that position, she was able to get on her knees, then twist around and sit up. The activity made her head pound, reminding her of the blows she'd taken to her forehead and left ear. What did he have planned next?

Sula considered the vehicle door. It was most likely locked; even if it weren't, she didn't think she could get it open with her hands taped behind her back. She twisted and pulled on her wrist binding, but it was as unyielding as ever. She decided her best option was to interfere with his driving, maybe make him crash and draw someone's attention. She decided to head butt him from behind.

As she scooted forward into position, the Jeep made another sharp turn. Sula rocked sideways but managed to right herself. Rudker's eyes caught hers in the rearview mirror. His were smiling. Sula looked away, so he would not see her intent. If she got the opportunity, she would kill the bastard.

As they passed block after block of dark houses, she tried to figure out where they were. Without streetlights, it was difficult, but that meant they were on a side street. She recognized a giant sequoia tree and knew they were traveling west on Twentieth Avenue. Rudker suddenly pulled into a driveway and stopped.

He crouched in the space between the front seats and faced her. Then he grabbed her shoulders with his huge hands. She tried to twist away, but it was a futile effort. She was a hundred pounds lighter, wounded, and trussed. With a small push, he flattened her against the seat. Sula's face pressed into the cool leather. She felt him groping around under her. He was looking for the seat belt.

Sula tried to roll toward the floor, but with her hands and feet bound, she had no strength. Rudker held her firmly in place. His hand came off her back long enough to loop the seat belt around her chest and snap it closed. Despair washed over her. She was completely captive and headed toward certain death.

* * *

Now that he had Sula bound and gagged in the back of his vehicle, Rudker knew he had to crystallize the rest of his plan. For the last few hours, he'd been operating on rage and impulse. He'd taken a few precautions about leaving evidence, but those were all common sense. The most important move was what to do with the body. He had already made the basic decision not to leave it in the house. Ideally, he wanted it to never be found. Without a body, there would be no investigation.

He drove slowly out Eighteenth Avenue, thinking about his options.

The night belonged to him; the rest of the city slept, unaware and unconcerned. He could drive up Wolf Creek, take off down a logging road, and hike into the woods a half mile or so. How long would it take to dig a hole big enough? If he didn't bury her deep enough, a wolf or coyote would eventually scatter her bones. If he didn't go far enough off the road, a logger or hiker could stumble on the freshly turned earth in the middle of the forest.

Rudker hated going into the woods. His sense of direction was inadequate and he was easily disoriented without recognizable landmarks. He'd quit Boy Scouts rather than go camping, and he had never hunted or hiked anywhere. What choice did he have now? He didn't want this body to turn up, ever. That was the best way to protect himself. Women disappeared all the time. Those who turned up dead were investigated. Those who didn't were forgotten.

Soon he passed Bertelsen Road and Rudker realized on some subconscious level he was headed for Prolabs. Then it hit him. The construction site. The new factory's foundation had been dug and the forms were built. Tomorrow or the next day, the cement trucks would roll in and start the pour. Piece by piece, the walls would go up. Whatever was in the ground underneath would stay there as long as the building remained. The whole area was freshly turned dirt. A grave site would not be noticed in the next twenty-four hours.

Rudker laughed out loud. Sula would be buried forever under a factory that produced Nexapra. A fitting end for a naive fool. It had been a long time since he'd let anyone get the best of him, and this little bitch should never have tried.

Remember Charlie Long from eighth grade? He used to kick your ass, steal your math homework, and put his name on it. Maybe we should look him up and set things right.

Rudker laughed again. What a thought. To go back and get even with everyone who had ever crossed him. It didn't necessarily have to be a violent revenge, just appropriately painful. Emotional or financial blows could be even more effective. He would start with Tara and give it some creative thought.

* * *

The tape across her mouth covered only part of her face and had not been pressed tightly. Sula discovered that the more she wiggled her jaws, the looser it became. When her jaws got tired, she rubbed her face against the smooth leather seat. She started vigorously, but it made her head hurt and emitted tiny little squeaks that she feared would draw Rudker's attention. She settled into a slow, steady rhythm. The movement was strangely soothing and helped keep her calm.

Sula still didn't have a plan for what she would do when she had finally worked the tape loose. Now, bound and buckled the way she was, all she could do was scream. And screaming inside the vehicle was pointless. It would only earn another blow to her head and more tape across her mouth. She would wait until they reached their destination—wherever the hell that was—and watch for an opportunity.

After a while, the combination of the motion and the pain made her nauseated. Stomach acid came up into her esophagus and scared her. Vomiting with her mouth taped could suffocate her. She held still and waited for the sick feeling to pass. The sense of being in the car and being scared and trying not to be sick brought back a vivid memory from her childhood.

Her family was on the way to the reservation to visit Aunt Serena. Dad was driving, Mom was in the front next to him, and she and Calix were in back—singing, chatting, and counting cars of a certain color. Sula always picked red. She and her sister paid no attention to their parents' conversation until they heard the tension. Then they half tuned in, picking up what they could while continuing their own chatter. Experience had taught them that becoming silent drew the tension their way.

Her parents argued about Daddy's job. He said he had to quit. "It's killing me," he whined. Her mother was unmoved. She said "no" and "not again" and "we'll starve." Back and forth they went until Dad finally shouted, "I'll kill us all, right here and now, and get it over with. It'll be better than the slow death we're living."

The old station wagon shot ahead and unexpectedly, they were zooming along, faster and faster. Mother screamed at her father to stop. Sula's stomach heaved and churned. She tried to be still, but before she could call out or roll down her window, she vomited right into her own lap, right into the pretty yellow dress she'd worn for the occasion.

Calix began to cry and yell at Daddy. Then it was over. The car slowed and they stopped on the side of the road. Mother helped her clean up with the jug of water they'd brought along to put in the radiator because it leaked. Daddy said he was sorry for scaring everyone. It was not the first time she'd heard the apology. Nor would it be the last.

Sula pushed the memory aside before it triggered others. She had to stay focused, to keeping working the tape and be ready for any opportunity.

Chapter 36

Rudker turned on Willow Creek, then started watching for the road to the construction site. The entry wasn't easy to spot in the dark. He missed it and had to turn around in the Prolabs' driveway. He drove back, pulled in, and started down the gravel road. A hundred yards in, a metal gate loomed in his headlights. Rudker hit the brakes. *Shit.* When had that gone up? *Shit. Shit. Shit.* He couldn't believe he didn't know it was there.

He put the vehicle in park and walked up to the gate. It didn't look particularly sturdy; he could probably run right through it. Nor would it present a problem to someone with a pair of bolt cutters. The construction people were probably just trying to keep teenagers from partying or four-wheeling on the site now that it was ready to build. Rudker ruled out crashing through the gate. He didn't want to draw attention to the fact that someone had been on the property. Scratches to the front end of his rig would look suspicious too.

A six-foot chain-link fence stretched out into the darkness on either side of the gate. Intuitively, he knew the fence didn't surround the entire site. It most likely bordered only Willow Creek Road and Prolabs' adjacent driveway. The rest of the property was open to the tree-covered hillside.

The sound of a car coming up the road made Rudker feel exposed, standing there in the beam of his own headlights. He ran back to his big Jeep and climbed in. A quick look over the backseat to check on Sula. Her eyes were closed, but her head was moving. He wondered if she was praying. If so, she would be disappointed. He put the vehicle in reverse and backed out to the road. Rudker gunned the truck and raced up to the Prolabs' driveway.

His short-lived mental peace exploded in a burst of rage. He hated being locked out. Hated it! It had happened to him over and over again as a kid because he couldn't keep track of his house key. This was his property, damn it, and he would access it if he wanted to. He raced down Prolabs' asphalt driveway, eyeing the fence that ran parallel about thirty feet behind the row of blooming shrubs.

He didn't slow down until he entered the auxiliary parking lot. No cars were in sight. The IT guy had gone home. At the end of the asphalt, Rudker kept going. Then he veered left and drove through a small grove of willow trees. On the other side, the fence appeared directly in front of him. Rudker shut off his headlights. A half-moon reflected enough light off the metal to keep him parallel to the chain link. The Commander rolled over the shrubs and bumpy terrain without much bounce. The fence ended abruptly about fifty feet later and Rudker came to a stop.

He decided not to drive onto the site itself. The Commander was big and heavy, and it would leave distinctive tire tracks in the wet dirt. In retrospect, it was a good thing the gate had been installed. It had kept him from making what could have turned out to be a serious mistake.

Rudker climbed out of the rig. The night had turned cool and he could hear the creek gurgling along the back of the property. The waterway was the only thing left on the ten acres that was still in its natural state. He took a leisurely piss, then opened the Jeep's back door. He hoped he would be able carry Sula all the way to the back of the site where the factory would be built. He had the physical strength, but maybe not the stamina. Exercise had never been part of his lifestyle.

First, he grabbed a flashlight from the jockey box. Before he could fit it into his pocket, the roll of duct tape had to come out. Rudker laid the tape on the front seat. He would toss it in a dumpster on his way home. Then he reached into the back storage area and pulled out the shovel he'd bought at Fred Meyer. He leaned the shovel against the truck, grabbed Sula by the ankles, and dragged her out. He would carry her as far as he could, then rest if he had to.

* * *

Robbie was unable to sleep. He'd dreamed for a while in a semi-wakeful state about going back to Prolabs, begging for his job, and being refused. In one dream sequence, his father came down from the executive suite into the factory to tell him personally to get lost. Each time, Robbie ran from the building and cycled away in shame.

Disturbed by the repeated dream rejections, Robbie got up and went out to the living room. He turned on the TV but couldn't focus on any of the inane middle-of-the-night programs. The shame of his dream stayed with him. He wished his mother would contact him. She always made him feel better about himself. Why hadn't she returned his call? His father had been as distant as ever.

Robbie felt himself sinking into despair but didn't know how to stop it. The trial drug he was taking clearly wasn't working for him, at least not yet. Some meds took a week or so to kick in. He would call the clinic tomorrow and tell them how he was feeling. Maybe he would drop out of the program and get back on the Zoloft.

In the meantime, getting a little nicotine into his system would probably help. It had in the past. Robbie looked for his cigarette pack but found it empty. He would have gladly walked the two blocks to the 7-Eleven store, but he didn't have enough cash even for a pack of generics. A trip to the ATM downtown was more of an effort than he had the energy for at this hour. He went out to the apartment's tiny deck and looked through the cigarette can for a decent butt. They'd all been smoked to the nub. Robbie shivered in the cold night air. It was officially spring, but you'd never know it by the temperature.

He grabbed a jacket and his cell phone and headed out the front door. Maybe if he walked around the apartment complex he would run into someone and be able to bum a smoke. He didn't believe he would get that lucky. It was three in the morning and even most students were in bed. The people who were still awake had better things to do than wander around outside. Yet on campus, anything was possible.

Robbie headed upstairs. A group of apartments on the fourth level always seemed to have a late party going.

Climbing the three flights of stairs took all his energy. He'd felt weak ever since his little overdose incident and tonight his legs felt like lead. The fourth floor was as quiet as the rest of the building. Not a single light shone behind the individual apartment blinds. Robbie was sorry he'd made the effort.

He remembered the guys in 404 often went up on the roof to smoke. They had nailed a couple of footholds to the side of the building at the end of the balcony. He'd seen them stand on the railing and use the footholds to push themselves onto the roof of the balcony. From there, it was a short scoot up to the flat roof surface, where he was sure to find a stash of cigarettes, maybe even a little pot.

Robbie shuffled to the end of the balcony and stared down at the street below. From this height, if he fell while trying to get on the roof, he would definitely die. He wondered why he hadn't thought of it the other night. If he had jumped instead of taking the stupid pills, it would be over now. There was no guesswork in jumping. And no one to stop him in the middle of a fall.

* * *

The girl's eyes were wide with terror as he lifted her over his shoulder. Rudker had never elicited so much fear in anyone before. He knew he intimidated, and sometimes frightened, his employees, and that had rather pleased him. This was different and disturbing.

He reminded himself that it was a one-time situation. He was acting in self-defense and he was in way too deep to stop now. He didn't believe in God or karma or have any concerns for his soul, but he would have to get back on his meds. He didn't want this memory to haunt him.

Sniveling coward. Never worry about the other person. Never show remorse. Didn't you learn anything from your daddy?

Oh yes. He'd learned quite a bit from the old man. Lesson number one? Never back down.

The girl didn't go easy at first. She twisted on his shoulder with a relentless fury for a minute, then seemed to give up. The terrain, although cleared of trees and shrubs, had not been graded yet. Rudker stumbled on a huge dirt clod and almost went down. After another ten steps, he was breathing so hard he had to stop. He kneeled and dropped Sula in the dirt. For a moment, she lay there unmoving. Rudker took a few deep breaths of air. Abruptly, Sula rolled away and split the night with a shriek.

Her cry shot through him like an electric jolt. Rudker lunged and landed on her as she rolled again. He covered her mouth with his hand and willed his heart to slow down. *Jesus.* What if he had a heart attack out here?

Sula finally stopped struggling and Rudker's pulse settled into a still-rapid, but steady rate. He pushed to his knees so he was straddling her.

Rudker used the flashlight to look around for the tape that had been on her mouth, but it was a pointless search. Even if he could find it out here in the dark, it would be covered with dirt and not likely to re-adhere.

Rudker squeezed her face and leaned in close. "You're not getting away. Diane Warner didn't get away and she was a better woman than you are."

In a quick motion, he pulled his hand away from her mouth and brought the flashlight down on her forehead. Sula's eyes closed and her head rolled to the side. Rudker peeled back a strip of the tape from her ankles, ripped it loose, and pressed it over her mouth. Letting her scream again worried him more than the possibility she could get away from him out here. He wasn't overly concerned about either. He had smacked her pretty hard. *If* she opened her eyes again she would be breathing dirt.

He heaved Sula's limp, heavy body over his other shoulder. Warner had been much smaller and easier to deal with. That had been an unfortunate accident. She had gone too far with her accusations and he had simply lost control. The fact that Warner had been dressed in jogging clothes made the *body* decision easy: Dump her near the bike path and hope some homeless crazy guy got blamed. It had worked too. This time he had to be more careful. A second death of a Prolabs' employee would draw police suspicion. A disappearance was another story.

With a new surge of energy, Rudker pushed to his feet. He had to get moving. He still had a grave to dig.

Chapter 37

Sula thought she was still in the vehicle, rolling down the road, but there was something wrong with one of the tires. It was making a rhythmic "chunk, chunk, chunk" sound. She fought to wake herself up. It was important to keep track of where they were going.

As she surfaced, the front part of her brain burned with raw pain. Her eyelids felt sticky, and she struggled to get her eyes open and keep them open. Darkness surrounded her, but overhead she could see stars. She was outside, not in the car. The ground beneath her was cool and damp even through her pants. Her arms, trapped under her back, ached from the strain and weight of her body.

How did she get here? Had Rudker carried her? Where was he? She inched her head forward off the ground. The steady "chunk" sound was louder and clearer now. About ten feet away, Rudker's form came into focus. He bent over, then straightened up.

Then did it again. As her eyes adjusted to the dim moonlight, Sula realized he had a shovel.

He was digging!

Her heart skipped a beat. The bastard was digging a hole to bury her in. Sula wanted to scream, but her mouth was taped and her lungs were paralyzed with fear.

No. No. No. She cried without sound, without tears. She wasn't ready to die. She wanted to see Tate grow up, even if it was from a distance. She wanted to have a real love affair. She wanted to write investigative journalism stories.

The chunk sound continued. She could hear Rudker's labored breath between digs.

A memory, dark and horrible, fluttered around the edge of her consciousness. Sula tried to push it away, but she had no strength, no reserve of mental health to draw from right now. At first, the memory floated in and out with brief hazy images, but the sound of the shovel striking the dirt reverberated in her brain. The past flooded into her consciousness in full, technicolor detail as though it were happening all over again.

Sula watched her father from her bedroom window. His tall, thin body hunched over the hole he was digging in the backyard as the wind tousled his collar-length hair. The cold evening air blew the tears off his cheeks as he worked. Sula had cried at first too. Mostly because her parents were upset and bad things happened when they got emotional.

Her mother had run over Patches, her daddy's dog, while coming down the driveway.

Mom had burst in as Sula and Calix and Dad sat at the kitchen table, eating cold ham sandwiches and corn chips. Her pretty face was twisted with liquor and grief. She slumped at the table and sobbed. All she would say was "I'm sorry." Sula and her sister refused to give their mother the attention she wanted, but her father, sensing it was more than just another missed dinner, ran out to the driveway.

A loud wail penetrated the thin trailer wall. She'd heard Daddy cry before, but not like this. This was distressing. Calix, older by a year and Dad's favorite, pushed past their mother and ran out to him. Sula followed, but with a wary caution. She'd learned to distrust high emotion, to shut down her own feelings so she would not be caught up in the drama.

Her father kneeled on the ground next to her mother's Oldsmobile and cradled the black-and-gray Australian shepherd in his arms. There was little blood, but Patches was clearly broken. The sight of the injured dog and her father weeping was more than Sula could handle. She and Calix cried with him.

Then abruptly, Dad stood. "Calix, bring my pistol.

Her sister's distress was visible. "Why?"

"I have to end his suffering. Bring it to the backyard."

Sula could not watch. She went to her bedroom, ignoring her mother's call for attention. Once there, she stood near the window and peeked out, watching to see if her sister would do as told. Calix, as stubborn as she was beautiful, often defied their parents. Sula preferred peace, even if it meant losing ground.

Calix came into the backyard, carrying the gun as if it were a poisonous snake. Her dad put Patches on the grass, took the pistol from Calix, then told her to go inside. Sula turned away from the window. The gun blast was a short, loud pop. Sula wondered if their neighbors had heard. The Crawleys were about a half-mile away.

Sula turned back and watched her father retrieve a shovel from the shed. He began to dig. The "chunk, chunk, chunk" sound seemed to go on forever, but Sula could not tear herself away. She wanted to know the minute he was done. She wanted to be ready for whatever came next. Part of her brain said to leave the house, to get far away, but she couldn't. She loved her mother in spite of her drinking and she would stay to protect her if she could.

She returned to the kitchen, where her mother sat at the table eating Sula's sandwich. She no longer wanted it, but it annoyed her anyway. Calix's dinner was also unfinished. Her sister was in the living room watching TV.

"Hi honey. I'm sorry about the dog. Was this your sandwich?" The smell of gin hung around her mother like a cloud.

"You can have it." Sula watched for signs of awareness or concern but didn't detect any. "Dad has been a little high strung lately."

"I know, honey. That's why I went to the bar with the girls."

"This may set him off."

"It's only a dog."

"Maybe we should go for a walk."

Her mother laughed. "No thanks."

As Sula started to sit down at the chipped laminate table, her mother jumped up. "I'm going to take a shower." She sashayed away, her jeans hugging her lithe body and her long hair gently swinging. She looked too young to have teenage daughters. People always said so.

The back door slammed. Sula jumped, then glanced over at Calix. Her sister's gaze never left the TV, but her eyes watched their father as he moved past both of them, gun in hand.

"Dad?"

"Not now, Calix."

Down the hall, he plodded. The muscles in Sula's back began to ache from the tension. She stood and started to follow.

"I wouldn't do that." Calix stood too.

"We can't let him hurt her."

"He's more likely to hurt himself." Calix moved toward the hallway as the shouting began. "Let me talk to him. Maybe he'll listen to me."

Sula stopped and let her sister move ahead of her. From the bedroom, their mother cried out. "Jake, no. Don't do this. Think of the girls."

Calix began to run. Sula followed.

The bedroom door was open. Their mother stood by the dresser in her underclothes, clutching a towel. Their father was a few feet away, the gun pointed at his own head. He didn't take his eyes from his wife as they entered.

"I can't live like this, Rose. I used to just hate myself, but now I've made you miserable for so long, I hate you too." He turned to look at his daughters. "I'm sorry, girls. I love you." He turned away and closed his eyes.

"No!" Calix lunged for their dad's arm just before the gun went off. She knocked him askew as the blast echoed around the room. Sula covered her ears, but she should have covered her eyes. At the edge of her vision, she saw her mother fly back against the wall. Her slender body slid to the floor and a hole opened in her chest. Blood, the color of summer berries, poured out of her.

Time and motion ceased to exist. The three of them were frozen, mouths open, as a dull hum filled the room. Their father broke free. With an anguished cry, he rushed to his wife. Sula edged in behind him. If she did not see the destruction, it would not be as real.

Her father was no savior. He could only weep as blood flowed from her mother's body. She tried to speak and a trickle of blood oozed down her chin. Her eyes closed and she slumped over.

Calix knelt down beside her body and wailed. "I killed my mother!"

Dad pulled Calix away. Grabbing both arms, he lifted her to her feet. The movements seemed slow and choppy, like an old reel film.

"It's not your fault." He shook Calix as he cried. Sula could see by his expression that he was shouting, but his voice seemed far away.

Calix would not be calmed. Sobbing hysterically, she jerked free and backed away. "You bastard."

Her father's face went slack. "Tell them I did it." He looked at both of them for compliance.

Sula was too numb to process what he meant or anticipate his next action.

He spun around and grabbed the revolver off the bed, where he'd dropped it in his rush to his wife's side. He put the gun to his head again. "Tell the cops I killed her, you hear me? I don't want Calix blamed for this."

He pulled the trigger.

Sula was still on her knees holding her dead mother's hand when she saw her father's brains spray into the room and fall to the white bedspread. She looked at her sister, as if to confirm it was really happening. Calix's face went deathly pale and her mouth fell open.

Sula felt numb, as if her brain had been injected with anesthetic.

Calix screamed. "Look at what I've done! I've killed them both." She pulled her own hair and began to keen, a never-ending sound that didn't seem human.

Sula wanted to comfort her, to say the right thing. Their parents had been headed for this tragic outcome as long as she could remember. Her father had craved death and her mother had no respect for life. When Sula envisioned her future, they were never there. Yet her mouth would not open; her body would not move.

Calix was alone in her guilt and it was more than she could bear.

All at once the wailing stopped. Before Sula could process why that scared her more than anything, Calix lunged to their father's body and pulled the gun from his dead hand. She shoved the weapon into her mouth, looked at Sula with eyes that begged forgiveness, and pulled the trigger.

The blast sent the room into a spin and Sula's mind went dark.

Chapter 38

For a few minutes, Sula's mind floated in darkness, unwilling to reenter either her present reality or the anguish of her past. Finally, the searing pain in her head and arms pulled her, trembling and cold, into full consciousness—where she was bound and gagged in the middle of an open dirt field with a madman nearby digging her grave.

For a moment, she lingered on that fateful day in her fifteenth year. Part of her had wanted to die as well, to join her family in their exodus, rather than live with the grief of losing them. Yet she hadn't even picked up the gun, nor had she managed to kill herself later with drugs and alcohol. She had clung to life, in all its anguish, again and again.

Sula listened for Rudker's activity. The digging sound had slowed and lost its steady rhythm. She kicked violently against the tape around her ankles. It gave a little bit. She realized the new strip on her mouth must have come from her leg binding, leaving it less secure. She kicked again. And again. She also began to inch away from Rudker, pushing with her feet and shoulders.

She kicked and pushed until she ran out of oxygen. A tremendous effort for such a small gain. With her mouth taped, she could breathe only through her nose, limiting her air supply and making her weak. Sula rested for a moment and listened for Rudker. She heard nothing except the wind in the poplar trees up the hill. In that instant, she knew where she was. She'd heard that musical sound many times while having lunch in the Prolabs courtyard. She figured she was in the open construction site adjacent to the factory. Fortunately, she had been inching herself in the direction of the road.

* * *

Rudker sat on his pile of dirt and took long, slow breaths. His heart pounded in his ears and he felt dizzy. He needed to lie down. Staring into the two-foot-by-six-foot crevice, he wondered what it would feel like to lay in a grave.

Do it. Get in there. Feel the terror…or peace. Death can be a release. See if you like it.

This voice was new and soft, perhaps even female. Rudker was surprised by its presence, but compelled to obey its hypnotic suggestion.

He eased himself into the hole and lay down. He didn't quite fit, so he kept his knees bent. Gazing up at the stars, he listened to his heart pound and felt the cool comfort of the dirt around him. He tried to imagine what it would be like to have it tossed on top of him, a shovelful at a time. *What would it be like to finally stop fighting?* He had lost Tara and he'd lost his position of power with JB Pharma. Even with Sula out of the picture, how long would it take him to get back on top?

He could not imagine his life without the struggle to be better than those around him, the need to make more money than he could spend, the craving for admiration and fear from others.

Death can be a release.

Rudker sat up and shook the new voice out of his head. He was not ready to give in or let go. He would fight his way back to the top. It was time to wrap this up and stop thinking about Sula Moreno forever.

* * *

The silence was disturbing. Where was Rudker? What was he doing? With a surge of adrenaline, Sula started kicking again. A small ripping sound pierced the night as her legs pulled free of the duct tape. A sob of relief rose in her throat. Arms still taped behind her back, Sula struggled to her knees.

The night air filled with the sound of his thundering footsteps. *He'd heard the tape give way!* Sula lunged to her feet and ran. Without the use of her arms, it was awkward and sluggish, and he would catch her soon. She scanned the area, searching in the dark for a place to hide.

The builders had leveled everything on the site, save for a few trees near the creek at the back of the property. For a moment, she regretted her direction. She should have run for the trees.

It was too late now. She kept running, with Rudker's footsteps gaining on her.

As her eyes adjusted to the moonlight, Sula realized she was down inside the massive footprint of where the new factory would stand. The perimeter of the excavated area was just ahead, a short wall that would have to be hurdled. If her arms had not been tied behind her, she could have easily leapt up and out of the two-foot-deep foundation. Without the swing of her arms, she wouldn't make it over in one leap.

Rudker was gaining ground. She could hear him breathing hard behind her, sounding like a sprinter at the end of a 440-yard dash.

Sula ran harder. Just before she hit the ledge, she threw herself forward. Her torso landed on the upper ground and knocked the wind out of her. Behind her, her legs stuck out over the recessed excavation, with nothing beneath them. Sula rolled on her side and pulled her knees to her chest. She started to roll again to get up on her knees, but Rudker's hands were there, grabbing for her feet.

She kicked viciously, landing both feet against his chest. He grunted and stumbled back. Sula got her legs under her and pushed up. Without her arms for balance, she stumbled on her first step and went down on her knees. Again, she pushed with all her leg strength to get on her feet and run.

* * *

Rudker wanted to shout, but he couldn't risk the noise. His heart hurt with the exertion of chasing her, and now he struggled to climb out of the foundation. Thank God for his long legs. He regained his footing and began to run again. The old familiar *other* in his head tormented him for letting her get away.

Incompetent fool. Lying in her grave instead of burying her! I told you, never empathize! What if she gets away?

"She won't!"

Rudker tried to speed up, but his arms and legs ached with fatigue. He wasn't used to digging and running, but Sula was also moving slowly and he would soon catch her. The farther the little bitch ran, the farther he would have to carry or drag her body back to its grave.

Bright little flashes of light popped behind his eyelids, as if he'd just taken a blow to the head. Was he having a stroke?

Rudker kept running, flashlight in hand. This time, he would take no chances. He would happily beat her with it until she was dead. It would serve her right for causing him this stress and pain.

* * *

Sula stumbled on a dirt clod and almost went down. A sob rose in her throat as she struggled to get moving again. She heard Rudker closing in. Her shoulder screamed with pain but she forced her legs to keep going.

In a moment, she heard traffic and looked up. She was near the road! She called on the gods to give her the strength and her pace accelerated. Headlights were coming in her direction. The cars were on Prolabs' property. If only she could reach them in time. Her legs and lungs burned with exhaustion, but she kept running toward the lights.

The vehicles came to a stop about a hundred yards away. Their headlights blazed across the opening between them. They would see her and help her. Sobs of relief choked her as she ran.

* * *

Cricket and his crew were prepared for the gate. Joe, riding shotgun, jumped out of the twelve-passenger van. With a sturdy pair of bolt cutters, he snapped through the small chain and pushed the gate open. Joe climbed back in. "That was too easy."

"We needed the break," Cricket said. "Daylight is coming, and we can't afford to waste time."

He put the van in gear and rolled forward. Another rig carrying their gear was bringing up the rear. Sandwiched in between was the KRSL TV news van. Trina Waterman had jumped at the chance to film his crew setting up their tents at daybreak on Prolabs' construction site. The company was hot news right now. Cricket hoped to have a chance to talk on camera about the environmental consequences of building on wetlands. Trina had made no promises other than to get up some footage.

This protest site would be more difficult than others. Typically, they built platforms in trees that were about to be logged. Cops and security guards couldn't get to them in their treetop perches. Sometimes they chained themselves to equipment or fences. This time, they would set up in the middle of the construction site and use long chains to secure themselves to the vans. Eight of them would stay for however long they lasted.

Cricket knew that eventually they would be dragged away in handcuffs, but that was the way it worked. Sometimes they managed to stall "progress" long enough for legal maneuverings to take place and change the course of events. Sometimes they accomplished nothing except a trip to jail, several court appearances, and a hefty fine. This was his life and he couldn't imagine living it any other way.

"Hey! What's that?" Joe shouted.

Cricket peered out beyond the headlights' immediate range. In the distance, someone was running toward them. It looked like a woman with no arms. He kept his foot gently on the gas, closing the gap between them. He pulled his cell phone from his jacket and pressed redial.

Trina answered immediately. "Yes?"

"There's something going on here. A woman running toward us. Just thought you might like to know."

He stopped the van and put it into park, unsure of what to do. The news van pulled up alongside. The woman stumbled into view about three hundred feet away. Duct tape covered her mouth and her eyes were wide with terror. Cricket jumped out and heard the other van door slam at the same time. He sprinted toward the woman, taking in the dirt on her clothes, the blood on her face, and the arms pinned behind her back. She had been held against her will and was running for her life.

Chapter 39

Trina took in the bizarre scene. Heart pounding with excitement at the strange turn of events, she shouted, "Camera!"

Chris was already right behind her. "Got it."

She heard the click and knew the tape was rolling. Together, they jogged after Cricket, Chris lagging behind with the heavy camera on his shoulder. A glimmer of early morning light peeked over the south hills.

A large man came into view from the dark dirt field. He thundered along, wheezing like someone with only one lung. Trina drew in a sharp breath. It was Karl Rudker, Prolabs' CEO. What the hell was going on here?

The news story played out in real time. As Cricket reached the running woman, Rudker began to shout. "Get away from her. She's mine!"

Rudker brought up his arm as he ran, as though it held a weapon. Cricket ripped the tape from the young woman's mouth, and she cried out, "He's trying to kill me."

Rudker bore down on them, shouting, "Death is a release! Let her go."

Three other protesters rushed past Trina.

Cricket pushed the woman in the direction of the road and shouted, "Get in the van."

Trina watched as the skinny environmentalist turned and faced Rudker, the madman who kept coming. She felt a pang of fear for their safety. What did Rudker have in his hand?

Hands still behind her back, the woman ran past the other protesters as they rushed to help Cricket. When they reached him, the dreadlocked men stood side by side, forming a narrow barricade. They were young and lean, and their presence gave Trina little comfort. Rudker kept up his charge, shouting all the while, "Death is release."

Trina tried to take it all in, but when Rudker barreled right through the protesters, knocking them to the ground as if playing Red Rover, her nerves frazzled.

"Jesus!" Chris swore as he stepped closer. The woman stumbled up to them, nearly collapsing into Trina. Her forehead was bruised and swollen and blood had dried on her face.

"Get my hands free!" She turned so Trina could reach the tape on her wrists. Then the woman saw Rudker still coming after her. She swore and raced toward the van.

Trina wanted to bolt after her and lock herself in the news vehicle, but she forced herself to stay put. This was the story of a lifetime. Rudker was clearly focused on the young woman. Trina figured as long as she kept out of his way, he wouldn't even see her.

Rudker kept coming, a massive man in a psychotic rage. Trina and Chris stood their ground, the camera still rolling.

As Rudker passed by, Trina took a step forward and stretched out her leg. She caught him at the ankle and he went down with a thunderous flop. Chris shoved the camera at her, then jumped on Rudker. He straddled the madman before he could catch his breath. Although not as tall as Rudker, Chris was two hundred plus pounds. Trina prayed he could hold him. Two of the protesters rushed to help hold Rudker down and Cricket ran for the van, calling "I'll get some rope."

Trina set down the camera, grabbed her cell phone out of her pocket, and dialed 911. Everything had happened so unexpectedly and so quickly, she hadn't thought of it before.

"What's your emergency?"

"Attempted homicide. Suspect detained, but still dangerous. We're on the Prolabs' construction site on Willow Creek Road. Between West Eleventh and West Eighteenth. We need police units here immediately."

Trina hung up before the dispatcher could ask her a bunch of questions. She wanted to interview the escaped woman.

* * *

Sula sobbed with relief as the young man with the dreadlocks cut the tape from her arms. Her shoulders ached from the hours spent in such an unnatural position. She wanted to feel safe, but Rudker was still only thirty feet away and the only thing standing between them was a beefy cameraman and a couple of skinny hippies. Sula heard Rudker yelling and cursing her with death. He was out of his mind.

She had no idea what all these people were doing out here in the construction site just before sunrise, but she was extremely grateful for their presence.

"I want to get in the van and lock the doors."

"Of course." The young man opened the side door and helped her into the van. She collapsed onto the backseat and fought for control. She was on the edge of hysterical sobbing.

"Are you all right?"

A lunatic had almost buried her alive. It would be a long time before she was all right. "I could use some water. Maybe some aspirin. And lock the doors."

"You got it."

He went to the other van and came back with a bottle of water. Sula opened the door for him. He shut and locked it behind him. As Sula gulped down the water, the newswoman approached with camera perched on her shoulder. Sula recognized her as Trina Waterman from KRSL. The young man let the newswoman into the van.

"What's your name?" Trina asked.

"Sula Moreno."

Sula did not want to be filmed. She knew she looked like hell and she might be too shaky to be coherent. Yet it was a chance to tell her story, to warn people who might be taking Nexapra.

"What happened here tonight?" Trina gently probed.

Sula took a deep breath and spoke slowly. "Karl Rudker kidnapped me, then brought me out here to bury me. He was digging my grave when I escaped. And all because I found out that his new blockbuster drug, Nexapra, has a fatal flaw that he doesn't want anyone to know about."

"What flaw?"

Before Sula could answer, a police scanner on the floor behind her squawked to life.

"Units 205 and 315. We have a possible suicide attempt at the Hilyard Street Apartments, 1560 Hilyard." The dispatcher sounded a little worked up. "The caller says the jumper's name is Robbie Rudker."

Sula and Trina stared at each other.

Trina asked, "Do you know Robbie Rudker? Is he related to Karl Rudker, the man who just tried to kill you?"

"He's his son."

"I do not believe this." Trina shook her head, stepped out of the van, and shouted at her cameraman. "Chris! I've got to go. There's another breaking story."

Trina climbed in the driver's side of the news van. Sula followed, glancing over at Rudker on the ground, then got up in the passenger seat. "I'm going with you."

Trina looked at her skeptically. "Maybe you should wait for the ambulance."

"I know Robbie and I think I can help him."

"All right then." Trina started the van and backed out through the gate. "The police won't like it that you're gone when they get here."

"I'll talk to them later."

They bounced along the gravel road and Sula experienced a new round of pain. Once they were on Willow Creek, the newswoman floored it.

"How do you know Robbie?" Trina asked when she had the van up to about fifty.

"He works for Prolabs, and I used to work for Prolabs."

"Did you know he was suicidal?"

"No." Sula thought about her last conversation with Robbie. He'd seemed wistful, but not depressed. She wondered about his mental health. Clearly, his father was psychotic. Had Robbie inherited a serious mental-health problem? Sula berated herself for the thought. It wasn't fair to make those connections. Her father had been unstable, and she took antidepressants. That didn't mean she was mentally ill.

"He seems like a sweet young man," she said. "He uses his mother's maiden name at work so no one knows he's Rudker's son."

Trina was too busy taking a right turn to respond. Sula grabbed the "oh shit" strap above the door and held on. Fortunately, there was no traffic this early in the morning, so they were unlikely to get into a collision. The thought made her laugh a little.

"What's funny?"

"Rudker tried to kill me twice in the last twenty-four hours. I feel amazingly lucky to be alive. It would be tragic to die in a car wreck right now."

"Sorry." Trina slowed down a little. "He tried to kill you twice?"

"He ran me off McBeth road yesterday. My truck landed on a tree and rolled."

"We're going to do a long and thorough interview in the very near future."

Trina turned right on Garfield, then left on Thirteenth without slowing down. Sula closed her eyes.

"What was that drug you mentioned? And what's the problem?"

Sula suddenly felt exhausted. She struggled to think and speak clearly. "It's called Nexapra. It's for depression. But it makes some people, some Hispanic people, commit suicide."

"And Rudker knows this?"

"Diane Warner, Prolabs' chief scientist, discovered the problem and told Rudker. He told her to forget about it and go ahead with clinical trials."

"Oh my God. Did he kill her too?"

"Yes. He bragged about it when he dragged me out to my burial site."

"Jesus. Who would have guessed he was such a psychopath?"

They were nearly downtown and the sun was just up over the hills. An occasional car appeared on the street and Trina flew past all of them.

"How old is Robbie?" the news reporter asked.

"Twenty or so. I'm not sure. Why?"

"There's all this data that says antidepressants are linked to teen suicide. I wonder if he's taking medication."

Sula wondered about it too. She thought about Robbie and how different he was from his father. He even looked completely different. He was lean, with light-brown skin and caramel-colored eyes. In fact, he looked Hispanic. Oh dear. "I wonder if he's taking Nexapra," Sula said, half to herself.

"It's not approved yet, is it?"

"No, but there are clinical trials going on right now."

"That would be ironic."

"To say the least."

They were in the campus area now and Trina slowed down. No students were out and about yet, but that would change soon. A moment later, they pulled up in front of the Hilyard Apartments. A small group of young people stood on the sidewalk and took turns glancing up at the roof. Some looked as if they had just gotten out of bed. Others seemed to be just getting in after a long night of partying. One girl had a blanket around her shoulders.

Trina parked across the street in a handicapped space. She grabbed the heavy camera and scooted out. Sula followed, moving more slowly.

Trina strode up to the group and began filming.

"Where is he?" Sula asked the girl with the blanket.

"There. On the corner." She pointed with one hand and held on to her covering with the other.

Sula saw Robbie on the edge of the flat roof. He sat cross-legged and stared off into the sky. He seemed oblivious to the group below. Sula wanted to get close enough to talk to him. He wouldn't be able hear her from the street.

She headed up the stairs. At the second landing, she had to sit so her head would stop spinning. Her body felt as if she'd been beaten with a bat.

On the third floor, three of Robbie's neighbors had gathered at the end of the balcony. Sula joined them. She couldn't see Robbie, but she assumed they were close enough to communicate with him.

"Is he responsive?" Sula asked a girl who looked too young to be in college.

"Sometimes." She turned to look at Sula. "Jesus! What happened to you?"

Sula reflexively touched her forehead, where Rudker had tried to kill her with a flashlight. "It's a long story."

The students all turned to stare.

"You can see it on the news tonight." She stepped toward the edge of the balcony. "What does Robbie say? Does he plan to jump?"

"He hasn't said anything in about ten minutes." The guy with the buzz cut looked as if he'd been downing whiskey sours. Yet he seemed genuinely concerned.

"I'd like to try talking to him."

"Be my guest." Buzz cut stepped aside so Sula could move up to the railing.

The other young man stepped back too and lit a cigarette. The enticing smell of an outdoor smoke on a cold morning flooded Sula with an old desire. "Do you have another one?"

"I don't. Sorry, man."

"It's okay." She was both disappointed and relieved.

Sula pressed against the railing and called out, "Robbie. It's Sula Moreno, from Prolabs."

After a long pause, he responded. "What are you doing here?"

"I have some information that I think will help you."

"I doubt that." His voice was quiet but Sula could hear the pain. "Why don't you and everyone else go away. I just want to die the way I lived. Alone."

"Are you in a clinical trial for Nexapra?"

A short pause. "How did you know?"

"The drug has problems. It gives some people strong suicidal thoughts."

Robbie laughed, a harsh sound. "The shrinks all say that isn't how it works. They don't believe a drug can make you commit suicide."

"Mental-health problems are complicated. And this drug has a genetic flaw that affects only Hispanic people."

Robbie unexpectedly scooted into view. Sula was glad to make eye contact, but she didn't like his proximity to the edge of the roof.

"Why would Prolabs give it to people if they knew that?" He seemed genuinely confused.

"There was some disagreement within the company. Not everyone believed Dr. Warner's findings." Sula wanted to keep the conversation away from his father if she could.

"Why should I believe you?"

"I've seen the data. I've talked to the wives of the men who committed suicide while taking Nexapra. I think it's the drug making you feel like this. If you stop taking it and start on another antidepressant, you'll feel better."

Robbie started to cry. Sula winced. What had she said? She wanted so badly to help him. She couldn't bear the thought that he would die as a result of his father's greed.

"Robbie, please come down. It's going to be fine. We'll get you some help. And a new prescription. Your world will look brighter, I promise." It was not a promise within her control but she believed it with all her heart.

Robbie continued to cry. After a minute, he stood and stepped toward the ledge. He looked over at her. "My father knows, doesn't he? He knows the drug has problems, but he doesn't care. Because it's going to be a big moneymaker."

Sula couldn't lie to him. The truth would be out there soon enough. "Yes, he knows."

"What a bastard. I am the son of a bastard. The world would be better off without either of us."

"No!" Sula couldn't stay calm. "You are not your father. Just as I am not my father. Or my mother. They were both unhappy and messed-up people. My father's selfish desire to end his life killed both of them. I know all about grief and depression. I lost everybody I ever loved. But I came through it. My life has purpose even though I don't always know what it is. Yours does too. You just have to give it time. Your life will be better if you fight for it. And if you stop taking Nexapra."

There was a long silence. The young girl behind her started crying. Sula felt like crying too. It had been quite a day. In the distance, she could hear police sirens coming their way.

"Robbie, come down. You can stay with me for a while. I'll help you through this. I know a great counselor."

"Do you have a younger sister?" Then he laughed, a quiet, beautiful sound.

"No, but I know a few young women." Sula was smiling.

Robbie stepped back from the edge. He moved out of view and they heard his footsteps on the walkway roof above them. He was coming down.

Chapter 40

Monday, May 3, 8:45 a.m.

Sula walked into the courtroom with Barbara at her side. Her lawyer's sharp black suit and confident stride failed to bolster Sula's nerve. Her heart quickened just at being there. Courtrooms tended to produce winners and losers, and today she didn't look or feel like a winner. She'd appraised herself in the mirror before leaving her house and was not pleased with what she saw.

Her dark-blue skirt and jacket looked as if they'd been borrowed from someone older and heavier, and the collarbone brace could be seen at the base of her neck. A thick slather of foundation across her forehead failed to hide the giant purple-and-yellow bruise, and the gash on her temple was still quite prominent. She looked gaunt from missing so many meals and her eyes were jumpy, like those of a stalking victim. Overall, she was not the picture of physical and mental well-being she wanted to project to the judge.

Barbara took her by the elbow and nudged Sula toward the front bench in the small, windowless room. This was a private hearing and only those involved were there. Tate's foster parents, Emily and John Chapman, were seated on the first bench to the right. Tate sat next to Emily looking very serious in his little grown-up courtroom clothes. He glanced up at her and waved, a bright boyish smile suddenly on his face. Sula's heart fluttered with joy. In his hand was a little blue transformer toy she'd bought him for his fourth birthday.

She tried to put her thoughts in order before the judge came in. Ever since Rudker had threatened Tate, Sula's feelings had been in turmoil. She loved her son more than anyone or anything in the world. All that really mattered was for Tate to be safe and happy. She didn't know if she was the right person to make him happy.

For the hundredth time, her mind played out the *what-if* scenario. What if the judge gave her custody? Would Tate go home with her today? Or would the judge give the Chapmans time to gather his things together and have a few days to say good-bye? Either way, what would it be like for a little boy to leave the people he thought of as parents and loved most in the world?

What would it be like for him to go live in a new home with a woman he had spent less time with than his daycare provider? How long would it take her to earn his trust? How long would he grieve for Emily and John? Could she bear to make him that unhappy? Even if it was only for a few weeks or months?

Everyone—her lawyer, her counselor, even Tate's caseworker—had reassured her that young children adapt to new family situations. Sula didn't know if she had the right—or the will—to make him unhappy, even temporarily.

It was so much more complicated than that. Most important, she couldn't provide him with a father, and little boys really needed a father. Especially in today's violent and mixed-up world. They needed, more than anything, a good male role model. Someday, she might find a suitable stepfather, but right now Tate already had a great father.

Sula grabbed Barbara's hand. "I want to withdraw my petition."

"What?" Barbara turned to her, stunned.

"I want to withdraw. I want to take the deal they offered. Unsupervised biweekly visitation."

Barbara locked eyes with her. "You remember that part of the deal was to give up your parental rights."

"I know. It's time. They are his parents. I can't undo that now."

"You should think about this."

"I've thought about it constantly for the last few days. I don't want to disrupt his life and take away his security. Long term, I think they'll be better for him."

"Are you sure?"

Sula nodded.

Barbara clicked into lawyer mode. "All right, this is what we'll do. I'll withdraw the petition and agree to meet with their lawyer in a few days to work out the new visitation arrangement. Giving up your custody will take a whole separate petition. This way, you'll have some time to make sure that's what you really want to do."

"All right." Sula felt a little numb as she watched Barbara approach Emily and John with the news. They both stared at her in disbelief. She smiled to reassure them it was real. Their faces lit up with joy. She stood and waved and left the courtroom. She knew she should have spoken with them, but it was more than she could bear. She was afraid if she started crying, she wouldn't stop.

It was time to put the tears behind her and move forward. Rudker had suffered a stroke while he was in police custody, and now he was in a coma. The doctors didn't think he would recover, and she would probably never face her tormentor again. She would start seeing her counselor again and stay with it for as long as necessary. She would also get to see more of Tate. She would be in his life for as long as he let her.

Sula planned to go home and tell Robbie, who had been sleeping on her couch for a week, that he could move into Tate's room. Then she would call Aaron and see if he still wanted to have that cup of coffee.

About the Author

Photograph by Gwen Rhoads, 2011

L.J. Sellers is a native of Eugene, Oregon, the setting of her thrillers. She's an award-winning journalist and bestselling novelist, as well as a cyclist, social networker, and thrill-seeking fanatic. A long-standing fan of police procedurals, she counts John Sandford, Michael Connelly, Ridley Pearson, and Lawrence Sanders among her favorites. Her own novels, featuring Detective Jackson, include *The Sex Club*, *Secrets to Die For*, *Thrilled to Death*, *Passions of the Dead*, *Dying for Justice*, *Liars, Cheaters & Thieves*, and *Rules of Crime*. In addition, she's penned three standalone thrillers: *The Baby Thief*, *The Gauntlet Assassin*, and *The Lethal Effect*. When not plotting crime, she's also been known to perform standup comedy and occasionally jump out of airplanes.

22144286R00177

Made in the USA
Charleston, SC
14 September 2013